I AM AUTOMATON 2
KAFKA RISING
Edward P. Cardillo

Acknowledgements

I would like to thank my wife, Sandra, who has been my editor, coach, and agent and never let me succumb to self-doubt. I would also like to thank Charlene Nunez, James Nunez, Alan Basso, Arno Kolz, Robert Rubicco, Jack Daly, and Jim Taylor for their feedback and support. Thanks again to Gary Lucas at Severed Press. Thank you to my son, Alexander, who keeps my imagination wild.

In memory of Genghis Cardillo

Prologue

Days passed and Captain Carl Birdsall was beginning to encounter more and more terrorists within the recesses of the mountains. He had seventeen more kills, bringing his total to fifty-two.

He came around a sharp bend, where there were bright lights and voices echoing off of the cave walls. Carl tightened his fist and telepathically urged the undead infantry drones forward. They began to pick up the pace, and as their footsteps thundered in the cavern, there were sounds of panic from the lighted area.

Gunshots rang out and people hollered. Carl turned the corner in his sea of undead drones, and as terrorists became visible, he took them out. Return volleys took down several infantry drones around him, but Carl was unharmed and unafraid. The drones swarmed the area, toppling over lighting, computer equipment, and a video camera.

Daylight crept in on the other side of the cavern from an opening to the outside. Several terrorists ran towards the exit, but Carl cut them down. After several minutes of gunfire and cries of terror, the room was once again silent. Carl rewarded his drones by letting them feed. This was the mother lode, some twenty odd terrorists, bringing his count to around seventy-two.

He saw the camera equipment lying sideways on the floor. Apparently, they were working on broadcasting something. They always did, to rally their men around the world or to claim credit for an attack.

Carl, worn out from wandering the caves for two weeks, picked up the camera on its tripod and righted it. The red light was still on. It was recording.

Carl backed up and stood in front of the camera, assault rifle pointed up towards the ceiling in bravado, and telepathically ordered some of the drones to stand behind him in the shadows.

Then he began to speak.

"This is a message to all of those who are enemies of freedom around the world. For decades, you have planned attacks on the free world while in hiding, cowering in these caves. You've massacred many men, women, and children in the name of your perverse ideology. It has been said that you do not fear death, as many of you have extinguished your own lives for your cause.

"All that has changed. I have found you in the recesses of these White Mountains, cowering like swine. You need not fear death, but you will fear me.

"I have come for your lives, and I have claimed many. There is nowhere you can hide that I will not find you. My men do not tire, they do not thirst, they do not sleep…but they hunger for your blood, and they will not be satiated.

"Heed this warning: disband, immediately. Your reign of terror is at an end. For every attack made on free soil, I will claim fifty of your heads. I will not stop until the attacks do, or until there are none of you left. I vow this from your own back yard. You will answer to the dead. Not only to your victims, but also to those in life who counted themselves amongst your ranks. You owe the free world a profound debt, and I am here to collect."

Then he lowered his rifle, trained it on the camera, and shot it to pieces.

Part I
Aftermath

Chapter I

The situation had spiraled out of control and Lieutenant Peter Birdsall felt powerless to help. There were tourists running around screaming as ravenous zombie infantry drones pursued them. Peter's infantry drones. The very infantry drones that he was now fighting.

The resort in Xcaret was in chaos, and Peter was trying desperately to organize his men. Without any firearms, they were backed into a mirrored workout room, barring the glass door against the undead onslaught.

Peter looked outside the room, and in the melee, he saw her. "Mom. MOM."

But she couldn't hear him. She was wandering around in between careening tourists and charging undead, like a lost child in the crowd at the mall searching for her parents, oblivious to all around her.

There was a flash of light…and she was gone. They were all gone.

The undead began to advance on the workout room, smearing torn limb and bloody jowls on the glass wall. A few began to pound their fists on the glass door, eager to claim their hot meal.

Peter looked around the room for an escape or anything they could use, but all he saw were the milky eyes of the undead gazing into him, unblinking and terrible.

"Barnes…BARNES."

Barnes didn't respond. When Peter called to him again, Barnes turned toward him, face mangled and hands reaching out as he moaned.

He turned to his brother. "Carl—"

However, Carl was peering at him with those glassy, clouded eyes, wheezing and gurgling.

Peter backed away towards the far mirrored wall, the waist high handrail jutting painfully into his lower back. He raised his baton in a futile gesture as his once human squad closed in on him, the others watching outside the room in fiendish bloodlust.

They all stopped a few feet away from him and stood there…waiting. Peter lowered the baton and waited for his demise, but they did not advance any further.

Something inexplicable, an inner voice perhaps or a feeling, made him turn around and look at the mirror. He looked at his reflection and shuddered in horror.

His reflection looked back at him with those cold, vacant eyes that he feared so much. His squad hissed and spat in mockery of their commanding officer. He smashed the mirror with his fist...

Peter awoke with a start in his bed. It took his eyes a few minutes to adjust to his surroundings and the stark realism of his dream to evaporate in the early morning air.

A nurse who was making her rounds entered the room. "Are you all right, Lieutenant?"

Peter blinked a few times and wiped the perspiration off his face with the palm of his right hand. "Bad dream."

"Can I get you anything?"

"May I have some water please?"

"Of course. I'll be right back." She left the room.

His mouth was dry as a bone. He saw on the clock beside his bed that it was only 02:00 HRS. The army base hospital was dark and quiet. He missed his own bed in the barracks. He was only there for observation, but he was looking forward to being discharged in the morning. There was so much to do. Carl...

The nurse returned with a plastic disposable cup of cool water.

"Thank you."

After the nurse left the room, he sipped the cool water. When he finished it, he placed the cup on his nightstand and lay back down, his body still aching from his ordeal with the Navajas cartel. He had escaped by the skin of his teeth.

When he turned the drones on them in one of their would-be training exercises, he had barely made it out of there in one piece. Nevertheless, that was what they got for holding him prisoner and actually trusting him to train them in using the infantry drones.

He remembered the video his one captor showed him of the drone in the wedding dress menacing his brother, their leverage to get him to comply with teaching them. He wondered what became of his brother after the botched mission.

After he escaped, he searched for Carl. When he found the shack where the video was recorded, he found the traitorous Sergeant Lorenzo dead inside, torn apart. His partner, Sergeant Lockwood, was in the same condition right outside. Those bastards got their just desserts for striking a deal with the Navajas. However, there was no sign of Carl.

He would have to wait until morning. He couldn't wait for his next therapy session with Fiona. He had more questions for her. Major Lewis was dead, apparently some kind of suicide. That son-of-a-bitch was in on it with Lorenzo and Lockwood after all, but she and Carl had seen to it that Lewis was dealt with. Now Carl was in Afghanistan.

Peter's mind raced with possibilities and he feared for his little brother, who was now out there on his own flushing terrorists out of caves with those monsters that turned on them in Xcaret.

He didn't understand much of what Fiona was telling him about Carl's new…what did she call it…*ability*. He had developed a brain tumor that afforded him some kind of understanding with the undead drones, and he was exploiting it at that very moment in Tora Bora.

Peter suddenly became exhausted and his body ached. He just wanted to close his eyes so he could pass the night quickly. In the morning, he would get some answers from someone. He would make sure he saw Fiona. She was sure to know more about this.

He closed his eyes, and within minutes, sleep took him.

***

Landi Kotal
Pakistan
07:22 HRS

Captain Carl Birdsall of the United States Army lay on a concrete slab in a decrepit cement parking structure, surrounded by his undead entourage of infantry drones. Somewhere between waking and sleeping, he contemplated his situation.

In quiet moments, his mind unfailingly drifted to memories of his mother. Her smile, her cooking, the way she nagged at him to soldier on when he felt like he was spinning his wheels, attending a college they could no longer afford.

However, Carl left that life behind, and although his departure was somewhat recent in the grand scheme of his life, it felt like another era. His childhood died with his mother, and that door could never be opened again. When the woman who brought you into the world dies, a part of you goes with her.

As a hot tear streamed down the dust on his stubble, he knew that everything he had done since was for her. She always told him that he would find his purpose, but in his innocence, he had never imagined that it would be hunting terrorists with army sanctioned zombie drones.

He thought back to his brother, Peter, and everything that happened during the Xcaret mission. Carl remembered the terrified look on his big brother's face in the exercise room of the resort, when they were surrounded by the reflections of those very undead drones

6

that now protected him…with those things that he now shared a psychic connection.

He found it ironic that he would find purpose in those *things* that took everyone he loved away from him. The reality of this filled his heart with a stony, bitter resolve. He still had his father left, but Carl was on the other side of the globe, unable to do anything to help him.

Nevertheless, he was helping him, wasn't he? That's what this was all about. Keeping the world safe from terrorists and drug cartels. Using monsters to hunt monsters, fighting fire with fire.

He slipped into a semi-conscious state and into a waking dream. He saw himself in front of Fiona London's office. He submitted to the retinal scan, and when he entered her office, the therapeutic ambience program conjured up the living room of his childhood home, a setting that filled him with warmth and comfort. Peter was standing behind her desk and Fiona was behind him with her arms around Peter's shoulders in an embrace.

Carl was immediately filled with jealousy at the sight, but Fiona spoke to him. "Open your eyes, Carl. You must open your eyes."

He opened his eyes and heard the staccato chopping of helicopters—Black Hawks he thought—in the distance, but rapidly growing nearer. His detection of the sound caused a ripple of response in the undead drones standing protectively around him. He felt eyes on him.

Carl craned his neck and looked between drones and out of the structure to observe his surroundings. As a tattered white tarp propped up by two wooden poles hung stagnant in the still air, the street beyond was quiet. Several broken down cars sat dormant in the middle of the street, strewn about as if the drivers had en masse suddenly decided to abandon their vehicles.

However, that was Pakistan. What Carl had seen of it reminded him of a set from an epic post-apocalyptic movie. The sounds of the aircraft were close, and the dust outside the three-level parking structure now rose up in dry clouds.

Carl stood up, his back and joints sore from the concrete floor, as soldiers slid down ropes from the craft hovering above. He could tell from their uniforms that they were American.

Carl did not have time to identify himself; the soldiers raised their weapons and began to open fire on the infantry drones. Before he could process what was happening or send a command to the drones, heads began to explode around him.

Why were they shooting at the drones? Did they realize who he was? He had been incommunicado with his team for days…or had it been weeks? They had to know he was out there.

Not taking any chances at the moment, Carl ran in the other direction. He instructed the drones to form a wall, but that was it. He didn't want innocent American soldiers hurt.

As he ran between cement pillars, dodging protruding rebar, he heard shouts as more soldiers began to swarm the complex. The drones formed walls, flanking Carl. He thought of his big brother playing football, running through lanes created by blockers.

He shot out an opening in the side and behind a deserted car. Looking back, he saw the last of the drones executed and the squad fanning out in his direction. That was it. He was now all alone, weak and fatigued from his ordeal in the Tora Bora cave system and the tumor working on his body.

He summoned the strength and, half crouched, ran from car to car. There were shouts behind him, but no one opened fire. If they were going to shoot at him, they would have done it by now.

He ducked into the bottom of an abandoned building, a primitive cement structure with the side blown out. He hurtled a half-crumbled wall and ducked down an alleyway, his dry throat choking on the dust.

He unslung his rifle from his shoulder and held it at the ready as he meandered from structure to structure, between pillars and behind piles of rubble.

It reminded him of how he and his Peter used to go paint balling. The course was similar to this, only the structures were made of plywood, but his brother was dead in Mexico and this was no game.

He heard more shouts and footsteps against the dry dirt and gravel all around him. It was only a matter of time before they were going to catch him. He thought it best to try to identify himself.

"I am Captain Carl Birdsall of the US Army!"

He heard more scurrying, and then a call from somewhere nearby. "Captain Birdsall, this is Colonel Betancourt. We have you surrounded. Lay down your weapon and surrender yourself to our custody. If you do not, we will use deadly force."

What? Why were they treating him like the enemy? Deadly force?

"Okay, Colonel," he threw his rifle down on the ground, "I am coming out unarmed."

He stepped out of the structure he was hiding in slowly. He saw several soldiers crouched behind cars and rubble, all with rifles trained on him. Boy, they caught up to him faster than he thought.

A large, rather stern-looking black man who could only be Colonel Betancourt stepped out from behind a pillar. "Captain Birdsall, we are taking you into custody. Do not resist."

"I won't resist."

Carl put his hands up as two soldiers cautiously approached him, rifles trained at his head. Colonel Betancourt approached with a small, odd-looking pistol and raised it, pointing it at Carl.

"Wait a minute," Carl blurted out in panic, "I said I wouldn't resist."

Suddenly the popping of gunfire erupted all around them.

"TAKE COVER!" Betancourt shouted.

He and Carl ran into the back of a building and took cover behind a wall pockmarked from a prior firefight.

"I told you I wouldn't resist," Carl barked.

"It's not us," Betancourt stated, "OIL has moles in the Pakistani Rangers. They must've gotten a tip you were in the area."

"Give me a gun," Carl insisted.

There were loud booms outside as grenade launchers blew holes in the already chewed up cover and the Americans answered with machine gun fire. Betancourt looked at Carl, sizing him up.

"I'm not the enemy," Carl said with urgency. If they were going to fight their way out, he didn't want to be unarmed.

Betancourt pulled his sidearm out of its holster and handed it to Carl.

"Are you kidding me?" Carl snapped.

"It'll have to do for now, Captain."

"I hope you have a plan since you executed all of my drones, sir."

"We'll stick to the natural cover and wait for air support. There are plenty of cars and trucks lying around out there. We have two Black Hawks in the area waiting for extraction."

Carl nodded, and Betancourt spoke into his mouthpiece attached to his helmet. "Sergeant Hill, column formation, two-by-two through the parking lot we have outside. Use the natural cover."

He waited for confirmation from Sergeant Hill, and then he turned to Carl. "Let's go."

Betancourt jumped up and began to run out of the building, weaving between the pillars and columns. Carl followed closely behind. They turned a corner and saw the street in front of them.

The street was lined on either side with one and two-level square structures jutting out unevenly with tattered fabric awnings. In the street was a traffic jam of burnt out shells of cars and trucks. It was like an automotive graveyard.

Betancourt nodded to Hill across the street, who began to lay down suppressive fire. Betancourt and Carl ran out amongst the wrecks, bullets flying around them and pinging metal.

Hill signaled to another squad, who then laid down suppressive fire from another angle, as his squad filed into the maze of cars. Then Hill's team reciprocated while the other squad followed suit.

Carl felt helpless and foolish with his little pistol as he crouched behind a blown out BMW. He felt vulnerable without his drones, whom he had grown accustomed to.

Betancourt was entering coordinates into his mini-com multitasker. "Now we wait."

Carl heard machine gun fire from the two friendly squads flanking them and the return fire from the OIL operatives. He tried to peek over, but Betancourt pushed him down. "Don't do that. Hold tight. We'll be out of here in a jiffy."

Carl was wondering how they were going to pull that off. While the cars provided cover, they also obstructed their vision. He couldn't tell where the OIL operatives were coming from.

Then he heard the Black Hawks. He looked up into the sky and saw one coming from behind their position and moving toward the center of the street. He grabbed a dangling side view mirror off the car he was leaning against and held it up, looking at the reflection. He saw another Black Hawk in the distance, coming from the other direction.

Bolts of red light began to shoot out of the Gatling guns on the Black Hawks and lit up the wreckages where the OIL operatives were positioned. Dust was kicked up everywhere, and there was wild gunfire from the opposition. Streams of light made Swiss cheese out of the dilapidated vehicles, igniting some gas tanks.

Carl looked up as a Black Hawk passed over them, the Gatling gun spinning, bullets flying out like a light show, the barrels buzzing loudly. He felt a stabbing on his thigh.

He looked down wondering how he was hit behind a car, but he saw a syringe sticking into his leg. Betancourt gave him a thumbs up when his vision shifted and he felt his eyes roll into the back of his head.

Chapter 2

Fort Bliss, Texas

Lieutenant Peter Birdsall stalked down the hallway towards Captain Fiona London's office. Ever resilient, his recovery at the base hospital was brief and he was anxious to speak to her. When he arrived, he found her door uncharacteristically open. He let himself in.

He found Fiona standing behind her desk working at her computer. She looked up at him startled. "Peter."

He looked around her office. It was empty and the therapeutic milieu program was deactivated. Normally, the retinal scan at her door would've registered his print and conjured up some fond setting from his memories in her office. However, the office was bare, and it was an unnatural sight given it was usually the only homey place on base.

"What's going on, Fiona?"

"Peter, I can't really talk now."

"You look like you're going somewhere," he realized that she was deleting psychotherapy files, "and fast."

"Peter, your brother opened up a whole can of worms with his broadcast. The Infantry Drone Program is being suspended, maybe even dismantled."

"On whose authority?"

"One Colonel Betancourt."

"Speaking of Carl, I heard he was picked up in Pakistan."

Fiona ignored his remark and continued to delete files furiously. He noticed that she didn't even flinch when he delivered the news about Carl, which meant she already knew.

"Fiona."

"What?" She sounded impatient.

"You know something about Carl. He's not in any trouble, is he?"

She stopped what she was doing and looked Peter directly in the eye. "Well, let's just say that the brass weren't too happy about his announcement to the world."

"But his mission in Tora Bora was a success, wasn't it? He has the Order for International Liberation scared. Have you seen the international press?"

"Peter, the world wasn't supposed to know about our infantry drones just yet. Then there was Major Lewis and Sergeant Lorenzo. There're going to be questions, investigations. And not just from within."

"What are you talking about?"

Fiona looked exasperated at his ignorance. "I am talking about the House Oversight Subcommittee for starters. The UN Security Council. I am talking prison time for those involved in the program and sanctions against the United States."

"Sanctions? For what?"

"Peter, there's something called the Geneva Protocol."

"What about it?"

"There's a provision against the development and usage of biological weapons."

"The drones are biological?"

She finished deleting files on her computer and began to delete files on her mini-com unit, a cellular communicator the size of a stick of gum. "Let's just say it's a grey area."

"So what's going to happen to Carl?"

"Peter, you know he played a significant role in all of this. It wasn't just his broadcast. It's his…ability."

"His link with the drones?"

"The brass doesn't want word getting out about his ability. They are afraid of how the international community will react. Such power in the hands of one man is frightening."

Peter read between the lines. "They're scared, too. The brass, I mean."

"Can you blame them, Peter? After what happened with Lewis, Lorenzo, and Lockwood? This project got way out of control. This is going to be worse than the Iran Contra scandal, or Fast and Furious."

"You didn't answer my question about Carl."

She finished with her mini-com and stepped out from around her desk. "Peter, I have to go. Word came all the way down from General Ramses that I am to disappear. There is to be no record of my involvement with the Infantry Drone Program."

Peter was stunned. "So you're just skipping out when things are getting interesting and leaving the rest of us to hold the bag?"

"Not exactly, Peter. I really can't tell you much."

She began to push her way past him, but he grabbed her shoulders and held her in front of him so that they were face-to-face. "Fiona. Please. What about the trust you always talk about in our sessions?"

"I am no longer acting psychotherapist. I have been reinstated to an old role, but it's nothing I can talk about. Please understand. I have my orders."

When Fiona told Peter of the role she played in Major Lewis' demise in collaboration with Carl, he realized that she wasn't quite the

Girl Scout as she presented herself. Now he really wondered. What was this 'old role' she was being so cryptic about?

"I want to know what's going to happen to my brother. Fiona, I know you know something."

She hesitated, torn between her apparent orders and something else…loyalty, honor?

"Let's just say that my new assignment will serve to protect Carl."

Peter squeezed her shoulders gently. "Protect him from what, Fiona?"

She looked deep into his blue eyes. "I really have to go, Peter. Let me go." There was urgency in her eyes. "Carl needs me, Peter. Let me go."

He released her shoulders and she left the office without another word. He stood there, his mind racing, wondering what was in store for Carl and how she was going to protect him.

Two MP's barged into the office. One barked at him, "You don't belong here. You have to…" they noticed Peter's rank. "Excuse me, sir, but you have to leave the office."

He stood there for a moment contemplating what was happening. They were going to clear Fiona's office. Strip it clean. The brass wasn't screwing around.

"Carry on, privates."

Peter left the office. The hydraulic door closed behind him and he heard the digi-lock engage. He stood there dumbfounded, completely out of his depth.

His mini-com unit sounded off. He had a message. As he began to walk back towards the barracks, he called up the message:

AS MY LAST ACTION IN MY CAPACITY AS PSYCHOTHERAPIST FOR THE ID PROGRAM, I PUT IN FOR A REQUEST FOR SOME LEAVE TIME FOR YOU THAT HAD BEEN APPROVED BY COLONEL BETANCOURT. REST UP, SEE YOUR FATHER, PAY A VISIT TO YOUR LOCAL WATERING HOLE. BEST OF LUCK. FIONA.

Peter found this message to be strange. This was an odd time to be granted leave, particularly when the shit was about to hit the fan. Somebody wanted him out of the way.

It could have been for any variety of reasons. He was probably going to be excluded from any hearings. The brass was going to spin their version of what went down, and it was a good assumption that they didn't want him getting in the way of a good lie. Maybe they didn't want him around for what was going to happen to Carl.

Poor Carl. As far as Carl knew, Peter was missing in action in Mexico. He couldn't wait to tell Carl that he still walked the earth.

Somehow, he thought he wouldn't get the chance. The whole program was going to be put under a microscope, largely due to Carl. He just hoped his little brother didn't dig himself into a hole he couldn't pull himself out of.

He found it interesting that Fiona referenced Frisky's (the local watering hole). He remembered unexpectedly bumping into her there once before, when she delivered the news to him that he had been approved for the Infantry Drone Program. He remembered the sexual tension between them—you could've cut it with a machete. Then he remembered her conspiring with Carl behind Major Lewis' back.

Did she want to meet him at Frisky's? It looked like she was going to disappear off the face of the earth. Maybe that was the perfect opportunity for a secret meeting at an inconspicuous place.

The idea sounded ridiculous to Peter the moment it popped into his head. She obviously had more urgent things to do. She wouldn't have the time to make a run to Frisky's. He silently chastised himself for such a ridiculous thought and was convinced that he was reading too much into her message.

He decided he would take the opportunity to see his father, who also thought him MIA. Since his return from Xcaret, he was forbidden to contact him. If he only knew what his sons were up to, saving the world from terrorists and cartels using rejects from a B-rated horror flick.

Peter wasn't sure how exactly he was going to break the news to his father that he wasn't missing or dead. The poor man had already been through a lot.

And maybe, just maybe, he would have a beer or two at Frisky's.

***

Barry Birdsall sat on his couch in his boxers and sweat-stained undershirt flipping through the channels. He settled on the Tyler-Skyler Show, the top rated docutainment show three years running.

The twins were sitting in their high chairs dressed identically with matching poufy hairdos and blond highlights. Barry thought they were so Nuveau Millenium.

"Skyler, word has it that the White House Press Secretary is going on the air in mere moments to make some earth shattering announcement."

"That's right, Tyler. And rumor has it that it has something to do with that mysterious broadcast from the Afghansistan-Pakistan border by that unidentified soldier."

"Skyler, perhaps the soldier was found."

"You mean apprehended, Tyler."

"Skyler, are you suggesting that the soldier in question is some kind of criminal?"

Gasps and boos from the studio audience.

"Tyler, the man is obviously some rogue assassin tramping his death squad all over Afghanistan supposedly taking out OIL operatives. Honestly, OIL operatives hiding in caves. How ridiculous!" He looked down off screen and then smiled. *"I just got one thousand and twenty-three hits on Skylerblog saying I'm right. What say you?"*

Oohs from the studio audience.

Tyler flipped his hair back, looking perturbed for the camera the best way he knew how. *"Brother, the soldier is a hero, risking life and limb to rid the world of those treacherous OIL terrorists."* Cheers from the audience. *"And moreover, I wouldn't be surprised if the soldier was one of ours…"* Skyler gasped and fanned himself with his hand. *"…and one thousand and thirty-seven hits on Tylerblog say **I'm** right. What say you?"*

The audience erupted into a combination of competing cheers and jeers as Skyler dramatically tried to compose himself. Tyler began to pick under his well manied fingernails with a self-satisfied grin on his face.

*"Tyler, I am horrified that you would even suggest that **he** is one of **ours**. He is clearly more of a terrorist than OIL. There are rumors in the international press that there is something quite…unnatural about this roving death squad. How else did they last so long in the Tora Bora caves? Those tunnels go on for miles and miles. Right? Oh, and Skylerblog just received eighteen hundred and five more hits that say **I'm right**. What say you?"*

Shouts and hollers from the studio audience in response. Tyler wagged a finger at Skyler and then the audience. *"Skyler, brother, I wonder if it ever occurred to you that our military may be unveiling a new technology of infantry that allows these men to wander the dark tunnels of Tora Bora for days. Perhaps they are some kind of robot or android. Nineteen hundred and eleven hits on Tylerblog say **I'm** right. What say you?"*

"Robots, Tyler? Really? You should know that there is no such thing yet as robot soldiers or androids. But you do have a point about the unnatural part. Doesn't he?" The camera panned to the audience stirring with excitement. *"I think that there is something unnatural about the captain of that murder squad who made the broadcast. No human could be so cold-hearted and callous. Four thousand two hundred and nine hits on Skylerblog say I'm right. What say you?"*

Some cheers from the audience. Tyler put his hand delicately to his chest and opened his mouth in an exaggerated expression of disbelief.

"Skyler, I shudder at the thought that you are suggesting that this hero is some kind of monster. Just what are you getting at? Six thousand four hundred and seventy-two hits on Tylerblog say we want to know."

The studio audience murmured in anticipation of Skyler's response.

*"Tyler, what I am trying to say is that maybe this soldier is some kind of...freak of nature. An abomination to be condemned, not celebrated. New technology, my eye. Alternative infantry or crimes against nature? If he is something different, maybe I don't want to know about it. He can keep it to himself. But he is no soldier in **our** army. Six thousand nine hundred and two hits on Skylerblog say amen to that."*

The studio audience was now on its feet, yelling in mixtures of support and condemnation of the statement just made. Studio security was standing by with tasers and itchy trigger fingers, not for the sake of safety, but the opportunity for even better television.

Barry rose from the couch shaking his head. They were talking about his youngest son, Carl, after all. He padded into the kitchen and pulled the refrigerator door open. He pulled out a cold beer and shuffled back into the living room, the refrigerator door half-closing behind him. He planted himself back into his seat.

Tyler was waving his hands to silence the audience. After a moment, the uproar began to die down and people began to sit back in their seats. When the noise dropped to dull murmuring, the co-host continued.

"We are going to our panel of celebrity experts to weigh in on this. This mysterious soldier: hero or monster? We go to hip pop music star, Murder Mouse, via satellite. Murder Mouse, are you with us?"

"Boo biggity, Tyler. You know the flow, son."

The audience cheered in response as the visage of Murder Mouse popped up on screen in the studio. Now Skyler spoke.

"Murder Mouse, I think that this so called 'hero,' likely the product of unnatural and horrifying experiments by our military, should be condemned and expunged. Ten thousand fifty-nine hits on Skylerblog say it is so. What say you?"

"Skyler, I say no frigiddy, you glean? This soldier of our fortune should be who he is, not who he is not, you feel my crux?"

Tyler applauded loudly, clapping his hands in a circle. *"Words of wisdom. I give this man a round of applause."* The camera panned to a woman who was dramatically gesticulating in the affirmative.

"Twelve thousand seven hundred and sixty-one hits on Tylerblog say they glean."

Skyler pursed his lips sternly until the audience quieted down. *"Well, I must say that I disagree most enthusiastically with Murder Mouse. So now we must hear from fashionista and heiress to the Mayberry snack cake fortune via satellite, Miss Glendella Mayberry."*

The audience applauded as her face popped up on the monitor. Her green hair was teased up in every direction, and her lips smacked as she sucked on a miniature couture lollipop.

"Like hi, Tyler. It's great to be here."

"It's Skyler, and you aren't actually here."

"Totally."

"Glendella, focus. What do you think of the mysterious soldier who broadcasted from Tora Bora? Friend or fiend?"

"Well, I think that any man who wants to wander around in caves all day is no real man at all. I mean, they're all dark and damp and sticky."

Skyler's face lit up. *"Caves aren't 'sticky,' but you agree that this death monger is some kind of cretin, an atrocity against nature herself. Twenty-six thousand and four hits on Skylerblog say that you are right."*

The audience burst into argument as the twelve-year-old heiress smacked her lips on the lollipop. Tyler stood up in protest and nearly fell off the stage as the screen went off.

"We interrupt this broadcast to bring you an announcement from White House Press Secretary, Bill Sayers."

A tall, balding man, thick in the middle, with round spectacles strode up to a podium bearing the White House Seal. His sandy hair stood out against the blue background.

"We are pleased to announce that we have located and taken into custody the soldier of Tora Bora. His squadron has been neutralized. He will be evaluated at one of our medical facilities at Guantanamo Bay..."

Guantanamo Bay. That was a detention facility. Why were they using words like *taken into custody* and *neutralized*? Why were they treating Carl like a prisoner of war? None of this made any sense to Barry.

Reporters began to ask their questions like impatient second graders in a classroom eager to get the teacher's attention. Sayers pointed to one reporter.

"Mr. Sayers, is this soldier indeed one of ours?"

Sayers kept his poker face and addressed the question in a matter-of-fact manner.

"I cannot comment on the nature of this soldier's affiliation at this time. He will be detained in the Guantanamo Bay facility for an indeterminate period of time where he will receive quality medical care and remain under observation."

Carl's father smiled bitterly. This son-of-a-bitch was purposely being vague and evasive. He mentioned that Carl's squad had been *neutralized* and that he was to be *detained* in Gitmo to throw the reporters off the trail that he was indeed an American.

He wondered if this was for Carl's own protection or if he was being disavowed and treated as a rogue soldier. He couldn't have imagined that Carl's superiors or the White House would have approved of his little broadcast that sent shockwaves throughout the international community.

Sayers pointed to another reporter.

"What was the nature of this soldier's squadron? Not affiliation, I mean nature. They were reported to have been wandering around the cave system in Tora Bora for weeks. How was that possible?"

Sayers, always the professional and not easily flustered, kept his composure.

"Again, I cannot at this time comment on the affiliation or nature of this soldier and his unit. As soon as we are able, we will provide you with more information. That will have to be all for now."

Just like that, Sayers nodded to the throng of now scurrying reporters and left the podium, disappearing behind a curtain.

Barry couldn't believe the way this was going down. Had Carl not told him everything, he would have been in the dark, wildly speculating like everyone else.

At some point, the White House would have to comment on this further. The media was already focusing a tremendous amount of attention on the subject. Now the focus and wild theories were going to go into overdrive.

The very next day, the press dubbed Carl the Soldier from Tora Bora, the Cave Man, and even the Automaton (based on speculations that he was not human but some kind of robot).

He was characterized as a hero and rogue, a villain by some, and just about everything in between. Some believed he was a mercenary contracted by the United States. Others believed him to be a Middle Eastern nationalist who was making a statement against the Order for International Liberation.

The docutainment circuit, like the ever-popular Tyler-Skyler Show, was making Carl out to be some kind of legend. The spin was mostly good, painting him as a do-gooder fighting against the forces of evil, but the opposing viewpoint was always included.

Carl's father was working at the hardware store taking inventory when he heard two men discussing his son in the plumbing aisle.

"Mercenary or not, the man's a hero. Someone needs to do something about OIL."

"But what if this pisses OIL off and they retaliate?"

"Retaliate? They've been quiet ever since Tora Bora. No more bombings on U.S. soil."

"Maybe because this man isn't one of ours. Maybe they're out looking for who is responsible."

"Either way, it works for me."

"We will never get rid of terrorism, you know. There have always been terrorists. You kill a few, or even a big wig, and more just take their place. And this ain't the days of al-Qaeda. OIL is organized and multinational. They're even all throughout Europe."

"Oh, Europe is a bunch of pussies. They don't have the sense to look after their own back yards. The UN will go after this Soldier of Tora Bora before they do anything about their own OIL problem."

Barry pulled into his driveway and turned off the ignition. He got out of the car, the sudden motion making his sinuses throb. Texas was going through a record draught, and the combination of the dryness in the air and poor air quality was wreaking havoc on his head.

He disengaged the digi-lock and entered his foyer. He threw his keys into the bowl on the small table by the door, shut the front door behind him, and stepped into the living room.

He turned toward the big screen television and was about to command it to power on when the reflection made him freeze in his tracks.

"Hi, Dad."

He turned around, and his eyes welled-up when he saw Peter. He stepped forward and threw his arms around his son. Last he heard from an officer who paid a visit to the house, Peter was MIA. The officer did not tell him where or anything else, but he knew from Carl that it was in Mexico.

"I'm glad you're okay, son."

Peter was relieved at his father's reaction. The last thing he wanted to do was give the poor man a heart attack.

"I'm okay. I got some leave time, so I figured I'd come and let you know I was still alive."

"How did you get out of Mexico?"

Peter was startled by this. That information was supposed to be classified.

His father saw the look on his face. "Carl told me."

"Carl...told you? He wasn't supposed to."

"I know, but he felt he had to tell someone. He's in trouble, isn't he, Pete."

"Yeah, I think so. He breached protocol with that broadcast of his and, apparently, he didn't stop there. He shouldn't have told you—"

"Pete, I'm glad he did. At least I know what you two were doing. Even though it sounded incredibly dangerous..." Peter huffed at the obviousness of the statement, "...at least I knew what you boys were working toward. I am proud of you both."

Peter didn't know what to say, exactly. He wasn't expecting this, and he felt awkward. He wondered if his father knew about the...

"Pete, what are they like?"

"What do you mean, Dad?"

"The...zombie soldiers."

...oh, there it was.

"The drones? Carl even told you about the drones?"

"It doesn't even seem real. It, quite frankly, all seems ridiculous."

"Dad, you know you can't tell anyone."

"Who the hell am I going to tell? Your mother is gone, and anyone else would think I was nuts."

"The press hasn't caught on to the drones yet."

"I know. They're focused on your brother right now. Are they really holding him at Gitmo?"

"It would appear so," said Peter gravely, "but I don't know any more about it than you do." He saw his father's expectant look. "All right, Dad. But I need a beer to wet my whistle."

"Oh, of course." His father gestured toward the kitchen. Peter led the way. He opened the fridge and pulled out two cold beers. He handed one to his father, and they each took a seat at the kitchen table.

Peter ran his hand through his hair, paused a moment, and then he began. "They're terrifying. I mean, we know what they can do to a person, but it's more than that. Their very presence is repulsive."

"Carl told me about Mexico and what happened."

Peter was staring off into nowhere. "Yeah...a lot went wrong in Mexico. I lost my whole platoon except for Carl, but I was separated from him. Once the drones turned on us, everything went to shit." He took a long sip of his beer. "They just kind of overwhelm you. They pile on in numbers, staring at you with those glassy eyes, reaching out for you. We started out with a whole platoon, but we had a weapon malfunction...

"We holed up in a gym at a resort, we armed ourselves with whatever we could find…free weights, bars…and they came in after us. We barricaded a stairwell with exercise machines and tried to take them out in a controlled fashion, one cluster at a time…

"But, as they were designed to do, they piled on in numbers, climbed over the barricade, and we began to fall back. We lost one or two men in the process…one had his fingers bitten off and then the rest of him chewed on…another tried to jump off the second floor…he broke his legs, and he became a hot lunch for whatever was waiting for him down there…

"We retreated to this exercise room, like where they hold aerobics classes, barring the door. But the wall was glass, and they pressed up against it, wheezing and snarling, snapping their teeth against the glass…" He recalled his nightmare. "…it was a mirrored room. I can remember their eyes, all around us. I began to lose my shit, but Carl broke the mirrors. I sent my team up into this vent that ran along the top of the gym and out. They went in one-by-one. I saw Carl go up and in...

"I was the last one in the room when they broke through. I was totally prepared to die. I grabbed a weight bar and began swinging wildly…crushing one skull after another. It's the only way to kill one of them. But then it was as if suddenly this great calm washed over me…you know, that feeling you get when you come to grips with your fate…"

His father had no idea what he was talking about, but he nodded in horrified fascination so Peter would continue.

"And my swings became less wild. It was like everything began to move…in slow motion. I was running in between them, like I could see every space, and I was taking them out one-by-one. Even so, they were too many. I worked my way over to the window when some debris from the storm smashed it open. It was as if some divine providence was giving me an exit…like it was telling me that it wasn't my time to die…

"I jumped out and landed in some bushes below. The wind was howling and pelting my face with all kinds of debris. I struggled to stand up; the wind was powerful, knocking me around. I tried to follow the outside of the building back around to where I thought the ventilation duct went and where my team was, but the wind was blowing me around.

"There were dozens of drones roaming about, and several caught my scent. It was ridiculous trying to make a run for it in one hundred plus mile per hour winds, but I half ran, half flew across the grounds and away from the hotel building."

Peter's father was entranced with a look of pain for his son on his face. This was the sort of stuff one saw in a blockbuster science fiction film or horror perhaps. "How did you get away?"

Peter took another swig of his beer and sat back in his chair pensively. "I was blown past the swimming pool. Nearly fell in it. One of the drones fell in the deep end. I got up and kept running, and those bastards…they were relentless. I remember running…and then nothing."

His father was confused. "What do you mean nothing?"

"I think something big hit me. A piece of debris. Next thing I remember, I was being dragged by my feet through the underbrush, my chest hurt and it was hard to breathe. I heard a loud explosion in the distance, but I was unable to regain my footing.

"I was dragged to a cartel outpost, a burlap sack thrown over my head, and I was tossed somewhere dark for a while. When I awoke, those bastards wanted me to teach them how to use the drones. I refused, but they showed me a video of Carl. They had him in a room with a drone dressed up in a wedding dress, sick sons-a-bitches. They told me that if I wouldn't comply, I'd watch her feast on Carl."

His father put his hand over his mouth, "Jesus. So did you do it?"

"Yes, but half-heartedly. I wasn't being extra careful, if you know what I mean. There were accidents, and some of the cartel had to be put down before they turned. What a pity. Then I noticed that after what must have been days, the video of Carl they kept showing me never changed. I mean it was exactly the same each time."

"So you began to wonder if Carl was still alive," his father finished the thought.

"Exactly. So that was when I was going to stage a big accident that would be enough of a diversion so I could escape."

His father was sitting forward in his chair. "What did you do?"

Peter sat forward in his, matching his father. "I told them I was going to show them the 'Circle of Covered Wagons' maneuver, because they wanted to learn more defensive maneuvers than offensive ones. They were planning to use the drones as security detail for their drug running.

"Well, there is no such thing as the 'Circle of Covered Wagons' maneuver, but it got me to put them in the center of a circle of drones who proceeded to surround them. As I heard the screams of cartel goons being eaten alive and gun shots from those watching trying to break it up, I ran.

"I ran as fast as I could until I flagged down a Mexican military jeep sweeping the area after the hurricane. They took me in and got me home."

"And Carl."

"As far as I knew, he was missing or dead."

His father chortled. "Funny, when he was here telling me everything, he told me the same about you. He told me that you sacrificed yourself to get your team out of harm's way. He told me how terrible he felt. Guilty."

"For what?"

"Because he felt that you've been looking out for him his whole life, Pete. And this particular time, he thought it got you killed."

Peter put his beer bottle down on the table. "Wherever he is now, he still thinks I'm gone. I don't think he knows I'm still alive."

"Well, I'm relieved, Pete."

Peter realized that he had been droning on about himself and abruptly changed topic. "How've you been, Dad?"

His father wasn't sure what he was supposed to say. He spent his entire parental life keeping his boys safe, and recently he finds out that they have been cowboys to a bunch of zombies, chasing enemies of the United States around the world.

"I've been okay, Pete. I've had to close the hardware store on the weekends, though. Not enough business. I'm mostly getting contractors during the week, but even that has slowed down."

"Do you need money, Dad?"

His father laughed. "I should be asking you that. No, I'll be fine. So how long is your leave?"

"One week. Enough time to catch up with you and pitch in at the hardware store."

"Pete, you don't have to."

"I want to. Besides, it'll be refreshing doing some work that didn't involve any zombies or Mexican cartels...that is unless the way you do business has changed."

His father smiled. "Nope. Business as usual. No zombies here."

"Dad, have you been doing anything else besides work?"

"I've been going bowling with the guys again on Monday nights. I'm in a league now. They are quite generous with handicaps."

"That's great, Dad. I'm glad. You need to come up with some new kind of routine." He looked around the kitchen. "I see you've been keeping the place up."

His father looked around the kitchen with something that looked a little like pride. "Well, that has been part of the new routine. Keeping the kitchen clean, the bathrooms, I've even been cooking."

"Oh, no. I hope your medical insurance is current."

"No, I hope *yours* is, son, because I'm going to subject you to some of it tonight."

They shared a laugh.

"So, you ever think of your mother?"

Peter's demeanor became a little more somber. "All the time. Poor Carl. He saw it all happen. He saw the suicide bomber. Passed him in the parking lot."

"Yeah, it really shook him up," said Barry shaking his head. "But then he became angry. Then driven. There was no talking him out of enlisting at that point."

"I guess Mom would've been pissed."

"No," his father blurted. "Not in the least. She was always proud of you boys. When you enlisted she was worried for you, but goddammit, she was proud. She told everyone that."

Peter was incredulous. "Proud? Really?"

His father put his hand on Peter's shoulder. "Absolutely, Pete. And I am too...of both of you. But I'm worried about your brother right now."

"Yeah, Dad. I know what you mean."

Chapter 3

Guantanamo Bay
Prison Facility
19:58 HRS

Carl awoke in his cell on the narrow cot. As his vision cleared, he began to see the skewed pattern of the cinderblocks that made up his walls. A naked light bulb burned overhead, casting a dim light into the small space.

He looked up and saw two dark eyes watching him through the small window. The stare was so intense it was unnerving. He rubbed the sleep out of his eyes, but when he finished, the eyes in the window were gone.

He sat up in his cot and smoothed his orange jumpsuit out. He had to be presentable. There was an interrogator coming to get the truth out of him. He was checked out medically and put through several physical stress tests. Despite the fact that he had a tumor the size of a kiwi growing in his skull, he performed very well on the tests.

In fact, he inexplicably felt great. When he slept, it was a deep sleep, and when he woke, he felt so refreshed that he thought he pulled a RIP Van Winkle.

However, this person who was coming tonight was different. Some kind of intelligence expert. He wasn't quite sure what this guy was supposed to be looking for. It wasn't as if he was hiding anything. He knew they were ticked off about the broadcast, but he was being poked and prodded like some kind of science project.

He figured it must've had something to do with his "ability." Maybe they wondered how he communicated with the drones. Truth be told, he wasn't sure how he did it himself. However, after flushing out the tunnel system in Tora Bora, he expected to be treated better.

Two guards came to the door of his cell. The waist-level trap door in the door clanged open. One of the guards addressed him.

"Captain Birdsall, please place your hands through the opening."

Carl stood up, walked over to the door, and placed his hands through the opening as instructed. He wasn't going to put up a fuss. They were, after all, on the same team.

One of the guards grabbed his hands while the other shackled his wrists.

"Captain Birdsall, please step away from the door, turn around, and face the back of the cell."

Carl did as instructed. He heard the digi-lock disengage, and then a manual lock (a failsafe in case of a power outage). The two guards entered the room. Carl heard the scraping of metal on the floor. A guard grabbed him by the shoulder and pulled him into a chair.

"Come on, guys. I'm not Hannibal Lecter."

However, they ignored him and fastened him to the chair with restraints. He guessed they weren't fans of pre-Millennial movies. Once secured, they dragged the chair out of the cell and proceeded to take him down the hallway.

As they made their way down a long corridor, he looked up at the light bulbs in their wired cages hanging from the ceiling. When they reached a heavy blue door, they stopped. One guard disengaged the digi-lock and then the subsequent three other manual locks. Apparently, there was something very important in this room. Carl felt honored that he was going to get to see it.

The guard who disengaged the locks swung the large door open, and the other dragged Carl into the room backwards. Once they placed him roughly in the center of the room, they turned and left. Carl guessed that they were in the corridor just outside the room, standing guard.

"Hello, Carl."

He knew that voice. It was like velvet on his brain.

"Why, Fiona, I had no idea that *you* were going to be doing the poking and prodding tonight. If I did, I would've dressed up a bit for the occasion."

Fiona stepped around the chair to face him, a wry smile on her face. "You know, you're no longer the timid Carl I met at Frisky's one fateful night. Back then, you would've nearly wet yourself in a situation like this."

"Who's to say I haven't now. I only have a small commode in my room. I really have to write a strong-worded letter to the management about the treatment of their guests."

"You're looking good," she said.

He smiled. "But things are looking up as we speak."

Fiona was a little flustered. "I mean your condition. For a man with a pretty advanced brain tumor, you are looking well." She looked down at her mini-com. "And it appears that you've performed above par on all of the tests." She scrunched up her face in deep deliberation.

"You seem vexed by the results."

"I am, Carl. It's almost as if the tumor was *helping* you, making you stronger. I want to give you some problem solving tasks with a motor component."

"I love it when you talk dirty like that."

She gave him a *come on* look.

"Well, I'm not going to perform very well strapped to a chair. Just saying. It might influence your results."

"Don't worry." She leaned over and undid the wrist restraints binding him to the chair. Then she produced a key and removed his wrist shackles, freeing his hands. "There."

"And what about the rest of me?"

"I just need your hands tonight," she smirked at him playfully.

"Oh, and I thought this was getting interesting."

Fiona wheeled a table over his lap and adjusted its height. Then she took out little blocks with various colors on different sides, some with two colors represented diagonally on one side.

"Gosh, Fiona, I haven't played with blocks since I was three."

"Well, I'm going to need you to play with them now. A pattern is going to flash on the screen. I want you to replicate the pattern with the blocks as fast as you can. The table will record when you are finished and flash the next pattern."

"My big brother always told me that women play games, but this is ridiculous."

"The patterns will get increasingly difficult. Are you up to the challenge?"

"Do I have a choice?"

"I have more interesting games once we're through with this one."

"Okay. Sounds good." He positioned his hands over the table. "Just say when."

"As soon as you see a pattern flash, begin." She pressed a button on the underside of the table.

The first pattern flashed and Carl went to work. It was the first, and therefore the easiest, and he finished it in seconds. The next one flashed, and he finished that one in seconds.

While Carl manipulated his way through the patterns, Fiona was making observations with a stylus on her mini-com. She said nothing as he worked his way through the patterns.

As the patterns became increasingly more complex, Carl did not seem to take much more time completing them. In fact, he was smiling as he worked, seeming to barely strain himself.

After he completed the fiftieth pattern, the screen flashed a TESTING COMPLETE message. Data was immediately fed to Fiona's mini-com, and she was pressing buttons on the screen with her stylus.

Carl sat back in his chair and put his hands behind his head. "So, how'd I do, Doc?"

Fiona was looking intently at her screen. "You did incredibly, Carl. You scored in the 99.9th percentile on all patterns."

"What, no hundredth percentile?"

"The computer program is the 100th percentile, and you almost matched it in completing the patterns."

Carl looked a little startled now. "It didn't seem like I was moving that fast. Fiona, how is that possible?"

"I don't know."

"It's the tumor. So I'm going to become a superhero before I die."

"That's just the thing, Carl. We've reviewed the brain scans and the growth of the tumor. The growth has stabilized, and the tumor no longer seems to be endangering your life."

"Wh-how is that possible? Does it still need to be removed?"

"That's the other thing. Its tendrils have fused with different parts of your brain. To remove it would be impossible and, frankly, dangerous."

"So let me get this straight, now it's dangerous to remove this tumor?"

"That's correct."

"But this is crazy. I am supposed to leave it in there now?"

Fiona suddenly looked awkward.

"Oh," Carl said, the truth of the matter dawning on him. "This evaluation has nothing to do with my health."

"Carl, the brass wanted to know if you are too dangerous to be kept alive."

"Oh. I see."

"Your abilities are expanding beyond the communication with the drones. You are becoming faster, stronger…"

"Smarter," he interjected.

Fiona nodded gravely, "Yes…there's another test I want to run."

"Wait a minute," Carl said with annoyance, "you are telling me that the army is considering putting me down like a sick dog because they feel threatened by me and you want to run another test."

"Carl, I'm doing my best to advocate for you, but you need to cooperate with these tests."

"You're trying to help me? That's what you've been telling me from day one in your therapy sessions, but that was when you were a therapist. Now you're in intelligence. Jesus, no wonder why you didn't flinch when I told you how we were going to deal with Major Lewis."

"Carl, I can't help it if there's more to me than you thought. Quite frankly, it was presumptuous of you to think I was a…"

"Nice girl," he interjected.

"Carl, I was never a 'nice girl.' In fact, if I wasn't looking for your brother that night at Frisky's, I probably wouldn't have given you the time of day."

"But you are a nice girl. Otherwise, you wouldn't have given me the time of day. You saw a nerdy guy and figured you'd give him a boost."

"Carl, I never meant to give you the wrong idea—"

"Oh, I think I got the right idea when you kissed me."

"Actually, I seem to remember that *you* kissed *me*."

"Hey, it takes two to tango, honey."

"You were leaving for Afghanistan. What was I supposed to do? Push you away and send you off so distraught that you'd get killed by the first guy to take a shot at you? And don't call me honey."

"Oh, someone really needs to get over herself. I don't think this room is big enough for you, me, *and* your ego. You were never like this in the program."

Fiona shook her head in exasperation and calmed herself. He was a test subject and she should not let him get under her skin. She needed to remain clinically dispassionate.

"Can I just run this other test? And then I promise I'll be out of your way."

Carl put up his hands in surrender. "Go ahead."

"Thank you."

She wheeled the table with the blocks away and wheeled another machine over. It looked like something an ophthalmologist would use. It had a chin rest for one's head and an apparatus for looking into one's eye.

"Change of subject," he ventured. She nodded as she set it up, so he continued. "So are you still a part of the Infantry Drone Program?"

"No, not any more. All records of my involvement have been expunged."

"Really. No records."

"None whatsoever. It's like I never existed in that capacity."

"So does this mean we can date now?"

She shot him a venomous look.

"Hey, just asking."

"Put your chin on this rest."

Carl shrugged his shoulders and did as he was asked, placing his chin on the rest. Fiona wrapped a strap around the top of his head, securing it in place. As she began to refasten his wrists to the chair, Carl began to get a little nervous.

"Say, Fiona, what is this neat little device anyway?"

She stepped behind him and began to press buttons on a larger device that was hooked up to the apparatus that his head was currently tethered to.

"I need to know what you know, what you've seen, what you've experienced. It may give me insight into how you actually communicate with the drones."

"That would be a neat trick."

"Actually, all I have to do is tap into your retinas and then follow the neural pathway to your brain from bottom level nodes up neural columns and into tertiary areas of your brain, interpreting the electrical impulse data using cortical learning algorithms."

Carl was quiet for a moment. "Okay, call me crazy, but that's all a little above the realm of psychology, isn't it?"

"It's not above the realm of human factor engineering, Carl."

Carl was fascinated and horrified all at once. "I didn't even know technology like this existed."

"Well, let's just say it's borrowed technology."

"And you are telling me all of this because I am probably never leaving this facility, am I?"

She didn't answer him. When he became tense, she finally offered a response. "Such little faith, Carl. This information can help me protect you."

"So, what exactly are you doing now?"

"Setting thresholds for spatial pooling. This helps me filter out all of the electrical noise from the more active nodes and columns."

"I have no idea what you just said, but I am very turned on right now."

"Okay, and we are ready. Carl, I want you to relax. That sensor right above your eye is going to read your retina and then feed the data into this other machine over here. It won't hurt at all."

Carl suddenly remembered his time in the MRI when they first wanted to get a picture of his brain. That machine banged a lot. He wondered what this one would sound like. He was glad he was out in the open.

She pressed a button and a bright light flooded his vision. The light was so bright that it gave him a headache. He heard the machine clicking and whirring behind him, processing and interpreting all of his sensory data.

The bright light triggered the memory of the flash of the explosion at the mall. One moment he saw his mother standing there beyond the glass door waiting for him, and then with a flash of light she was gone, snuffed out in a hot second, erased from the earth. He remembered waking up, upside down in his father's car, broken glass in his hair. Everything sounded like he was underwater. Then the sound began to rush back...

After a brief but indeterminate amount of time, the light turned off. Consequently, his headache began to subside. "Well, you were right. That wasn't so bad."

No response.

"Fiona..."

Something was wrong.

"FIONA..."

She began to unfasten the strap around his head. He sat back and squinted until his vision began to clear. "So, did you find what you were looking...for?"

She looked like she'd just seen a ghost. She was pale and very startled.

"What? What did you see?"

She wouldn't answer him. She was lost in some kind of private deliberation, as if she had no idea what she just saw.

"Well, Carl, let's just say that I think the brass will want to keep you around. That's all I can say for now, okay?"

He was getting the willies at her sudden change in demeanor. She was spooked, really spooked. "Okay."

"Carl...why did you broadcast out of the cave?"

He wondered why she was asking this now. "I'm not sure what you mean."

"Surely you knew you weren't authorized to make that broadcast. Didn't you think about the consequences?"

He thought about this for a moment. Now that she mentioned it, he didn't actually remember thinking it through. "It just felt like the right thing to do. Why do you ask?"

"I ask because you should've been smarter than that. It just doesn't add up."

"So, what now?"

"No more testing for today," she said with a haunted look.

The two guards re-entered the room and dragged Carl back out into the corridor fully strapped to his chair. Fiona turned the equipment off and locked it with a security code. She then left and locked the room.

She walked the other way down the corridor towards her new office. She disengaged the digi-lock with retinal and fingerprint scanning, and then rounded her desk. As she sat, the digi-locks re-engaged.

This office wasn't equipped with the therapeutic ambience program, of which she was the author. It was a Spartan military office, bare bones and functional with no touch of comfort.

She sat at her desk stunned by what she just witnessed. As the machine read his retina using the same technology as her therapeutic ambience program and interpreted the images, the images flashed up on a screen.

At first, they were normal. The barracks, base, and then Xcaret, Mexico. She saw everything that happened. Then the images got strange whenever he appeared to be communicating with the drones.

Something began to flicker on the screen in between frames. She barely noticed it at first. She only felt an inexplicable feeling of being ill at ease. Then it began to increase in frequency. When she isolated the interstitial frames from the rest of the images, what she saw on the screen was horrifying.

She picked up the phone.

"Colonel Betancourt, Captain London reporting."

"How did the assessment go, Captain?"

"The apparatus picked up on something, sir."

"Why wasn't this picked up by the therapeutic ambience program? It's the same technology. We installed it to monitor the participants in the program for something like this."

"Sir, I don't know why the therapeutic ambience program didn't detect it. All I can think of was that it was just a screening program. The assessment I conducted today was more thorough."

"Did you find the mechanism behind his ability to communicate with the infantry drones?"

"Sir, I think I found the original author of this technology."

"Original author? What do you mean?"

"I have some concerns, sir. Perhaps our finding this technology wasn't an accident."

"Of course it was, Captain. You aren't suggesting that it was planted here purposely. There was a crash and wreckage."

"All I'm saying, sir, is that we have been using this technology to watch our men, but what if its author has also been using it to watch our men."

"Say no more. I want a copy of the data and video streaming on my desk ASAP. Am I clear, Captain?"

"Yes, sir. And what about Captain Birdsall?"

"Do you believe he is dangerous?"

She took a moment to word her opinion carefully.

"Not of his own accord, sir. He is psychologically stable. His physical and cognitive acumen has improved beyond normal limits, but there is no instability at the moment."

Betancourt was silent for a moment on the other end.

"Let's reinstate him into the program and see what he can do in training exercises, but I want him on a tight leash. Have an amygdala inhibitor installed into his brain, just like the ones in the drones. This way we have an off switch should we need one. We have the House Oversight Committee and the UN Security Council meetings coming up shortly, and if the Infantry Drone Program is shut down, we won't have a chance to learn more about this connection you discovered."

"Yes, sir."

"I'll put through the paperwork. He will be demoted. His captain status was a field promotion based on the erroneous presumption that his brother was dead. Besides, I don't want him to have that much power. He's stable now, but we're not sure for how much longer. We'll promote his older brother to captain."

"Yes, sir."

Betancourt terminated the phone call. Fiona sat at her desk and began to think about the ID Program, specifically about the undead drones. She remembered *The Art of War*. Sun Tzu mentioned something about rather than destroying your enemy's soldiers, make them your own soldiers.

The undead drones did both. They either ate you or turned you into one of them. Either way, the enemy would lose a war of attrition by design. What if this was the design of its original author? The Tutsi-Hutu Virus was found in the vicinity of the crash site.

What if the application of this technology was broader in its intent? The purpose of the infantry drones was to clear an objective. She took this assumption to its furthest conclusion: what if the objective was more than just a cave or a terrorist bunker? What if it was entire nations and eventually continents?

A chill went down Fiona's spine, and she began to wonder if using the technology to begin with was a mistake. She was haunted by what she saw on that screen and, for some strange reason, she felt that it was looking back at her.

This was, of course, ridiculous. The monitor was a one-way output apparatus, but its image on screen left an indelible mark on her that was terrifying.

She wasn't sure how she was going to convey this in her report to Betancourt, and she wasn't sure he would even care. He would be more interested in studying the connection, which at the moment, kept Carl alive. She just wondered at what cost in the long run.

Chapter 4

Security Council Chamber
United Nations Conference Building
09:09 HRS

"Colonel Betancourt, I understand that you are now overseeing the Infantry Drone Program under the oversight of General Ramses."

"That is correct, Inspector General."

"Then perhaps you can elaborate on the nature of these *drones*, and how they are not a violation of the Geneva Code regarding the use of Biological or Chemical Weapons."

Betancourt looked at Ramses, who nodded, and then began to address the assembly of fifteen nations. "Well, the infantry drones do not fall under the category of biological weapons, as they are not biological."

Asad Javaherian, the representative from Iran, was glancing over a report through reading glasses. "In your report, it appears that these *drones* were created using the Tutsi-Hutu Virus."

"That is correct," Betancourt stated.

"Viruses are, by definition, biological, yes?" Javaherian prodded.

"That is correct. But the end product, after the virus has died from a lack of live tissue, is an undead drone."

"Undead? Define undead, Colonel," said Secretary General Ellis.

"Undead, as in not alive, yet not dead."

"Secretary General," blurted Javaherian with an obvious tone of irritation, "this is exactly the type of semantic gymnastics we have come to expect from the United States."

There were murmurs of agreement from Hsin Shen and Gregor Vasiliev of China and Russia respectively.

"The drones are not alive. They do not exhibit consciousness or cognitive ability as living humans would. There are no vitals...no pulse, respiration," Betancourt continued.

"Yet, they move and they eat," challenged Vasiliev. "If they are not alive, then why do they need to eat?"

"The drones have a condition known as Kluver Bucy Syndrome," General Ramses interjected. "It is a condition that makes them hyper oral and hyper aggressive."

"Yes, this Kluver Bucy Syndrome...how can dead men be afflicted with a syndrome?" Javaherian asked.

"Once again, Mr. Javaherian, they are not dead. They are undead," stated Betancourt.

"And what is the nature of this undead state, if you please?" asked Secretary General Ellis.

Ramses took this one. "It is a reanimation of a body and it's tissues as the by-product of exposure to the THV virus. Reanimation is defined as autonomous movement of muscle tissue."

"And could this state indeed be called life?" Shen asked.

"Once again, not without vitals," Ramses responded.

"What about the transmission of the virus through bites? Isn't that a delivery mechanism for the virus?" Vasiliev asked, switching to a new line of attack.

"The THV virus expires at reanimation, Mr. Vasiliev," Betancourt answered. "The THV virus that is transmitted is not active, much like an influenza vaccine."

"But exposure to this *inactive* form of the virus can result in the death and reanimation of the bitten," Vasiliev continued.

"That is correct," said Betancourt.

"So then, this does indeed fall under the category of biological weapons, Secretary General," said Javaherian with exaggerated outrage. "Once you get past all of these semantic distractions, we are left with a biological agent delivered through *undead* means. The delivery itself is irrelevant. What matters is that the agent is biological in nature."

"But that is not how the drones are used, Secretary General. Their primary purpose is not to deliver the agent to convert targets into additional drones. The purpose is to neutralize them," explained Betancourt.

"But if some of your *targets* are converted through exposure to the inactive form of THV, that would be advantageous to you, yes?" said Vasiliev.

"Actually, it wouldn't," said Betancourt. "These drones are controlled through amygdala implants. Any targets turned in the field would not be subject to these kinds of controls and would therefore be a liability, as they were in Xcaret, Mexico. We lost an entire platoon that way. But, there are frequent hiccups when new technology is first implemented."

"Yes, according to your report, the botched operation in Xcaret, Mexico was quite the hiccup," commented Ellis.

"The only casualties in that operation were army, Secretary General," said Betancourt. "No civilians were harmed."

Ellis was glancing at the report. "There was one survivor. The one the press calls the Man from Tora Bora."

"Yes, sir," answered Betancourt.

"It says in your report that he can coordinate the drones through what is assumed to be a telepathic mechanism."

"The precise mechanism is yet unknown, sir. We believe it to be the byproduct of an inoperable brain tumor," explained Betancourt.

"If he can control the drones due to a brain tumor, then the weapon is biological," interjected Javaherian eagerly.

"First, there is no conclusive evidence that the tumor is the cause of the link," argued Ramses. "Second, telepathy is psychological, not biological."

"We are now splitting hairs," said Vasiliev.

"This is a great deal of power in the hands of one man that isn't even understood," said Ellis frowning. "What safety measures do you have in place?"

"We are working on measures, Secretary General," said Ramses. "But with all due respect, that is an internal matter. I thought we were here to discuss the infantry drones."

"I would like to discuss the targets of these drones and *how* these targets are neutralized." said Vasiliev. "They are eaten alive, yes? Not very humane."

"They are absolutely humane, Mr. Vasiliev, because they can infiltrate inaccessible terrain and spare countless American lives in the process," retorted Samuel Bixby, the American representative. "In war, soldiers are shot, stabbed, blown up…is that humane?"

"What I am more interested in," interrupted the Secretary General, "is how these drones are used. Some would say that your activities in Afghanistan and Pakistan are unsanctioned acts of aggression."

"It was a response to the OIL attacks on U.S. soil, as well as their involvement with the drug-running activities of the Navajas cartel in Mexico," explained Bixby.

"Pakistan has no problem with the United States' activities within our borders or their enforcement of our boundaries with Afghanistan," said Imran Mahmood of Pakistan.

"Nor does Mexico have a problem with their activities in conjunction with our government," added Roberto Achai of Mexico.

"Wasn't it the American involvement in your cartel problems that resulted in your military running security for the cartels rather than stamping them out?" said Agathe Marchal of France reproachfully.

"And isn't it *your* country's financial involvement in the Middle East the reason why we have an OIL presence in Europe, Madame Marchal?" answered Achai.

Secretary General Ellis banged his gavel before Marchal could respond, "Enough. I want order." The room settled down. "The question is whether or not these drones constitute a biological weapon, and if they were then used in an act of unwarranted aggression."

"Well I think that these drones are an abomination and demonstrate just how low the United States will sink to rattle its saber," blared Javaherian. "Dead or undead, these monsters are the results of obvious experimentation, much like the Nazi doctors of World War II."

"As indicated in the report," Ramses declared, "the donor bodies were obtained from death row inmates—"

"And some from political prisoners in your Guantanamo Bay facility," Javaherian added.

"Who are convicted terrorists and enemies of the State, as processed by our justice system and none of your affair," Ramses added. "Their bodies used after-the-fact to fight the very organizations that they represented in life that murder around the globe. Secretary General, our judicial system is not under investigation here—"

"Frankly, I am concerned that this technology is only in the hands of one power," Vasiliev said. "What about the rest of us?"

"Some of the nations at this table have nuclear capability," said Bixby, "I don't see any of you relinquishing it to those who do not."

"But in this case, the United States is the only one who has this technology," Vasiliev replied. "And might I remind you that, like in the case of these drones, the United States is the only nation ever to have used the atom bomb, and without consequence may I add."

"We rebuilt Japan," said Bixby, "and as a result, it is a major economic power."

"*Was*," taunted Marchal from France.

"So, are you saying that these undead drones will be a tool for nation building?" asked Vasiliev. "And how does the United States decide who gets to be rebuilt?"

"As far as I know, we haven't tried to rebuild Afghanistan, Pakistan, or Mexico—all locations where the drones have been applied," answered Betancourt. "All locations where we were tracking the Order for International Liberation. The drones are designed to go where our men cannot, to pursue OIL. They save American lives."

"And what about your nation's tendency to destabilize dictatorships it finds unpalatable?" asked Javaherian. "Who is next?"

"Our objective is not to topple regimes," said Ramses. "It is to hunt down and kill terrorists. If you are not involved in terrorism, then you have nothing to hide, Mr. Javaherian."

"Secretary General Ellis," said Javaherian throwing his hands up in indignation, "will you allow the United States to make veiled threats at this meeting against fellow Security Council members?"

"I didn't hear a threat," stated Ramses. He turned to Betancourt, "Did you hear a threat?"

"No, sir. I heard a promise…to wipe out OIL."

"I would like to hear more about the origin of this THV virus," said Ellis.

"With all due respect, we are not at liberty to discuss that, Secretary General."

"It will be difficult to determine the nature of this virus and its effects if we cannot know where it comes from," said Ellis.

"I am afraid that I cannot discuss that matter further," insisted General Ramses. "All I can say is that the drones are not biological. They are reanimated necrotic."

"I guess the question is whether or not there is a ghost in the machine," said Ellis. "These drones may not have vitals or show consciousness in the traditional sense, but they move with purpose. They are not random."

"Now you're getting into metaphysics, Secretary General," pointed out Ramses, "which is not the focus of this group. These drones are merely tools. Equipment, if you will."

"I have heard enough," announced Secretary General Ellis. "We will deliberate on whether or not this undead state falls within the parameters of either biological or chemical weaponry. I am afraid that there are no precedents on this matter. General Ramses, Colonel Betancourt, I thank you for your testimony and now excuse you from the proceedings while we deliberate on these matters."

Ramses and Betancourt stepped out of the crucible and into the hallway and entered a separate room. There was a small table with a pitcher of water, glasses, and six chairs. Neither man sat.

"It was a mistake to let Iran into the Security Council," said Betancourt with exasperation, thankful to be out of the pressure cooker. "They are often the instigators of trouble, and they have no place on the council."

"Their inclusion was good PR for the council, so it didn't look biased."

Betancourt sucked his teeth at this.

"Hey, they're better than North Korea or Afghanistan," Ramses added. "Besides, we have our allies in that room.

"But we also have plenty of detractors in there, Colonel. France is in bed financially with OIL, and Russia is noncommittal which makes them a threat. And wait until they all find out that Carl Birdsall was reinstated."

Betancourt raised his right forefinger to his temple thoughtfully. "He was court marshaled for his lapse in judgment, and consequently demoted. His involvement in neutralizing some traitors within the Program...within *our* military was a hell of a mitigating factor. And there's another, sir, discovered by our intelligence officer, which suggests that Sergeant Birdsall was not operating under his own volition. But he now has an AI chip in his head that we can activate at any time and from any distance via satellite. If he were to get out of hand, he could be taken out with the push of a button."

"Good. We need to take precautions, especially now."

"Besides," Betancourt added, "this program just altered the war on terror. No other nation in that room is equipped to handle the Order for International Liberation. As always, we alone bear the responsibility of cleaning up their mess."

Ramses chortled, "While it's true the UN hasn't been much of a help in the past, they usually stay out of our way."

"I hope you're right, sir."

"Besides, this technology is just the beginning. There is also the related technology regarding intelligence gathering. It has applications for the field as well as a home. Imagine every home, every office being fitted with the therapeutic ambience program. Under the Second Patriot Act, it's all legal and would provide unprecedented surveillance."

"And what about our intelligence officer's concerns?" Betancourt broached.

"What, about the original author of the technology?"

Betancourt nodded.

"There is no evidence that there is something else out there using the technology to watch us," said Ramses. "And until there is, the development of this technology will continue. With all of its applications, we'd be foolish not to. As far as we know, no one else has anything even close to it. It's a gift."

"But sir, there's that saying about looking a gift horse in the mouth. There's that image that she saw during her assessment."

Ramses waved his hand dismissively, "A random image, the equivalent of a brain fart, an artifact of some perverse fantasy of his."

"I hope you're right, sir."

"Please, Colonel, don't tell me you're spooked, too."

"No, sir. Of course not."

About two hours later, there was a knock at the door. Betancourt answered it. It was Bixby.

"They've come to a decision."

Betancourt looked at Ramses, who nodded in response. They both followed Bixby back into chambers.

After they took their seats, Secretary General Ellis spoke. "We, as a council, have come to a decision after much deliberation."

Betancourt looked around the table. Vasiliev looked sullen and Javaherian looked livid. This was heartening.

"We have concluded," Ellis continued, "that the Infantry Drone Program does not violate the biological weapons clause of the Geneva Code and, regarding the activities of the program in Afghanistan and Pakistan, the United States acted appropriately in response to attacks on its soil by the Order for International Liberation."

However, Betancourt noticed that Bixby didn't look satisfied either.

"In addition," Ellis continued, "it is the concern of the council that the infantry drones have the potential of being used aggressively in a manner unsanctioned by this council and its members. Therefore, it is the strong recommendation of this council that the United States use the drones strictly for matters of defense only, or face sanctions imposed by members of this council."

Betancourt and Ramses looked at each other. Defense? What was that supposed to mean, that the United States was to maintain a standing militia of zombies to defend against invasion from Canada?

"The objections," Ellis continued, "of the representatives of Iran, China, and Russia are duly noted and will be recorded in the minutes. This investigation regarding the American infantry drone program is closed, and this meeting is adjourned."

For weeks after, there were shockwaves in the international press. England, Canada, Australia, Italy, and Japan reported the story in a favorable light. North Korea, Al Jazeera, and the French and Russian media condemned the program as American imperialism at its worst, calling it an atrocity against human rights. They blasted the UN Security Council's decision not to call for its termination and accused the UN of being a puppet of the United States.

The House of Representatives Oversight Committee was compelled to launch an investigation into the ID Program. However, as it was directed by Arnold Wilkins, a conservative from Iowa, it was pro forma. No wrongdoing was found, and no funds were redirected.

The American mainstream media was a bit more critical, calling the program expensive and unmanageable. There were calls from the Left for the criminal prosecution of now Sergeant Carl Birdsall. The talk radio circuit deemed the program a prime example of American exceptionalism and hailed Carl as a hero and true patriot. The nation was yet again polarized, with some positing the truth to be somewhere in between.

***

Biggs Army Airfield
Fort Bliss
13:59 HRS

Captain Peter Birdsall and Lieutenant Nolan Kettle sat in the debriefing room awaiting Colonel Betancourt.

"So you went through Basic with Carl?" Peter asked.

Nolan nodded. "He's a good man, your brother."

"How did he handle Victory Tower? I mean *really* handle it?"

"He actually handled it so well that he was made platoon leader by Maddox."

"Really." Peter was impressed. Victory Tower was the bane of every cadet's existence. So was Drill Sergeant Maddox for that matter. "And you were there at Tora Bora."

"Yes, sir. Your brother was my commanding officer. Permission to speak freely, sir."

"Go ahead, Kettle."

"Your brother is a real badass. The way he went into those caves with the drones. He tore through there and out the other side. I heard it took two squads to bring him in at Landi Kotal."

Peter was smiling. Apparently, his nerdy little brother had blossomed into quite the warrior while he was being held captive by the Navajas in Xcaret. He wasn't used to hearing about Carl in these terms.

"It's a shame he was demoted to Sergeant," Kettle added. "He is a hero. A true patriot."

"All right already. Jesus, I can't handle this anymore. My little brother is a badass. Just remember, now this badass answers to me. Got it?"

"Yes, sir."

When Betancourt entered the room, the men stood and saluted.

"Be seated," Betancourt said.

They both sat.

"Gentleman, it has come down by executive order by the President that the Infantry Drone Program be relegated to defense only. The President himself thought that it might be a good idea to use the drones as boots on the ground along the Mexican border."

Betancourt gestured for them to open their holo-desk panels and, as they did, three-dimensional tactical plans flashed on the screens.

"You will be split up into squads," Betancourt said, "with a twenty-klick spread. Camouflaged in your homeostasis suits, the drones will zero in on any other movement in the area. They will swarm any targets, and you will hit the Amydala Inhibitor switches before they can do any damage. You will then proceed to apprehend said subjects."

He pressed a holo-button, and images of a large, car-sized apparatus flickered on the screen. "The function of the Sweepers will be different. They will no longer be running alongside structures to scan for the neutralization of targets. We are defense now. So they will be miles out, using radar mounted on vehicles to scan the area and help direct your efforts. Any questions?"

"So the point is not to let the drones actually eat the subjects," Peter reiterated.

"Yes, that is correct, Captain. Lieutenant Farrow in engineering has some new toys for you guys that should assist in your efforts."

Betancourt stood up and Peter and Nolan followed him out of the debriefing room. When they reached the airfield, Lieutenant Farrow was waiting for them. He saluted Betancourt and Peter. Peter had recently been promoted to captain and still wasn't quite accustomed to the rank.

"Lieutenant Farrow, would you like to show these men the new equipment they'll be using?"

"Yes, sir," answered Farrow. "Remember that signal that the drones responded to that we used to help get them back into the crates?"

Peter and Nolan nodded.

"Well, I designed a tag that can be fired out of a rifle. And this tag," Farrow picked it up off a table and held it up so they could see it, "emits the very same frequency. All you have to do is shoot the tag at a target and the drones will follow it. This will provide some order to the assaults."

Betancourt cleared his throat. "Ah-hem, you mean defensive maneuvers, Lieutenant."

Farrow looked a little flustered. "Yes, of course, sir." He picked up a rifle, a sniper rifle with a large scope for long distance shots. "This ammo clip contains tags. Allow me to demonstrate. Sergeant Torres, the pig."

"Oh boy, here we go with pigs again," Peter cracked. "What does the army have against pork?"

Torres opened the door to a small crate, and a pig came waddling out. He applied an electrical prod to its rear end and it took off like greased lightning.

"Sergeant Torres, release the drones," Farrow commanded. As Torres opened the door to a second crate, Farrow raised the rifle, took aim, and fired a tag into the pig, which had slowed down to a trot. The tag caused it to run a little faster and further away.

Several drones came shuffling out of the crate, sniffing the air. Peter and Nolan, who were only about thirty feet away from the crate and the drones, staggered backwards.

"Don't worry," Farrow reassured them, "the tag's signal is so strong they won't even notice you."

Sure enough, the drones got wind of the signal and started staggering towards the pig. Deciding that it put enough distance between itself and danger, the pig came to a halt a half a klick away. The undead drones were in their relentless pursuit, driven by the call of the tag.

As the drones drew close, Nolan started to shift back and forth on his feet.

"Something wrong, Lieutenant?"

"I was wondering if Lieutenant Farrow was going to stop the drones, sir. I mean, we've got the point. The tag works."

Peter shared a furtive smile with Farrow, who gave no indication that he was going to halt the drones. Nolan started to squirm as the hungry undead began to close in on the unsuspecting pig.

Peter nodded, and Farrow hit the AI kill switch just as they began to reach out for the pig. The pig sidestepped the now frozen throng of killers.

Nolan let out a sigh of relief.

"And you were in Afghanistan with my brother?" Peter teased. "You're a little green for such a mission."

"Your brother handpicked me, sir."

"Oh, relax, Lieutenant, I was only joking. You stay in this outfit and you'll see your share of action soon enough."

"Yes, sir."

"Well, if by action, you mean bagging illegals crossing the border, Captain Birdsall," Betancourt warned.

"Yes, sir. That's exactly what I meant."

"I know Major Lewis was your commanding officer. He ran a sloppy outfit. A bunch of goddamned cowboys. I run a tight operation. Either you adhere to my parameters or you're dog meat. Got it?"

"Yes, sir," Peter replied, his back rigid at attention. "Zero distortion."

"You'll begin training with your platoon this afternoon, Captain. I'll expect a full report on my digi-desk this evening detailing your progress. We go operational on the border in 48 hours. Your men have had prior training with the infantry drones. You will only be drilling modifications for border control."

"Yes, sir."

"Oh, and one other thing…"

"Yes, sir."

"Members of the press will be at your training today."

Peter's eyes bugged out of his head, "Sir?"

"You guys are an international sensation. The President thinks the ID Program is good press. He wants to make the most of it politically, both within and outside our borders. And your brother has become something of a lightning rod. Everyone wants to see the Man from Tora Bora…the Automaton." He sniffled derisively at that last nickname.

Kettle didn't quite know how to process this latter detail. Peter straightened up, "Permission to speak freely, sir."

"Oh, go ahead, Captain Birdsall," he said impatiently.

"Sir, do you think it's a good idea for the press to broadcast the images and…activities of the infantry drones? And what about our identities?"

"You will all be wearing masks," Betancourt explained. "I'm not crazy about this myself, Captain. If it were up to me, your brother would be cooling his heels in Gitmo for eternity for the stunt he pulled in Tora Bora. But it's not up to me, Captain. This comes straight down from the President himself. Am I clear?"

"Crystal, sir."

Betancourt saluted, and Peter, Nolan, and Farrow all saluted him back. Then Betancourt strode off.

"What a hard-on," Peter murmured. It reminded him of how he learned Barack Obama used Seal Team Six for good PR, turning them into celebrities. The only problem was that it compromised their tactics and eventually rendered them less effective. "Hey, Farrow, these tags look cool. Does this mean no more dogs?"

"Oh, no sir. The army zoo is still open," Farrow quipped. "You'll need them to herd the drones along the border fence."

"Excellent. Thank you, Lieutenant."

Peter saluted Farrow, who saluted back.

"Let's go, Lieutenant," Peter said to Nolan. The two men headed back to the barracks.

"Sir, I don't know if we are going to need the dogs with your brother," Nolan ventured.

"Ah, yes," Peter said, "Carl's new ability. I haven't seen it in action yet."

"It's really quite remarkable, sir…Is it true?"

"Is what true, Kettle?"

"Is it true that he has a…chip in his brain? An amygdala inhibitor like the drones?"

Peter hesitated for a moment. "Yes, it's true, but it's not an inhibitor. It's more of a self-destruct measure. And I'm supposed to have my finger poised over the button."

"What effect will the button have on him, sir?"

"It'll fry his brain I suppose."

"I-I don't think it'll be necessary, sir. Carl isn't…dangerous." Nolan practically choked on the last word as if it were painful for him even to utter.

The truth was that Carl's mystique amongst the men turned to something of suspicion and caution. Word had it that his ability was no longer limited to subliminal communication with the drones. Rumor had it he had become faster and stronger.

Peter had heard the rumors as well. Not only had his brother seen his whole platoon die in front of him and evolved into a hardened warrior, but there were these strange abilities. He hadn't seen them in action yet, and since his brother returned to Fort Bliss, he didn't have any real indication of these abilities.

Peter smiled pensively. "I suppose it would make good television, seeing my brother's brains fried, but don't worry, I think he'll put on a better show alive."

Peter would see these abilities in action soon enough if they were indeed real. He had been instructed privately by Betancourt to utilize Carl's abilities to communicate with the drones, but not to rely on him. Betancourt seemed to believe that Carl's abilities were real, and he must be concerned because he told Peter not to hesitate if Carl became dangerous.

There was that word again. Carl's psychological profile indicated profound resilience in the face of adversity and loss. His mood and behavior appeared stable, although Peter sensed that he was a bit miffed about his demotion and Peter's own subsequent promotion.

With everything that Carl had been through, Peter had earned his rank of Captain. He had been taken captive twice by the Navajas cartel and survived to tell the tale without compromising the program or his men. He had seen a lot of action and completed many successful missions.

Carl had persevered through a lot, but he was still green. Then there was that stunt in the cave. Peter could not fathom why Carl had made the broadcast. He chalked it up to inexperience and bravado, but something nagged at him. He had an uneasy feeling in his gut that he couldn't articulate.

Betancourt handed him what amounted to a kill switch for his brother. It was a hell of a thing, to be given that kind of responsibility, but Peter told himself that he would never let things come to that. He would look after his brother as always.

He thought of Fiona. She was gone. No record of her having been in the program. He could've used her insights in session right about now. She was replaced by some quack, but this one was very formal. He had a normal office, no therapeutic ambience program. No folksy demeanor, no creature comforts. Peter was introduced to him briefly and had forgotten his name a few minutes later.

Whatever her new role was, Fiona delivered on her promise to bring Carl back. Peter wasn't exactly sure how safe his brother was walking around with a kill chip in his brain. He wondered about this tumor Carl supposedly had. Normally, when people had brain tumors, it made them weak and eventually killed them.

There were so many things that didn't add up.

When he reached the barracks, Peter found Carl lying on his bunk with his eyes closed. He looked like he could've been sleeping, but Peter knew better.

"Carl, assemble the men. Lieutenant Farrow has some new toys for us."

Carl opened his eyes and sat up, fingering the large scar on his left temple. "Yes, oh fearless leader."

Kettle looked at Carl and then at Peter uneasily. Then he nodded to Peter and moved on to assemble his gear. Peter shook his head at Carl.

"Carl, when I give you an order, you carry it out."

"I see that you've got my men running around for you now."

"Carl, they are not *your* men, and I am not your brother here. I am your commanding officer."

Carl stood up. "Permission to speak freely, *sir*." He said that last word with more sarcasm than Peter was comfortable with.

Their reunion had been touching but short-lived, and Carl was bitter about Xcaret and his demotion. Peter wanted Carl to fall into line. The sooner they re-established some kind of order, the better. He knew that if they didn't have it out now, at this very moment, it would only cause more problems.

"Go ahead, Sergeant."

"I think that it's wrong, given everything I have been through, that I have been stripped of my Captain status…and that it be given to you."

"Carl, first of all, it was Colonel Betancourt's call. Secondly, you are still green. You can't just expect to be given Captain's status so quickly. Besides, you used coercion on Major Lewis to obtain it."

"Pete, I saw everyone die in Xcaret. I thought you were dead. Where the hell were you when I was running for my life?" The other men started to hear Carl's voice gradually elevating and were beginning to clear out. "Where were you when I had to kill those monsters all by myself? Where were you when Lorenzo and Lockwood were ready to feed me to the drones?"

"I did my best to keep you safe. It wasn't like I was on goddamned holiday, Carl. I was taken by the Navajas. They wanted to coerce me into teaching them how to use the drones. They showed me a video of you and some drone in a wedding dress…Jesus, Carl. You heard the story."

Carl shook his head. "Just because you're my older brother, does not mean that you are best at everything, Pete. I lead those drones into Tora Bora in a way only I could. We cleared the mountains. Maximum penetration. It had never been done before. Because of me, the attacks on our soil have stopped."

Peter put up his hands in exasperation. "But that's exactly it, Carl. It's not about *you*. It's what's best for your country. You have to take ego out of it."

Carl stood up and faced away from Peter. "Oh, this is rich, considering you have an ego the size of Texas. You always say you're looking out for me, but you want to control me. For shit's sake, you have a kill switch to take me out if I get too uppity."

"Carl, that's not what it's for, and I never asked for it."

"No, you never asked for any of this, right? But I don't see you complaining either."

Peter stepped closer to Carl and put his hand on his shoulder. "Think of the men. You aren't ready to lead yet. You completed the mission in Afghanistan, but then you made that broadcast. Why, Carl? You had to have known you'd get into trouble. You were never authorized—"

"Given the situation, I didn't need Lewis' authorization," Carl said defiantly.

"Do you think that this was all between you and Lewis? There are other people in this great big army. You, I, we are all blunt instruments, and our job is to carry out our orders. I heard about your little arrangement with Lewis. You did the best given the situation.

Lewis was rotten. Because of him, many good men were sacrificed to the Navajas." He thought of his best friend Delroy Apone.

Carl turned around to face Peter and chortled, "Arrangement you say. That man was dangerous, Pete. The only way I could keep him at bay was with my control of the drones. Hell, it was the only way I got Afghanistan green lighted…and in the end, it was the only way to get rid of Lewis."

"I know, Carl. That whole scenario was wrong. Now, Betancourt is trying to re-establish proper order. You served as leader when you were needed; now, it's time to step down. It's not about you or me or me being your big brother or my enormous ego. We have a job to do. I need your gift, Carl. Your country needs your gift."

"It doesn't feel much like a gift. I have the army poking at me like some kind of lab experiment."

"It's keeping you alive, isn't it?" Peter pointed out.

"And your kill switch?"

Peter looked down at the floor. "I have no intention of using it. But you need to show Betancourt that you are stable, Carl. You have to keep your temper in check, follow orders."

"Why do I feel like the enemy, Pete?"

"You're not the enemy. The brass is just not sure what to make of you and your emerging abilities. No one does. But if you start losing your shit in front of the men and start making people nervous, it may be back to Gitmo for you…or worse."

"Why the hell would they give *you* the kill switch anyway?" Carl asked. "You're my big brother. Doesn't that serve as a conflict of interest or something?"

Peter had already thought of this. "They want me committed to keeping you functional. They don't want you dead, Carl."

"I think that the late Major Lewis would disagree with that statement."

"Major Lewis was a traitor, Carl. So were Lorenzo and Lockwood. The country is a hot mess. Morale is low, but I think Betancourt is a good man."

"I hope you're right, Pete."

"Now I am asking you, as my sergeant, to go round up the men. We have to train for border patrol, and we go online in less than 48 hours."

"Yes, sir."

Carl went off to round up the men. Peter was definitely concerned about his brother's stability. The transmission out of Tora Bora was a definite lapse in judgment. Carl possessed great power but lacked the judgment that came from experience, and Peter was afraid it would corrupt him if left unchecked. The brass must've felt this way too, hence Carl's demotion.

Truthfully, Peter understood Carl's resentment. He had survived a botched mission in Xcaret. He saw his whole unit murdered by malfunctioning drones and the Navajas. By process of elimination, he had become captain. However, Peter had returned, which precluded Carl's promotion. In fact, Carl's resentment at his demotion registered as disappointment in Peter's survival. Peter felt a little stung by this, but he knew that wasn't how Carl meant it or how he really felt.

Peter knew he'd have to keep him in line. Disciplined. The world was watching them. Hell, their own country was divided regarding the Infantry Drone Program. He had to run a tight operation, or the consequences would be dire for everyone involved.

Chapter 5

When they reached the airfield, several members of the press were waiting, digi-cams and media multi-taskers in hand. Peter saw one reporter wearing a Fox News logo, another wearing CNN. There were a few local stations represented.

They began to stir as Peter marched forward with his company in ranks behind him.

"Company halt," Carl barked.

The company halted in organized rows. The reporters were taking video and still photos of the soldiers in the curiously sci-fi looking uniforms and masks concealing their faces. Peter knew they were trying to figure out which was the Automaton.

"Company, atten-tion," Carl barked. He found it amusing that he now served as Peter's mouthpiece. Everyone stood at attention.

Lieutenant Farrow was standing next to Kettle and Peter. Peter began, "As you know, our objective is now to patrol the border with Mexico." He looked directly at the reporters. "Strictly defensive." He looked back at his unit. "Lieutenant Farrow has been kind enough to whip up a few more toys to help us accomplish this. Every squad will now have a spotter who will be equipped with a precision rifle. This rifle will contain rounds that serve as tags."

Peter picked up the rifle. "Your job will be to identify targets and tag them. This will, in turn, draw the infantry drones to the signal emitted by the tag. The infantry drones will pursue until the targets are apprehended. Casualties will be avoided when possible. The Sweepers will be roving, radar mounted on jeeps to provide remote surveillance." He nodded to Carl.

"Company, break into squads," Carl barked.

Seven squads of ten were formed. Spotters were assigned and equipped with said rifles and tags. Each squad leader was equipped with an amygdala inhibitor kill switch for their fifty infantry drones.

The drones were stored in crates, sitting ominously off to the right of the men. The reporters had not yet taken notice of them.

Peter turned to the reporters. "In this exercise, we are going to simulate border patrol and practice tagging bogies. Once tagged, we will coordinate the pursuit of the infantry drones."

At their mention, the reporters stirred excitedly. This was going to be the first time they saw them up close. This was the first time any civilians were going to see them up close…and live to tell the tale.

Peter continued, "The targets are out there on the outer perimeter of the airfield." He gestured with his hand. There was some murmuring from the reporters about the pigs being positioned on the far side of the airfield.

Peter nodded to Kettle, who disengaged the digi-locks on the three large shipping crates and stepped away cautiously. The reporters were looking at the crates with morbid anticipation.

As the first drones stumbled out, dogs ran up along each side of the crates and funneled the undead out into the airfield. Each squad of human soldiers ran up alongside its cluster of drones. The reporters gasped at the sight of the undead.

Perhaps the reporters expected some kind of android or robot. To their shock and horror, there marched the drones in all of their putrescent glory. Their decomposition was largely camouflaged by their own futuristic looking black suits, but their shambling, hissing, and clouded eyes gave them away.

They weren't mechanical…at least not in the inorganic sense. No wires, no motors. Just shuffling bodies moaning with what could only be interpreted as feral hunger.

Kettle blew a whistle and the dogs began to fan the squads out. He then raised a Sweeper in the distance operating radar mounted on the back of a jeep. "How's the picture?"

A voice answered back on his mini-com, *"Crystal clear, sir. I'm registering a dozen bogies. The drones are closing in."*

The undead staggered across the airfield at a staccato but steady clip. The pigs in the distance had no idea what was coming for them.

Peter spoke into his mini-com, "Cronos, start to tag the targets."

"Yes, sir."

Peter now spoke to the reporters. "And now our Spotter will begin to tag the targets so that when the drones close in and they begin to run, the drones will be able to track their movements."

Cronos raised his sniper rifle, rested it in in the crook of his shoulder, and located the pigs in his scope. He made adjustments for distance, wind speed, and direction. Then he fired the first tag.

He nailed the pig right in its rump, and it jumped and took off. The other pigs shifted about uneasily, alarmed by their compatriot's flight. When Cronos tagged another, and then another, they all began to scatter like greased hogs at a rodeo.

"Tags deployed," Cronos informed Peter.

The Sweeper in the jeep began to coordinate the movement of the squads to engage the bogies. The reporters were pointing and whispering as they saw the dogs begin to fan the drones out across the width of the airfield by squad.

Then, coming within range of the tags, the undead began to pursue the bogies in a self-directed fashion. The pigs ran, and the drones followed. A pig would stop to rest, the drones would catch up, and the pig would begin to run again.

"This is the advantage of our drones," Peter said to the reporters. "Unlike their targets, they never tire, they never lose focus, and they never give up."

There were gasps from the reporters as it became evident, even from a distance, the pigs were beginning to tire. The squads of undead were closing in on them in their relentless pursuit.

Peter spoke into his mini-com, "Squads, ready your AI kill switches." Then he turned to the reporters. "Each squad leader is equipped with a kill switch that will deactivate the drones."

One squad of undead began to reach out for its exhausted prey. "Tango squad, hit it." Suddenly the drones in that squad became perfectly motionless. No twitching, no chest heaving from breathing. They looked like statues. The reporters began to stir as they instructed their cameramen to zoom in.

Another squad of undead ran down another pig. "Alpha squad, hit it." And just like Tango squad, the drones became motionless.

One-by-one, as each pig was caught, the infantry drones were immobilized, the terrified pig caged in the outstretched arms of the undead.

Peter spoke into his mini-com, "Sweeper, scan for casualties."

There was a brief pause. *"Zero casualties, sir."*

Peter was relieved. The training exercise had gone off as planned. None of the pigs was harmed. It was a successful demonstration of the non-lethal force of the infantry drones.

He turned to the reporters, "As you can see, all of the targets were apprehended, and there were zero casualties."

The reporters were dumbfounded. They were apparently in awe of what they just saw. Then one of them began to point. It was the reporter from CNN. He looked horrified. "Look!" The others began to panic. Peter heard shrieks from behind him.

Confused, Peter turned to look at the airfield. The drones of Delta squad were tearing its captive pigs to pieces.

"Delta squad, report."

"The AI switch is malfunctioning, sir. The drones are mobile."

Then one-by-one, the undead from each squad began to move and rip its hog to pieces. The screams of the mortified pigs filled the airfield, and within each cluster of drones, there was a frenzy of blood and guts.

Peter was barking commands into his mini-com.

"Alpha squad, engage kill switch."

"Negative, sir."

"Delta squad, engage…"

"Negative, sir. The drones are autonomous."

The whole exercise was falling apart in front of him, and he was powerless to do anything about it. The reporters were shooting everything. It was a disaster.

Then Peter turned and glared at Carl. "Make them stop. NOW."

Carl stood there looking at his big brother. If Peter wasn't mistaken, he would have sworn Carl was smiling under his mask. He appeared to be looking off to the left, but no one was there.

"NOW, Sergeant."

Just like that, the drones ceased their frenzy. They were statues once again.

The reporters were going wild, blurting out questions.

"Is that what the drones are designed to do?"

"What *are* these drones, Captain?"

"Is that what's going to happen to illegal border crossers?"

"That soldier you ordered to stop them, is that the Automaton?"

"How does the Automaton control the drones?"

"Who controls the Automaton?"

"The exercise is over," Peter announced to the reporters. "No questions at this time."

Peter had Carl round up the men and the drones were being directed back towards their respective shipping crates as MP's escorted the reporters off the airfield. They were shouting protests as they were driven off.

***

At home, Barry Birdsall was watching Channel 8. The young female reporter was shouting into her microphone as she was being jostled off the airfield.

"You saw it yourself, the drones mauling their targets…blood everywhere…there must have been some kind of technical difficulty…the soldier, who must have been none other than the Automaton, was instructed to stop the murderous assault of the infantry drones."

He sat there dumbfounded in his recliner, wondering how it all could have gone so wrong so quickly. He wondered why Carl had allowed it to go so far without stopping it sooner.

Channel 8 cut to anchors, Mark Wasserman and Lisa Gorton.

"There apparently was some kind of accident on the airfield. The drones weren't supposed to attack the targets," Wasserman pointed out.

"It makes you wonder if the program is ready to be used on the border," Gorton speculated. *"From the looks of it, the answer appears to be NO."*

"Imagine if those poor pigs had been actual border crossers, Lisa."

Lisa pantomimed a shudder, *"I don't want to, Mark."*

Barry began to flip through the channels. CNN had captions flashing at the bottom of the screen:
BORDER DRONES: DEFENSE OR OFFENSE
POTENTIAL HUMAN RIGHTS VIOLATION?

The pundit, Rand Hubel, was commenting on the spectacle, *"Just moments ago, an army training exercise at the Fort Bliss Airfield in Texas showcasing the infantry drones went horribly wrong, the targets being mutilated. One must ask the question: Are these drones safe?*

"There were rumors about drones going rogue in Xcaret, Mexico, but the reports are unsubstantiated. The soldier, whose identity remains a secret, dubbed the Man from Tora Bora, ended this catastrophe. But it is unclear how he did it.

"There was apparently a malfunctioning of an electronic restraint that activates and deactivates the drones. This Man from Tora Bora was apparently ordered to stop the drones, and he did. We go to our panel composed of Gary Hauser, our senior military correspondent..." an older, slightly pudgy, grey-haired man appeared on screen, *"...Senator Michaels of Massachusetts, who is opposed to the House of Representatives Oversight Committee's conclusions to allow the Infantry Drone Program to continue..."* a tall, thin man with slicked back hair appeared on screen, *"...and human rights expert, Dr. Roman Spencer from Harvard University,"* a tall, bald, professorial black man with glasses appeared on screen.

"Senator Michaels, let's begin with you. Is this what you expected from the Infantry Drone Program?"

"Yes, Rand, this is exactly what I expected. Given all of the technology at the army's disposal, there is no way that these undead drones can be controlled properly. They don't think, they have no judgment, and they are driven by pure instinct."

"But, to play devil's advocate, isn't that the nature of a drone, Senator?" Rand asked.

"*Drones have traditionally been mechanical, smart weapons over which we exercise complete control,*" Michaels explained. "*These are some kind of necro-mechanical drones that are guided by dogs and handlers. They were designed to infiltrate cave systems, not patrol a border.*"

"*But our traditional airborne drones are designed to use lethal force, which would make them inappropriate for border patrol,*" Rand pointed out.

"*Well, as we just saw, I think that these infantry drones are quite lethal as well. They were intended to be boots on the ground, but I don't think the mutilation of border crossers was a part of the plan,*" Michaels added.

Rand turned to Spencer, "*Which brings us to an interesting human rights question, Dr. Spencer: Is it a human rights violation to use deadly force on border crossers?*"

"*Absolutely,*" Spencer declared. "*These are mostly people who are leaving behind their birthplace, their homes, to sacrifice all to find a better life in this country. They don't deserve to be torn to shreds like that.*"

"*But some would argue that some of these border crossers are Mexican drug cartel or terrorists masquerading as Mexican emigrants,*" Rand said.

"*Absolutely,*" Spencer retorted, "*but does that justify tearing apart every border crosser to catch the one or two criminals in every ten or twenty? I think not. Besides, there is a thing in this country called due process.*"

"*This raises another interesting question,*" added Rand. "*Are we empowering our military to be judge, jury, and executioner in addressing these border crossers? Does every border crosser face a brutal death sentence if caught?*" He turned to Hauser, "*Gary, is this the proper use of our infantry drones?*"

"*This was obviously a program designed for offense,*" Gary said. "*After the UN Security Council threatened sanctions, we shifted to defense. But are we trying to force square pegs into round holes?*"

"*So the question is,*" Rand added, "*why wasn't this program dismantled? Why are the President and our military determined to make use of these infantry drones?*"

"*Perhaps a great deal of money was invested into this technology,*" Gary posited. "*An awful lot of necro-mechanical research went into the development of this technology, and we don't fully understand its potential yet. Supporters of this technology will tout how it is saving the lives of countless U.S. soldiers. But what about the lives of border crossers?*"

Spencer jumped in. *"Exactly. Most of these border crossers are tradesman—tile workers, builders—who are looking for opportunity in this country. They are not terrorists. Yet, we are willing to slaughter them like animals. I definitely think there is a xenophobic undercurrent to this program that frankly is un-American."*

"What about this Man from Tora Bora we keep hearing about?" Rand asked. *"He somehow controls these drones. Is this too much power in the hands of one man? What is the mechanism that we aren't seeing?"*

Barry switched to Fox News. There was a panel already under way.

"Illegal border crossers represent a major threat to national security," said a very polished looking middle-aged woman with a retro 2017-esque hairdo.

"Are you saying that border crossers deserve to be met with lethal force?" asked the host, Efram Peabody.

"I am saying that maybe these drones will serve as a powerful deterrent to those considering entering our country illegally."

"That's preposterous," blurted a Latino man, who must have been the token Democrat on the panel. *"The punishment doesn't fit the crime."*

"Well, nothing else seems to be deterring these illegal immigrants," said a portly man with glasses. *"Our government refuses to build a wall. So what else are we left with? Besides, we tried to put cameras on the border fence, but they were shot to pieces. Should we place live soldiers on the ground to be shot at, too?"*

"These people want to get in because America is still the greatest country in the world," said the woman with the retro do. *"And they want to take advantage of all of our entitlements. Welfare, food stamps, Medicaid. Why wouldn't they want to come? Our government insists on expanding entitlements. It's like a magnet to these people. And now you have the President using this infantry drone unit to try to make us think he's trying to do something about illegal immigrants."*

"Oh, come on," said the Latino man, *"I thought you were all for these drones."*

"I am all for fewer entitlements," retorted the woman, *"but since our government doesn't want to do that, yes, I'm for these drones. Enough half-measures. Something needs to be done."*

"So placing man eating zombies along the border is the answer," challenged the Latino man. *"You are a Christian woman. How do you reconcile using such atrocities? It's unnatural."*

She leaned forward in her seat, *"Placing live soldiers—our sons and daughters, brothers and sisters—on the border to be shot at is unnatural."*

"There is no question," added the portly man with glasses, *"that these infantry drones save lives."*

"Where do these drones come from?" demanded the Latino man. *"Notice how the military is so hush-hush about that little detail."*

"What are you suggesting?" Efram accused more than asked. *"That the government is harvesting innocents to create these drones?"*

"Perhaps I am. The point is, we don't know, and the military isn't being forthcoming."

"Carlos brings up a good point," said Efram, glossing over the man's implication. *"Are these drones unnatural? How do religious groups feel about using the undead?"*

Pie charts started to appear on the screen.

"Although 85% of those who identify themselves as Christians do not agree with the technology of using undead," Efram continued, *"92% think it is necessary to combat enemies of the United States, 98% of those who identify as Jews disagree with the technology, but 66% think it is necessary; 99% of those who identify as Muslim disagree with the technology, and only 3% see its utility."*

"That's probably because of the heavily radical Muslim influence in the Order for International Liberation," the portly man with glasses speculated.

"Good point, Pat," said Efram. Mr. Birdsall then recognized Pat as Pat Endicott, Conservative radio host.

"Or maybe," interjected Carlos, *"Muslim groups tend to be the targets of these infantry drones."*

"Don't be ridiculous," spat the woman. *"Cartels and OIL have been the targets of these drones. The cartels are Mexican, and OIL is a diversified group of terrorists. But the fact that there is a heavy radical Muslim influence speaks volumes."*

"And what of this Man from Tora Bora?" asked Efram, changing the topic. *"Patriot or pariah?"*

"The Automaton? Oh, I think he's a hero," said the woman. *"A true patriot protecting our interests. I don't care how he does it."*

"How can you not care how he does it?" asked Carlos in disbelief. *"Talk about unnatural. They say he can communicate with the undead."*

"Carlos brings up a good point," said Efram. *"How does he do it? Some in the media are painting him to be some kind of freak."*

"Maybe he's God's answer to all of the chaos in our great land," said the woman. *"The economy's in the toilet, unemployment is through the roof, our enemies grow stronger every day...this Automaton is someone with a gift to help us, someone we can all get behind."*

"A gift?" Carlos said with exasperation. *"You call communicating with the dead a gift from God?"*

"Jesus Christ raised Lazarus from the dead," she retorted.

"Yeah, but Lazarus didn't then go around eating people," Carlos chided. *"Is this woman for real?"*

"The point is," said Pat Enicott, *"since this Automaton came on the scene, the attacks on U.S. soil have stopped. He had our enemies watching their own backs. However, with the UN Security Council's resolution, our enemies will only be emboldened. Our hands are tied. Now the Liberals want to tie our hands with border defense. Why don't we just open up our borders and let everyone in to destroy our country?"*

Barry switched to the Celebrity Channel. Docutainment Now! was on.

"Who is this Automaton, the latest sex symbol to hit our military?" asked a young woman in a scanty outfit. *"Women want to know."*

He turned off the television and sat there in silence, catching his breath. What can of worms had Carl opened? He was anything from a hero to an abomination to a sex symbol. The country was going mad, and Carl was stoking the flames.

The truth was Barry was worried for Carl's safety. Not just from terrorists, but from the media and his own government. The already polarized country had become even more divided. Although OIL attacks had ceased, there were riots breaking out over the country. The unemployed were stuck on welfare, the middle class were being taxed into oblivion, and people were losing their homes...

Barry was wondering what was preventing the government from using the drones on its own citizenry. It was a time of great civil unrest. Alaska and Texas were filled with Separatists, and the specter of revolution loomed on the horizon. He didn't want to think what would happen if the drones were used to restore order.

The President was issuing one executive order after another, skirting Congress for the supposed greater good. This was a man who was willing to use a strong hand in uncertain times.

Since Carl's scourge in Tora Bora, things have gotten out of hand. Barry wondered how Carl was doing, and if Peter was looking after his brother.

***

Peter slammed Carl into his locker, "Are you out of your frakking mind?"

Carl's back caved in the locker behind him, but he appeared unfazed…amused even.

"Oh, come on, Pete. I was giving them good television, showing them what the infantry drones can do."

"What you did was make it appear that we weren't in control," Peter scolded. "Someone could've gotten hurt."

"By the way, who was the weird reporter off to the side by himself?" Carl asked.

Peter was startled by the question. "I didn't see a reporter off to the side by himself, Carl."

Carl looked sheepish. "No one was going to get hurt…besides the pigs that is."

Peter went nose to nose with his little brother. "It's not funny, Carl. Betancourt is going to have our asses for this. We made the President look like a fool."

"The President is a fool, Pete."

"Don't talk like that," Peter pointed an admonishing finger.

"Oh, come on," Carl said. "The country's a mess. He's a weak President, and the world is laughing at us."

"And now they're afraid of us, Carl. If they become afraid enough, we are going to have problems."

"What, the UN?" Carl snickered. "They're a bunch of pansies. They don't give a shit about America."

"Carl, we are soldiers. It is not our place to make policy. We carry it out, even if we personally disagree with it."

"So we're just blunt instruments, is that it?"

"Yes," Peter shouted, "it's the way it's always been. It's what you signed on for when you enlisted, like it or not. You've become drunk with power. Just because you ran all over Major Lewis, doesn't mean that you are above the chain of command. Just because you are all over the news and Docutainment Now! doesn't mean you are a celebrity. You are a soldier."

Carl smirked. "Oh, come on, big brother. Are you sure you aren't jealous? Now I'm the popular one, and it's burning your ass. I'm stronger now and you can't handle it."

"It's not about that, Carl. I know you had it rough growing up."

"Rough, Pete? I was beaten up and ridiculed most of my childhood, and where was my big brother? You were too busy with your friends."

Peter, frustrated, ran his hands through his hair. "That's not what this is about, Carl. The army isn't a place to resolve your childhood conflicts, and it's certainly not a place for ego. If you have issues, you need to discuss it with the shrink."

"That asshole? You've got to be kidding."

Peter was about to retort when Kettle barged in.

"What is it, Nolan?"

"Betancourt wants us to report to his office. He's mighty pissed, sir."

Peter stood there glaring at Carl, his mind racing. "Okay, let's go gentlemen. Time to face the music."

Kettle left the locker room. As Carl passed Peter, Peter put out his arm to stop him. "This isn't over."

"Let's not keep the Colonel waiting, Pete."

Peter removed his arm and let Carl pass. He didn't know what got into Carl, but he was scared. Carl was behaving recklessly. He was losing his discipline, and Betancourt had Peter's finger over Carl's kill switch.

He knew Carl had issues. He was the nerd who was always picked on, but he kept his nose in the books through it all with the promise of success. That promise went unfulfilled when he dropped out of college, and his dreams of becoming an engineer were on hold.

Then there was Xcaret. Peter knew what it was like to lose your entire unit. He wondered if Carl had become unhinged from his traumatic experience. Then there were these abilities. Peter cursed them.

Why had Carl been singled out? Peter didn't see these abilities as gifts. They were eating away at his brother, changing him. He was becoming more powerful, and the only check and balance was the kill chip in his skull.

Peter followed behind his brother and dreaded what Betancourt was going to say. They screwed up big time, and Carl's life was up for grabs and he didn't even seem to care.

***

"Goddammit, what in the hell were you thinking?" Betancourt boomed sitting forward in his chair behind his desk.

Peter looked at Carl. "There was a…miscommunication, sir."

61

"A miscommunication, Captain? Please, enlighten me. What was the nature of this miscommunication?"

Peter cleared his throat and prayed Carl would behave himself. "Sergeant Birdsall thought that we were supposed to demonstrate the drones' full capability, sir."

"Oh he did, did he? By tearing live hogs apart in front of reporters?"

"Yes, sir, apparently."

"And did you issue that order or elaborate such instructions before the training exercise, Captain?"

"No, I didn't, sir."

"And *you*," turning to Carl, "what in the hell were you thinking, having those drones attack the pigs?"

Peter held his breath awaiting Carl's response.

"Sir, I was operating under the assumption—"

"I'm sorry, son, under the what?"

"The assumption—"

"Sergeant, we don't *assume* in the army."

"Yes, sir."

"We follow orders. Did Captain Birdsall order you to override the AI kill switches and have the drones attack the pigs?"

"No, sir. He didn't."

"Did he make it clear that, during the training exercise, you were to simulate apprehending targets without casualty?"

"Yes, sir. He did."

"Then at what point," Betancourt's voice began to rise and his face turned purple, "did you think it was a good idea to put on a horror show for the press? You, of all people, who helped fight to make this program what it is today."

Peter bit his lip. Carl looked the Colonel in the eye, "I guess I wasn't thinking, sir."

"Oh, you were thinking all right, Sergeant, but you aren't paid to think. Thinking is above your pay grade."

"Yes, sir."

"Don't interrupt me, goddammit. You are a soldier. You are paid to follow orders without thinking. Am I clear?"

"Yes, sir."

"One more stunt like this and you're getting a one-way ticket back to Gitmo. Don't forget that I have my finger poised over *your* kill switch."

"Yes, sir."

"One week in solitary should remind you of what your priorities are. You can think all you want there. Get it out of your system."

After Betancourt said that, he pressed a button on his desk and two MP's came in. "Any trouble out of you and I'll press that button without hesitation, am I clear?"

"Crystal, sir."

One of the MP's gestured for Carl to stand up, and he did. They shackled his hands and feet. Carl found it amusing since the threat was not from his limbs but his mind, but he played along.

They marched him out of Betancourt's office. Peter and Nolan looked at each other nervously.

"Had to be done," Betancourt declared. "He's undisciplined and he's dangerous. We need to keep him focused…we wouldn't want to have to pull the trigger…" He let those words hang out there in space like the threat it was intended to be.

"Yes, sir. I understand," answered Peter. However, the truth of the matter was that he didn't understand. He didn't understand any of this. He didn't understand what was happening to his little brother. He didn't understand what the brass was doing with him.

He didn't understand why Fiona wasn't there. Of all the times she was needed…

"You go operational as scheduled with or without Sergeant Birdsall. Understood?" demanded Betancourt.

"Yes, sir."

"Dismissed."

***

Carl sat in his ten-by-ten cinder block cell alone with his thoughts. After his mother was murdered in the explosion at the mall and then he lost his entire unit in Xcaret, it was if he had suddenly developed a kind of clinical detachment, as if his feelings had been boxed up and shoved into the back of his consciousness to collect dust. It was what got him through the fiasco at Xcaret.

However, now emotion came in waves, lapping at the shores of his sanity, eroding it slowly. He wasn't sure what he was supposed to do. He didn't know what his purpose was.

He wasn't destined to graduate college or work as an engineer. His whole life he had been an outsider, the underdog, and now when he thought he had finally found purpose, that he was doing good for the world, his own government treated him like a recalcitrant child.

He thought he deserved some recognition. He survived treasonous agents from within the military, he survived the Navajas cartel, and he hunted OIL. He thought of his brother, who had his share of suffering and survivor's guilt. He, too, was a hero.

However, Carl knew that he could do things his brother couldn't even imagine. He was getting faster and stronger every day. He could coordinate the drones better than the shepherding dogs or radio signal tags ever could. He had OIL on the run.

Yet, here he sat with a kill chip in his head, the thanks he got for a job well done. To add insult to injury, he had to report to his older...weaker brother, because he was still "green." He killed more terrorists in Tora Bora than a whole squad of Seal Team 6. They couldn't have achieved maximum penetration of the cave system. No one could have.

He knew that the only thing keeping him from being locked away permanently, or worse, was all of the media attention. He supposed he had the President to thank for that. After the successful operation in Tora Bora and the attacks on U.S. soil ceased, it would be a tough case to persecute the Automaton.

Yet he knew that Betancourt and Peter were right about his lack of discipline. He couldn't explain it, nor could he help it. The broadcast from Tora Bora, how he had the drones attack the pigs in front of the reporters, his snarky attitude...it was like he was an unruly teenager with raging hormones that at times made him irrational.

Ironically, when Carl was a teenager, he was a model son and student. He didn't have any angst or rebellion in him. He always did what he was supposed to...what was expected of him.

Now he was departing from what was expected of him. Hell, he didn't know what to expect of himself. This was all new to him, and the army was treating him as if he was some kind of science experiment.

Once again, rationality gave way to rage in short order, and he punched the cinder block wall of his cell. Pain radiated from his knuckles up his arm, and the feeling synergized with the fury in his brain.

He held up his hand to the light and saw that his hand was busted. His fingers were beginning to swell, and some of them were dislocated at the knuckle, jutting out at odd angles. Panic began to wash over him at what he had done, and he stifled a scream.

He gingerly took his dislocated index finger between his index finger and thumb of his other hand and began to pull it back into place. The pain was sharp and the feeling of the finger shifting back into location peculiar and unnerving. It slid back into place.

He felt the pulse of his blood vessels in his hand and wrist. At first, he thought it was the throbbing of pain, but then he realized it was something else...something more. He could sense his own rhythm...feel it, like he never could before.

Curious, he began to pull his other fingers back into place one-by-one, swallowing the pain in the back of his throat. When all of his digits were back in place, the swelling in his hand went down. It wasn't possible, but then again, none of his other "abilities" were possible either.

He wondered why all of this was happening to him. It was as if his body had a mind of its own, and he was along for the ride. Was he sick? Was this some kind of rare illness? The tumor couldn't have anything to do with his joints.

Just as the rage and fury came on, it receded almost as quickly, leaving him with that clinical detachment he had become familiar with. He sensed the guards down the hall from his cell. He felt their electrical activity...neurons firing in sequence, exciting some while inhibiting others. Their heartbeats were like the rhythm of a primitive beat, a tribal drum.

He couldn't help but view them as weak...almost insects, unaware of his detection like prey unaware of a lurking predator. It was then that he realized that his humanity was slipping away from him. He was becoming something other than human...more even. It was a feeling he had that he could not articulate, as if a sentiment had been downloaded into his mind from a remote collective unconscious.

He lay back on his bunk and closed his eyes, the rhythm of the guards lulling him to sleep. Their presence was comforting from his being in tune with their vitals...from the heightened awareness of everything around him. He felt plugged into his surroundings, and the stimulation was soothing.

That night he dreamed that he was running down streets, his undead guard around him. He hacked, slashed, leapt, pounced, and shot. Bodies fell all around him. He felt pulses cease as the undead took to their grisly task of consuming lives.

The feeling was exhilarating, all set to that tribal backbeat. He ended lives as if it was second nature to him. His bloodlust raging, the killing was like sex. In his dreams, he knew his purpose, and it gave him power. He was the harbinger of death, the bringer of doom to his enemies, a general of an undead army...

...a pathfinder.

Part II
Metamorphosis

Chapter 6

Mexican Border
Nogales, Arizona
22:14 HRS

It was a brisk, clear night. The sky had transitioned from deep purple and red at the horizon to pitch black up above. Peter's Alpha Squad clung to the chain link fence reinforced with corrugated tin at the bottom, the only membrane between Nogales, Mexico and Nogales, Arizona.

The drones shuffled in almost single file in the dry dirt. Cronos followed behind, carrying his sniper rifle with night vision scope loaded with tags. Peter looked at the crudely fashioned crucifixes affixed to the border fence as he picked up his mini-com.

"Sweeper One, any activity?"

After a brief pause, there was an answer. *"Negative. No activity in your sector."*

This was the job. It was slow…painfully slow at times. When their unit first began border patrol, they caught dozens of jumpers a night. Then, as word got back that the United States had undead patrolling the border from the few that narrowly escaped, things began to slow down. Either that or the jumpers got sneakier. Peter figured the latter.

There was a big business in Nogales, Arizona and the neighboring town of Patagonia for "coyotes," those who harbored border jumpers. Both were sleepy towns with small one and two-story buildings that looked innocent enough, and that was the point. There were safe houses, guides who exploited gaps in the fence, and those who provided counterfeit documentation.

The United States was as much at war with these coyotes as they were with the jumpers. What made matters worse was that these coyotes on the American side were supporting drug smugglers, gunrunners, and terrorists. The jumpers weren't all immigrants looking for a better life.

"Delta Squad Leader, report." Peter waited for Kettle's response.

"Delta Squad Leader reporting. All quiet on the Western Front."

Peter smirked at Nolan's movie reference. He liked Nolan. He was a wise ass, but a good soldier and a natural leader. He had a way with the men that almost made them forget that they were herding zombies, or at least laugh about it.

Delta Squad was roving somewhere in Nogales. There were mostly factories on the American side of the fence in Nogales, and it was usually quiet.

The Mexican Nogales, on the other hand, was a hotbed of illegal activity, which is why he stationed two roving squads there. Speaking of which, it was time to raise Carl on the mini-com.

"Beta Squad Leader, report."

"Beta Squad Leader reporting. No activity in our sector. Sweeper gave the all clear."

"Roger that." Peter kept Carl on a tight leash. His little brother had calmed down significantly after his stint in solitary. He dropped the attitude and followed orders to the nine, which pleased Colonel Betancourt. It also kept Peter's finger off the kill switch for the moment, for which he was also grateful.

He sensed something different about Carl…something that made him uneasy. It was as if he went from very arrogant and unruly to very compliant, quiet even. Peter recalled that saying about still waters running deep.

Carl had apprehended the most jumpers out of any squad, many of which were OTM's (Other Than Mexicans)—al-Qaeda, Hezbollah, etc. His squad was a well-oiled machine and a tribute to the program. It was good press for the President, and therefore, good for the program.

Of course, Carl had the distinct advantage of being able to communicate with the drones. He was faster and stronger than any of the other soldiers or border jumpers, and his senses were beyond acute. He often spotted jumpers and apprehended them before his Sweeper could spot them with the radar.

Peter was proud of his brother, who appeared to have a new perspective on his role. Carl no longer seemed to care one way or another about the media. Monster, hero—it made no difference to him. He appeared to have a renewed focus on their mission.

Carl was strolling with his unit of undead shambling in the desert. He enjoyed the cool, winter air. It was crisp and electric. He sensed the unique rhythm of his undead entourage and then that of his live assistant, Private Mackler.

He snorted at the crucifixes lining the American side of the border fence. Peter said that it was to protect the jumpers, but Carl knew better. It was to keep the undead out.

Carl sensed the buildings on the other side of the horizontally mounted corrugated tin panels. They were squat, spaced far apart, and dilapidated. Once in a while, he sensed a small animal scurrying, a night predator. Once he even sensed a man, but the man was moving in the opposite direction of the border fence.

He came upon a small house in poor repair a distance away from the border fence. He sensed dozens of people in the house, feeling their numerous rhythms in a symphony of vibration. He halted his squad to get a better feel.

"What is it, sir?" Mackler asked.

"There's a small house about 200 feet away from the fence with a lot of activity in it," Carl responded coolly.

Mackler wasn't with the unit long, and he was unaccustomed to Carl's…talent. He raised his rifle. "Are they moving towards the fence, sir?"

Carl put his hand up to silence Mackler. "Sweeper two, report."

"No activity in your sector, sir."

"He can't detect it," Carl said thinking out loud. Carl hesitated for one last feel of the house and then decided to command the drones to continue.

Then he felt it. They were gone.

He halted the squad again.

"Sir?" Mackler looked confused.

"They're gone," Carl stated.

"They probably just left, sir."

"No, they just…disappeared," Carl corrected. "One minute they were there, the next they were not."

"Are they moving towards the fence?" Mackler asked again.

"No. I do not detect any movement whatsoever."

Mackler awaited Carl's next instruction.

"Wait here, Private."

"Sir?"

Carl turned to face the fence. "I'm going for a quick stroll."

Mackler looked uneasy. "With all due respect, sir, should we radio this in to the Captain?"

"I won't be but a moment," Carl said with his back to Mackler. Then he leapt up into the air and grabbed the top rim of the uppermost corrugated tin panel. It was an incredible jump.

Mackler looked on in utter disbelief. He had heard rumors of Carl's unreal physical prowess, but he still didn't believe it when he saw it.

Carl pulled himself up and hoisted himself over the top of the fence. He moved so deftly that he was up and over before any Mexican snipers could sight him.

He landed on the other side, his knees dislocating from the impact and quickly resetting, and he sprinted in an uneven line towards the dilapidated house.

The air was still and the night silent. He made it to the house quickly, and he breached the front door without raising his rifle. He trusted his senses, which told him that the house was empty.

Inside, the house was completely empty. There were cracked walls, holes in the walls and ceiling, and absolutely no furniture. Yet, he could see multiple sets of footprints in the dust on the wooden floor.

The floor creaked as he moved around the house, and he reached out with his senses around the outside searching for humans. There was nothing.

He picked up his mini-com. "Mackler, any activity on your side?"

"Negative, sir."

Carl put down his mini-com and thought. Something didn't add up. Those men just couldn't have disappeared into thin air.

"Sir?"

"Yes, Mackler. What is it?"

"The Sweeper detected you jumping over the fence and is inquiring as to what you are doing?"

Carl wasn't supposed to cross to the Mexican side. His jurisdiction ended at the fence, and any breach of jurisdiction could cause headaches for the State Department, who already had a tenuous relationship with the Mexican government.

"Tell, the Sweeper that I am investigating suspicious activity…"

"Sir, the Sweeper already informed the Captain."

"Carl, what in the hell are you doing?" It was Peter's voice.

"I'm investigating suspicious activity," Carl replied.

"On the Mexican side? You know full well that we cannot cross the border," Peter reprimanded.

"There was a shitload of activity in this house, and then they all just up and vanished," Carl explained.

"Maybe you're mistaken," Peter offered impatiently. However, Carl knew that Peter knew that this wasn't possible.

Carl was looking down at the floorboards when he saw it. There was a faint hairline gap in the shape of a rectangle in the floor. He reached down, found the edge of the panel with his gloved fingers, and he pushed. The panel popped up and he pulled it up all the way. A dark tunnel yawned just below the floor.

"Carl, get your ass back to American soil, pronto."

Carl lowered himself into the tunnel. "Yes, sir. Heading back now." The tunnel stretched out in the direction of the border fence. Carl knew it had to have gone way past the fence. There was nothing in close proximity on the other side to cover the exit point at the other end.

He raised his automatic assault rifle and peered down the tunnel. He mildly regretted the fact that he didn't have his undead tunnel rats with him.

"Mackler, look around. Do you see anything in the distance? A building, a garage, or a shack?"

There was a pause, as Mackler was likely scanning his surroundings.

"There's nothing around for miles, sir."

Carl stopped and thought a moment. If he were to cross the border underground in this tunnel, there was no knowing where he would resurface and when. No, this wasn't the right time. He had to get back across to the American side.

Carl hoisted himself back through the opening in the floorboards, gingerly closed the panel, and swept the dust on the ground with the palm of his hand.

He looked up and saw a dark shadow in the window. Someone was watching him from the outside. He flung open the door and burst out of the house. He looked around the outside, but there was no one there. The strange thing was that he hadn't sensed anyone.

He stalked the stretch of dirt and dust to the fence like a predator in the night air, undetectable. If there were snipers or sentinels, they were either asleep or unable to see his movements. Either way, it worked for him.

When he reached the fence, Carl scaled it in short order and startled Mackler when he landed with a dull thud on the other side.

"Sir?" Mackler said expectantly.

"There's a tunnel stretching out from that house I told you about under the fence," Carl said looking around. "I don't know where it goes, but a whole bunch of people just disappeared into it."

"Beta Squad Leader, report." It was Peter.

"I am back on U.S. soil, sir," Carl said into his mini-com.

"I want a full report at the rendezvous point, Sergeant."

"Yes, sir."

***

Miracle Valley Camp
08:17 HRS

"What were you doing, Carl? You know we're not supposed to cross the fence," said Peter disapprovingly, his voice echoing off the circular dome of the abandoned church. There were soldiers operating equipment along the walls. The brothers were seated in the few pews left in the middle of the room.

"There was this house, Pete. One minute there were a bunch of people, and then they vanished."

"Whatever happens on that side is none of our concern," interrupted Peter.

"I found a tunnel under the house," Carl continued patiently. "It looked like it stretched pretty far out onto our side of the fence. There was nothing for miles, so it must be a long tunnel."

Peter finished Carl's thought, "Not something immigrants or even coyotes would likely construct."

Carl shook his head. "No, this is something different. Drug runners, weapons smugglers."

"How did you get over the fence?"

"I climbed and jumped over."

"Right. Stupid question," Peter said sarcastically. "Well, there's really no way we can track where this tunnel leads. It can go anywhere, and searching basements from town to town will be a waste of time."

"I think we have some time," Carl said. "Whoever dug the tunnel doesn't know that we know about it, and after digging a tunnel like that, they're not just going to abandon it. But you're right about canvassing towns."

"There's the radar," Peter offered. "We can use it to track the tunnel and follow it on the jeep."

"I'm not sure if the radar can penetrate the ground," countered Carl.

"Let's see," said Peter. "Sergeant Harley!"

The Sweeper looked up from his instrument panel and walked briskly over to where Peter and Carl were seated. "Yes, sir."

"Can the radar be used to track movement under the ground?"

"Under the ground, sir?"

"Yes, Sergeant Birdsall discovered a tunnel stretching under the fence that runs deep into U.S. soil." Peter glared at Carl, "We don't have access to its start point because it's on the Mexican side."

"I suppose it's possible, sir. It depends how far under the ground."

"We'll have to try it," said Peter.

"I want a Spotter with me next time," Carl said.

"What are you talking about?" asked Peter. "You never needed one before. I thought you can direct the drones without using tags."

"I have an idea. Call it a backup plan." Peter looked at him expectantly for an explanation of this statement, so Carl explained. "The Spotter can be positioned at the fence, sighting the house."

"Carl, if you tag someone, I think they'll feel it."

"Not if we tag a piece of equipment, or a bag or something. Then the drones can follow the signal up top. If we use the radar mounted on the jeep, they will feel the jeep following them up above. A squad or two of drones travelling on foot travel lighter. They won't hear us."

"He's right," said Harley. "Even if the radar can penetrate the ground, they will hear the jeep following them and get spooked."

"I'm just not sure a Spotter can tag something from that far away and a piece of equipment no less. You are both assuming that we are going to get a clear shot at something like that."

"We can use Cronos," Carl said. "He's the best shot around."

"If we are going to do this, I want three squads in on it. Yours, Kettle's, and mine. If these are gunrunners, we may be in for a hell of a fight. One unit can carry provisions."

"Even better," Carl said, "we can strap provisions to the drones. I did it in Tora Bora. They never tire, and they're coming with us anyway."

Peter smiled at his brother. "Good idea, Carl. We'll need all of our men available for firepower. I have a feeling we're going to need it.

"We'll wait for Kettle to rendezvous here, which should take a day. Then we'll back track to Nogales to the coordinates that Carl provided. We'll stake out the house while having a squad pass by on patrol so that everything appears status quo on our side. Cronos will be on the fence and tag something. If by some miracle this works and they go under, we'll follow them to wherever they resurface."

"I can amplify the tag's signal," said Harley, "so it'll be easier to track underground."

"Excellent," said Peter. "Carl, ready the drones with our supplies. I'll send a report of our change of plans to Colonel Betancourt."

Everyone nodded.

"Dismissed."

Harley walked off to work on Cronos' tags. Carl stayed.

"Something on your mind, Carl?"

"Permission to speak freely, sir."

Peter smiled at Carl's formality and nodded.

"Do you really think it's wise to inform Betancourt of our every move?"

"Carl, he wants to be apprised of everything that we do. I'm just following orders."

"I don't trust him."

"Listen, he's no Major Lewis. I know that you're not his biggest fan since he had the kill chip implanted in your skull, but I believe he's honest. He's keeping a close eye on our operations and, given everything that's happened, I can understand why."

"What if he doesn't go for this, Pete? What if he wants us to continue our patrol with the original nav points?"

"He'll go for this, Carl. Something this big. This tunnel is bad news in a big way. It needs to be dealt with."

"There's only one problem," Carl said frowning.

"What's that?"

"What if he asks how we found the tunnel?"

Peter thought about this. Carl was right. If he told Betancourt that Carl hopped the fence, Carl would be in deep shit. "We'll tell him the radar picked up on the tunnel."

"But Harley said it might not be able to penetrate the ground," Carl retorted.

"Betancourt's no engineer. He'll believe it."

"I hope you're right, Pete."

"Your lack of faith is staggering," quipped Peter.

"Hey, you're not the one with the kill chip in your brain."

"Good point."

***

Carl was chasing a woman through the woods. He didn't know who she was or why he was pursuing her, but he knew she had to die.

He glided through the underbrush, dodging trees large and small by mere centimeters. At first, it felt as if he were moving at a velocity that exceeded his mind's ability to process his surroundings…like someone "out driving their headlights."

Yet, his body had the confidence in where it was in space to operate autonomously from his mind. His mind was focused on other, related things. He knew that the woman was tiring, because her pace was uneven and she would stumble every so often, and with increasing frequency. He felt her pulse like a drum beating in his soul, her panting like the steam engine that was his body.

He decided to close the gap. He began to leap into the air, like an astronaut hopping on the surface of the moon. He was glancing the forest floor, hurtling through time and space and, oddly, the sensation was familiar to him.

His pulse accelerated as he gained on her, her sobbing egging him on. He tasted her imminent death on his tongue, bittersweet as he reached out for her.

She stumbled and fell face first into the leaves. He stood over her imperiously, savoring the brief moment before he ceased her existence in the world, his bloodlust climaxing.

She turned around to face him, and he gazed down at none other than Captain Fiona London. He was filled with a chaotic ambivalence, torn between what must have been something like pity and a yearning for satiety.

She looked at his face knowingly, as if an acceptance of her reality washed over her. He wanted to help her achieve that reality in tune with her new acceptance. He wanted her to fulfill her destiny to fall under his strength.

Frenzy rattled his body and he reached for her...

Carl awoke with a start on his cot in the abandoned church. He was sweating and panting, as if he really had been sprinting through the woods, and he absentmindedly fingered the scar on his head.

He stood and walked over to a small flat screen that blared, unwatched by the others in the room. The news was just finishing a story on rampant premature balding in young men and cut to a commercial.

Uncle Sam wants YOU to join the fight against terrorism (a particularly muscular version of the iconic figure with torn off sleeves was pointing out at Carl). More than ever, the military has OIL on the run, and YOU can be a part of history as they rid the world of enemies of freedom. (It cuts to a dark silhouette framed in heroic fashion against a backdrop of what are unmistakably undead drones) Join the Automaton as he hunts down OIL operatives and vicious drug cartels to make the greatest nation on the planet safer for our families (cut to children of various ages posing with senior citizens).

Carl huffed at the advertisement. Now they were using his likeness for recruitment videos. Even he was starting to think that this whole thing was getting out of hand.

The whole country was in turmoil, and everyone was so desperate for something positive that he had become something the whole country could get behind, a symbol of American exceptionalism.

Carl wondered how his legions of fans would feel if they knew he dreamed about stalking and killing people every night. He couldn't even call them nightmares because, in the dreams, he enjoyed it. The thrill of the hunt, the rapture of the kill.

He wondered what Peter would think. In Afghanistan, Carl was looked up to as a leader, admired for his strength and ability. Now the men in the unit kept their distance from him, as if what was happening to him was contagious. For all he knew, it was, but no one else appeared to show signs of any of his symptoms.

He thought about what Peter said and thought that maybe he was right. He had to take ego out of the equation. It wasn't about being loved. It was about duty. It was about the good he could do to make America safer.

He thought about his mother. She didn't want him to enlist because she feared for his safety. She had no idea of the kind of monster he was to become, so feared by his own government that they placed a kill chip in his brain and gave his brother the button.

He knew how Peter felt about him. He did his best to try and hide it, but he was also afraid of Carl. Not so much Carl's abilities, but his change in demeanor. His arrogance, his recklessness. Peter knew the price that was paid for recklessness, and he was tired of losing good men.

However, that was what Carl and the infantry drones had to offer. Good men, Americans with families, no longer were fodder for the battlefield. Carl was sure that he was doing something good, but something on a visceral level didn't feel right.

The dreams, which were becoming more frequent, were leaving him with a bad taste in his mouth, and the exhilaration they gave him was beginning to creep into his waking experience. He savored the thought of tracking those Mexican smugglers in the underground tunnel...hunting them, wiping them and their evil off the face of the earth.

The more he thought about it, the more he searched his feelings; he was startled by the dawning realization that it had nothing whatsoever to do with good or evil, freedom or democracy...

It was the thrill of the hunt and the rapture of the kill.

***

Fiona knocked at the door of her grandmother's house. It was a rundown Victorian with a dilapidated wrap around porch, the kind old Southerners in the movies sat on in rocking chairs, sipping sweet tea.

Twilight was falling, but she figured she'd pay her Nana a visit. It had been a while, and her work keeping tabs on the Infantry Drone Program from a distance and developing the Retinal Gateway Technology had occupied most of her time.

Her Nana opened the door and smiled when she saw her. She gave her a hug and gestured for her to enter. Fiona was used to the silent treatment since the stroke. Nanna didn't speak after that, but she understood everything.

They traversed a long hallway past a staircase leading upstairs, their footsteps echoing off the walls. The house had three floors. Her Nana lived, at this point, exclusively on the first floor, using the dining room as a bedroom. The second was no longer used. The third floor, once rented to tenants and those passing through Abernathy, had been abandoned for years.

Fiona grew up spending many a hot summer day at that house. Her little brother had once dared her to go up to the third floor when Nana was napping. She was around eight years old. He was seven. She had gone, but he chickened out as usual.

She remembered spending what was probably only a few minutes, but felt like an eternity, up there. It was a dark, creaky, dusty place. The stale scent of mothballs wafted in the air and the shadows played tricks on the eyes.

As they now passed the staircase leading up, Fiona smiled to herself nostalgically. They passed through a door, passed by the dining room, and entered the kitchen.

Nana hugged Fiona again and took a good look at her in the light, appraising her from head to toe. Then, apparently liking what she saw, she gestured for Fiona to sit at the kitchen table.

As Fiona sat, Nana went to the fridge and opened the door. She grabbed and held up various beverages: milk, diet soda, iced tea. Fiona nodded at the iced tea. Her Nana had always made the best iced tea.

After she had fixed Fiona a glass, she held up one finger telling Fiona to wait. Then she disappeared into the bathroom across from the dining room.

Fiona sat there holding her cold glass of iced tea. She took a sip and it brought back memories of long summers from an almost forgotten period in Fiona's life. She was glad that it was still there, buried in her subconscious.

Her life since that time had been filled with tragedy. Her brother's death when she was in college from an acute asthma attack. Her father's heart attack and death shortly thereafter. That was right about the time she had enlisted.

Her father was a major in the army. He was a proud man, but he had never wanted the same for his daughter. Not his princess. After the loss of her brother and father, Fiona's life had lost its direction. She had taken all kinds of tests. She scored in the superior range of intelligence, and she was a high 4-9 on the Minnesota Multiphasic Personality Inventory, the 4 being the Psychopathic Deviate Scale and the 9 being the Hypomania Scale. The 4 referred to what the shrinks called "moral flexibility." The military saw her scores and immediately recruited her into Army Intelligence.

A high 4-9 was the profile of a psychologist, so she attended a graduate program in clinical psychology and the army paid for her Ph.D. Her "moral flexibility" made her ripe for shadow ops, and she was trained in gathering intelligence on terrorists. She showed a particular talent for interrogation, and she collaborated with human factor engineers in developing the Retinal Gateway Technology, which made waterboarding and such obsolete.

She grew distant from her mother over the years, as if the distance would bury the pain of losing her brother and father. In Army Intelligence, fostering relationships was not a priority and frankly discouraged, particularly for the type of work Fiona was involved in. Connections to others were a liability that could be exploited by the enemy.

Fiona had left her entire young life behind. She imagined her classmates from high school settling down, getting married and having children. In the meantime, she was figuring ways to penetrate the minds of terrorists to keep American families safe.

Nana came out of the bathroom and made her way back into the kitchen. She poured herself some iced tea and joined her granddaughter at the table. She held Fiona's hands in hers.

"I've been fine, Nana. I've been very busy with the army. Nothing I can talk about," and she winked at Nana. Nana smiled in delight and shivered in excitement.

"I've been meaning to visit."

Nana waved her hand dismissively and made a gesture that Fiona understood to be happiness that she was there now.

"So how have you been?"

Her Nana made a so-so gesture, turning her hand over and back.

"Are you taking all of your meds?"

Nana put her hands up in the air in exaggerated exasperation, indicating that she was taking too much medication in her estimation.

Then she put her finger up in the air again.

"Okay. What is it?"

Nana rose from her chair and gestured for Fiona to follow her. She had something to show her. Fiona stood and followed her. Nana walked to the dining room, opened the door, and pointed inside.

Fiona caught up and looked through the doorway into the dark dining room. She saw a dark outline of her Nana's bed and the outline of the dining room table pushed to one side with irregular piles of what were likely papers on top. Then there was a dark shape, tall and thin, like a coatrack.

"What is it, Nana?"

Her Nana pointed insistently into the dark room, her face glowing with excitement.

"I can't see in here. Let's turn the light on," Fiona reached for the light switch.

As the dim light went on, she was confused by what she initially saw. The coatrack wasn't a coatrack at all. It was an adolescent boy just standing there still as can be. His face looked pale and the skin around his eyes dark.

Then her eyes widened in horror as she recognized the boy.

Her Nana put her hand on Fiona's arm and, for the first time in years, spoke clear as day.

"Fiona, your brother's here."

Fiona backed out of the room, nearly tripping over her own feet, her back hitting the wall behind her. Her brother reached out for her, baring broken yellow teeth.

She opened the door to her right and ran back through the hallway towards the front door. She slid the deadbolt and pulled on the handle, but the door wouldn't budge. She heard her brother clawing on the door behind her as her Nana laughed in maniacal delight.

The door creaked open slowly, and the doorway was dark. Her brother was no longer there. But she heard scratching on the kitchen floor, a scurrying, and she saw a small shadow creeping along the floor.

It stopped when it reached the doorway and just paused there on all fours, waiting. Her heart pounding in her chest, Fiona strained her eyes to make out the small figure. It was oddly shaped, its head disproportionately larger than its body, its rear end up higher than the rest of its body.

"Nana..." she called out tentatively.

The thing in the doorway cooed back at her. Horrified, she yanked on the doorknob, but the front door wouldn't open.

"Stay away from me," she called out to it. It hissed at her in response and began to scurry towards her.

She ran up the staircase, rounded the second floor landing, and continued up to the abandoned third floor. She heard scurrying on the steps below. It was coming after her.

She opened the old wooden door to the third floor apartment and ran into the dark room closing the door behind her. She engaged the lock and backed away from the door, listening.

She heard more scratching and scurrying as it climbed the second flight of stairs. It stopped right outside the locked door and cooed at her. It knew she was in there.

"Leave me alone," she called out, and it began to scratch at the door.

"I said GO AWAY."

It hissed at her through the door and continued to scratch.

She thought of the fire escape. She groped in the darkness and stumbled uncertainly into the next room. The moonlight shone through the window and she lurched towards it, feeling for the latch at the top of the windowpane.

It was painted over and, as her fingers struggled to unlock it, she realized that it was painted shut. She searched the room for some large piece of furniture as the thing on the other side of the apartment door clucked and gurgled horribly.

She found an old wooden chair and picked it up. She brought it to the window and pulled it back to take a swing when she saw it in the darkness of the other room. The eyes she saw when she used the RGT on Carl Birdsall, the face she had seen in her nightmares ever since, glared at her in the black void.

Her body became frozen in terror and she dropped the chair. Behind her, she heard keys jingling and her Nana talking to the thing scratching at the door. "It'll only be a moment, dear. Don't worry, I have the key."

"Nana, DON'T," she called out desperately, sounding like a frightened child.

However, it was too late.

The lock disengaged and the door swung open. She heard scurrying in the other room behind her as the eyes in the room in front of her glared menacingly. She screamed as the scampering horror brushed up against her leg and sunk its teeth into her ankle.

Fiona awoke with a start, dripping in sweat, tears streaming down her hot face. Another damned nightmare. She looked around her room and it dawned on her with some relief that she was still on base.

She wiped her face with the back of her right hand and got out of bed. She turned on the light and walked over to the window. She saw herself in the reflection from the light. She looked terrible. Ever since that day the RGT revealed a glimpse of that face, she had been stricken with these nightmares.

They were very personal. In one, Carl was hunting her down viciously, and this one…she hadn't seen her Nana in years. This was something she had felt guilty about, but she was busy with her work. She no longer felt any connection to her family.

Her brother…that really got to her. She missed her brother terribly. Why did he appear in the nightmare? What was the purpose of these nightmares?

The brass didn't take what she saw that day seriously, and they chalked her nightmares up to stress. They ordered her to see one of the other shrinks, but it was all pro forma. The psychologist made obtuse interpretations about guilt in giving up a normal life connected to family and a fear of settling down and having children.

Fiona knew her life didn't follow a traditional path, and there was some guilt about that. However, she had never been plagued by nightmares like this before. In every dream, there was that face…

She mused about what her life would've been like if she'd settled down, but she couldn't imagine the man she would essentially settle down with. The Birdsall brothers popped into her head. There was Carl, the younger brother. She understood what it was like to have lost purpose and why he enlisted. Then there was Peter. He was strong and heroic. She didn't deny that there was an attraction there. She had to tune it out during her sessions with him. However, she was no longer his therapist, and any record of her therapy had been erased.

She shook her head, dismissing the fantasies as foolish. She went over to her computer and powered it on. She called up the files on the RGT data collected on Carl and reviewed the files on the crash site in the Congo. There had to be a connection. Nothing in the files explained that face she saw in the nightmares.

She couldn't help but think that, while the government was using the Retinal Gateway Technology to spy on others, something else— the technology's creator—was watching them.

She knew there had to be a connection between the RGT and the THV virus. The virus was found in villagers near the crash site. They died, reanimated, and tried to eat the other villagers.

Then there was Carl's unique situation. His body was going through changes. Was it because of his proximity to the undead drones? If that was the case, why didn't any of the other soldiers develop tumors or any of Carl's abilities?

He was becoming the perfect soldier—fast, strong, more acute in his senses. He had the ability to communicate with the undead drones. It was as if he was their commander. They obeyed him without question.

She had wondered if he had the same nightmares…if he saw the same face. None of the data she had indicated so, but she wondered if he was being influenced somehow.

An epiphany hit her like a freight train. He was the perfect soldier, the commander of an army of undead. All they appeared to do was kill, eat, and make more zombies. In a war scenario, it was the perfect battle of attrition. Whoever wasn't killed was converted. Sun Tzu would've been proud.

With such an army, one could conquer a nation. Moreover, she thought about what happened in Xcaret, Mexico, and how they had lost control of the drones which turned on Peter, Carl, and their platoon.

She played out the scenario in her head to its ultimate conclusion. If the drones couldn't be controlled, the virus would spread, killing and converting anyone in its path. From an epidemiological perspective, it would become an epidemic, and eventually a pandemic.

A pandemic was an infectious disease that spread across large regions or worldwide. So then, the THV pandemic would, in effect, wipe out the world population through attrition.

Carl could control it, somehow, for some reason, but what if he wasn't meant to control it…

What if he was meant to direct it…?

***

Nogales, Arizona
05:04 HRS

Carl lay on a mound of dirt with a receded, sparse hairline of grass a hundred feet away from the border fence, the deep purple sky yielding to burnt orange on the horizon. There was a drone lying motionless next to him. Cronos was literally hanging on the fence covered in corrugated tin for camouflage.

They had been staking out the house through the night. Carl detected activity inside, a significant gathering of some kind, but there was no movement from the house.

Cronos was motionless, hanging on the top of the fence with his night scope on the house, his limbs falling asleep. He waited as man after man entered the house with large black duffle bags. He tagged two of them undetected, and he wanted one more shot just in case. It would've been foolish to rely on one tag alone. Tags could fall off, bags can be left behind.

A final man walked over to the house, looking around. For a moment, he gazed over at the border fence, but Cronos' corrugated silhouette still blended with the retreating dark sky. He didn't have much time left. Soon he would be visible against the dawn.

The man turned to enter the house, and Cronos took aim. He exhaled and held it to steady the shot, and he squeezed the trigger. He hit the man's backpack. The man entered the house completely unaware. There didn't appear to be another soul around.

Cronos shouldered his rifle and began to lower himself from the fence slowly. He slid down to the ground and crept his way over to where Carl's mound was, chasing the pins and needles out of his legs. He gave Carl a thumbs up and then three fingers.

Carl nodded and whispered into his mini-com. "Three birds away."

"Copy that," Peter responded.

Now they waited. Peter was with Carl's and his squads in a nearby abandoned factory. Kettle's unit passed by a few hours earlier on patrol and waited further west. Carl reached his tendrils across the fence and into the house. He silently hoped that the tags wouldn't be discovered, which would be the next possible wrinkle in the operation.

After approximately a half an hour, Carl sensed movement in the house and, just like that, the group vanished from his detection.

"The birds have flown the coop," he whispered into his mini-com.

"Copy that."

Carl rose and commanded the drone to do so with him. As they walked over to the fence, he commanded it to follow the signal of the tags. The drone gave no outward recognition of its silent command. It only turned and began to walk a path that must have been that of the subterranean coyotes.

"The bloodhound is loose," Carl said into his mini-com.

In the defunct factory, Peter pointed his right index finger in the air and made a circular motion. Soldiers hopped into three trucks loaded with drones, which Peter thought would be the best way to mobilize, and engines fired up. Peter hopped into the first truck. Mackler was driving.

Peter pulled out his mini-com multi-tasker and began to track the drone with Carl, as well as the three signals coming from the tags. Carl was going to feed him coordinates as Peter followed from a distance, and Peter would track the tags' signals as a backup contingency, extrapolating a vector from the tags' movement. From this, he would be able to predict possible destinations where the coyotes might surface. At least that was how Lieutenant Farrow had explained it. It was all Greek to him.

Mackler followed the coordinates Peter collected from Carl, and Peter used his multi-tasker's mapping function to cross-reference towns with the probable vectors of the tunnel.

"Sergeant."

"Yes, sir."

"I think I know where your coyotes might be headed."

"Yes, sir."

"The most likely destination is a ghost town approximately 18 miles east of the start point in Nogales, called Lochiel."

"Got it. What's next?"

"Veer away from the signals. We'll swing by and pick you up. I want to get there before they do."

"Yes, sir."

Peter spotted Carl and Cronos walking along the side of the road. Mackler pulled along side them.

"Where's the drone?" Peter asked.

"He's following the signals in case you're wrong," Carl answered.

"Carl, what if it—"

"It won't hurt anyone," Carl interrupted. "Trust me."

"Get in," Peter frowned.

They took an alternate vector to Lochiel. There was a wide dirt road leading into what barely qualified as a town. There was a lot of dirt and tall grass with a wide smattering of abandoned buildings and half-erected wire fences running throughout.

Peter figured they arrived there before the coyotes with plenty of time to spare. "Mackler, stop here."

Mackler stopped the truck by an old house with a front porch enclosed with heavily corroded metal screens. The other two trucks stopped behind them.

Peter grabbed his mini-com. "Kettle, block the road and establish a perimeter."

"Copy."

"Carl, assemble Alpha and Beta squads. We're going in on foot."

"I don't understand," said Carl as they flanked the dirt road, "there's an abandoned border station right here in Lochiel. Why not just cross here?"

"That's what we'd be expecting," said Peter. "Besides, the Mexican government has stepped up security on their side, so it is assumed that Lochiel is covered on their end."

"And so we turn a blind eye," added Carl.

"Something like that. It's all about misdirection."

They made their way around thick bushes and found what looked like an old white church at the crest of a hill. It was a long building with a crucifix above the front doors.

"There," Carl pointed, "that church."

"It's a post office," Peter said consulting his min-com multi-tasker. "What makes you think—"

Then Peter saw what Carl saw. It was the drone Carl had trailing the underground coyotes. There were shouts from up the hill. A couple of sentries spotted the drone staggering along.

"Shit, they spotted your drone," whispered Peter.

One of the sentries shouted something to the other and then to the drone. The drone ignored the order, and the sentry opened fire, dropping the drone.

"Make it stay down, Carl. We don't want to make them too suspicious."

Carl nodded. "Hopefully, they think it's some homeless guy or drifter."

"In a hundred-thousand dollar sci-fi suit," Peter added sarcastically.

They watched as both sentinels went over to investigate. One stooped down on his haunches for a closer look at the drone. There was a conversation, and then a debate.

"This is it," whispered Peter. While they are busy trying to figure out what the hell our drone is, we're going to move in. The coyotes must be surfacing within the post office. A nice, strong building for a rendezvous."

Carl saw one of the sentries pick up a mini-com. He sent a message to the drone, which reached up and grabbed the man by his throat so hard that he didn't have the chance to yell.

"Carl, what the—"

"He was going for his mini-com," Carl responded.

When the other man realized what was happening, the drone was sitting up and had pulled him down. His windpipe was crushed before the poor bastard could yell out a warning.

"Nice work, Carl," said Peter patting his brother on the back. "That'll buy us enough time."

Peter motioned with his hands and the squads fanned out. Cronos and Rayburn, the other Spotter, remained under the cover of bushes while the undead advanced on the post office.

Peter and Carl brought up the rear, training their weapons on the post office. Someone inside must have heard the first drone being shot. There were the sounds of shattering glass and gunfire erupting out of the windows of the post office.

"Fall back!" Peter commanded as they let the drones advance to take the post office.

Several of the drones were hit in the chest and limbs, but kept coming. So far, there were no headshots. There were panicked shouts from inside as the undead that were shot got up and continued their assault as if nothing had happened.

Suddenly, gunfire erupted from behind them as more smugglers joined the party. Peter, Carl, and the others took cover.

"Shit! They must've been hiding in some of the nearby shacks," shouted Peter as he returned fire. "Kettle, we're being ambushed from behind."

"Copy that. En route."

Cronos and Rayburn were tagging the party crashers. As they were tagged, the smugglers grabbed their chests where the barbs of the tags dug in and looked at each other in confusion.

Then drones started stumbling in from behind them and were lunging for them. The terrified smugglers began firing at the frenzied undead, but no headshots. The gunfire subsided and was replaced with screams of pain and horror as the drones did their dirty work.

This gave Peter and his men the opportunity to focus on the church.

"Carl?"

"Some of the pulses are disappearing, Pete."

"They're going back into the tunnel. We need to get in there."

Carl stood up and jumped behind five drones that formed a wall in front of him. Peter knew what Carl was doing. "Give him some cover," he shouted. They all opened fire on the windows of the post office.

Bullets whizzed by Carl's head and his undead wall staggered and stumbled as they advanced on the post office. He pressed on their backs as they were hit, pushing them forward with body and will. Friendly suppressive fire erupted all around him, forming a corridor of bullets as they pushed their way forward.

Carl made it with his entourage to the front of the post office and they began to push their way in. The rest of the drones were clawing their way in through the tall, narrow windows on each side.

Most of the gunfire from within was focused on the drones coming in through the sides. Carl parted his undead shield and began picking off gunmen one-by-one.

The ones that saw Carl tried to fire back, but taking their attention off the undead coming through the windows proved to be a fatal error. Carl didn't even need to waste a single bullet on them.

"Carl, find the tunnel. We only have 18 miles to catch the others before they reach the border."

"Copy that." Carl frantically looked around for the hole to the tunnel. There was a mess of bodies with drones feeding on them and bullet casings everywhere. The gunmen in the window were well armed. These were gunrunners after all.

He hopped the counter and saw it. A large gaping hole in the tile floor. He commanded the infantry drones to abandon their feast and come behind the counter.

He looked around and saw a couple of stray black duffle bags. As he rifled through them, he found assault rifles, Mac-10's, and...

He jumped into the hole first, and the drones fell in behind him like carnivorous lemmings. Carl crouched down and scurried as fast as his legs would take him. He knew they had a head start on him.

"Carl, we're in the post office. We've found the tunnel."

"Stay out of the tunnel, Pete!"

"Please repeat. It sounds like you said—"

"You heard right. Stay out of the tunnel, Pete. Trust me."

"Copy. You better get those coyotes."

"I'm working on it," Carl said with irritation as he scrambled down the tunnel. Fortunately, his enhanced speed allowed him to gain on the fleeing coyotes, but it also meant leaving his undead bodyguards behind.

He scampered down the dark tunnel, sweat dripping down his face. Time was slipping away, and he still had more tunnel to cover.

"Carl, you only have ten more miles before you reach the fence." Peter was tracking Carl's mini-com from the surface with his own multi-tasker.

Even with Carl's enhanced speed, these bastards were fast. Their head start really paid off, and Carl was running out of tunnel before the border. As he scurried, he thought of Tora Bora. Those caves were bigger. These were large enough for bodies to pass through almost in single file, and just tall enough for the diminutive smugglers. Carl was scraping the top of his helmet.

On the surface, Peter was back in the truck following Carl from above. He had caught up and was directly above him when the road veered to the right.

He turned off the road to stay on top of Carl. Carl was moving quickly, but it didn't take much for Peter to keep up in a moving vehicle. Carl curved now and then, the tunnel winding under the ground.

"I am now directly above you," Peter shouted into his mini-com.

"I don't see them, Pete."

"Six more miles till the border fence, Carl."

"You're not helping, Pete."

Peter's mind raced. He saw the border fence in the distance. He thought of firing his grenade launcher at the ground, but the tunnel wound too much and he would have no way to pinpoint the coyotes or even guarantee penetration.

"Do you have eyes on the targets yet?"

"No. I don't suppose they took any of the bags that were tagged with them."

Peter had thought of this before. "No such luck."

Carl hurried along, frantically reaching out and down the tunnel for a pulse. He began to pick up on something faint. He was closing the gap. He heard distant voices as he rounded another bend.

"Two more miles, Carl."

The tunnel began to straighten out, and he could see the coyotes running in the distance ahead of him. It looked like a straight run, which made sense. The coyotes would want to get across and away from the border as quickly as possible. Once far enough away, the turns in the tunnel would throw anyone above off track.

"Pete, it's a straight run from here."

The coyotes must have heard Carl. The one bringing up the rear began to open fire on Carl. There was nowhere for Carl to go in the narrow tunnel, but the distance was too great and the smuggler's aim too poor. The bullets never reached Carl.

Carl slowed his pace and returned fire. The coyotes were panicking and firing wildly back down the tunnel at Carl. He stopped and knelt on one knee.

He grabbed an RPG-7 out of the black duffle bag he brought with him and took aim. He lined up the end of the tunnel in his sights. This was going to be close. He had to aim the blast on the American side of the tunnel. It was going to be a wild guess in the best of all possible scenarios.

He squeezed the trigger and the rocket whistled down the tunnel. The coyotes disappeared in an explosion as flames shot back down the tunnel...right at Carl.

Carl was too far away. The flames raged down the tunnel and then evaporated with the souls of the coyotes it consumed.

***

"This is Olivia Friend with Channel 8 News at the U.S.-Mexican border, where apparently some big smuggling operation was stopped by the United States military.

"This is as close as we are allowed to get at the moment, but if you look you can see backhoes working overtime starting almost right at the fence to reveal an underground tunnel likely built by smugglers.

"Word from local officials is that the tunnels stretch miles into U.S. territory. Local authorities have also converged on the ghost town of Lochiel, which may or may not be related to what has transpired here in Nogales.

"Locals reported hearing a muffled boom and the ground shaking. First thinking it was an earthquake, they later spotted what looked like soldiers dressed in futuristic black suits, some of which, to quote a local onlooker, 'Didn't look so hot'—this after reports that gunfire had been erupting in Lochiel.

"Who are the men in black? Most likely these were the Infantry Drone Program, and they have apparently stopped something here. It is unclear at the moment if any of the coyotes were taken into custody. We will stay with the story and fill you in as we obtain more information. This is Olivia Friend for Channel 8 News. Back to you Mark and Lisa."

"Well, it appears that someone was trying to cross the border illegally," Mark said. "Smugglers likely, as Olivia said. The question is: what was being smuggled?"

"We now go to Katrina Zeta Torres, on location at Lochiel, with information about what locals described as gunfire…"

"Thank you, Lisa. Local authorities converged on the sleepy ghost town of Lochiel this morning when they received reports of gunfire coming from within the town.

"They quickly converged on the town, sealing it off. A border ghost town, Lochiel used to be a bit of a tourist destination. When the Rollercoaster Recession hit, it lost federal funding as well as tourist traffic and consequently closed.

"The Mexican government in cooperation with our government stepped up security, establishing a checkpoint on the other side of Lochiel. But it appears that the ghosts of Old West shootouts have returned to this deserted spot.

"There might be a connection to the underground tunnel discovered in Nogales at the border, and the gunfire may have been the Infantry Drone Program intercepting smugglers at this spot here.

"Local authorities are remaining tight-lipped about what transpired in both locations this morning, leaving the rest of us, for the moment, left to guess. We expect the local sheriff to go public with an official statement as to what happened sometime this afternoon.

"This is Katrina Zeta Torres for Channel 8."

Peter was riding back in a truck with Private Jonas driving. Carl was in another truck with Beta Squad. He was reflecting on how very fortunate they were that Carl got the coyotes less than a mile from the fence on the American side.

If it were a mile more, this would have been an international incident and they would be in very deep shit. However, as it were, Carl got them on the right side. There were no prisoners, but they fired at him first. Carl did the right thing by taking them out.

Now they had to report back to Colonel Betancourt. Peter imagined Betancourt would be happy, as this was a successful operation. They stopped a rather ambitious group of weapons smugglers and uncovered a significant tunnel system. This was even better PR than stopping immigrants, because the smugglers were true threats to national security.

The anti-gun folks on the Left would be all for what happened—stopping the influx of illegal assault weapons—and they would have to say something nice about the program for a change. The President would get a much-needed boost in the polls, and the program itself will have established its niche.

They couldn't have done it without Carl. Peter didn't know how his brother sensed the house on the other side of the fence when the radar didn't register squat. Other than making a quick hop across the fence (which no one needed to know about), Carl was cool, collected, and damned effective.

Only he could have caught up with those coyotes in the tunnel, and they had one heck of a head start on him. Carl was becoming some kind of a super soldier. On top of all that, he seemed to calm down. He wasn't brash or reckless. Maybe he was evening out and everything would be okay.

Carl sat in the truck with Mackler driving. Mackler seemed upbeat with the success of the mission and less weary of being near Carl than usual. If he knew what was eating Carl as they drove back in silence, he wouldn't have been so comfortable.

Carl was thinking back to the moment when he caught up with the coyotes in the tunnel, when he raised the RPG-7 and took aim. When he pulled the trigger and the rocket whizzed down the tunnel, it was a sensation that he could only describe as pure exhilaration.

It wasn't the adrenaline or the excitement. Hell, he didn't even think he was actually pumping adrenaline. He experienced a clinical kind of calm, like a skilled hunter confident in his craft. The excitement was the knowledge that the coyotes were going to be snuffed out within seconds.

When they were, it was like a violent orgasm that racked his mind, body, and soul. It was satiety from a thirst for blood and death, and he drank deep in their demise by fire.

He knew this sensation was on some level...no many levels...wrong. True, they fired at him, and he returned the favor, but it was unnatural for him to savor these kills.

He thought about telling someone about these feelings and the dreams. The company shrink was a hack. He wouldn't know what to do with this. He considered telling Peter, but things had gone so well. Peter had finally relaxed his finger over the button of Carl's kill switch.

Carl showed them all that he wasn't a danger to them. Betancourt would be happy. No, he decided he wouldn't tell anyone about these sensations. Not just yet, anyway. If the feelings got worse, if he felt he couldn't control them...then he would tell Peter.

At the moment, he felt in control.

At the moment.

***

"So, what you are telling me is that Sergeant Birdsall's ability to communicate with the drones may be deliberate, by design, for the purpose of wiping out the human population all at the behest of this face you saw when you used the RGT on him at Camp X-ray?"

Fiona cleared her throat. "I know it sounds speculative, sir—"

"Speculative isn't the word," said Colonel Betancourt.

"But, sir, we don't fully understand this technology or who created it. We don't understand why Sergeant Birdsall is becoming an enhanced soldier from his brain tumor or why he can communicate with the drones."

"So you think that our finding the crash site in the Congo was no accident."

"There's that distinct possibility, sir."

"But there's no evidence of that, Captain. In addition, we can't jeopardize this program and the RGT technology based on something you thought you saw and your nightmares. Do you know how important RGT will be for national security when applied under the Second Patriot Act?"

"But, sir, with all due respect, you are assuming that this technology was found, rather than planted."

"Planted in a crash? That's preposterous. The crash clearly indicated that an accident had transpired. Besides, we've taken precautionary measures. Sergeant Birdsall has a kill chip in his head.

If he starts to direct the extinction of the human race, we'll just flip the switch. Once RGT is ready to go, we can discard the drones. They've been more trouble than they are worth anyway."

"Regardless," Fiona continued, "I believe that we are taking an awful risk with technology that we don't fully understand from an unknown entity."

"Captain, we've had this technology for decades and no space aliens have come looking for it. We will stick to our objectives until I say otherwise, or Congress yanks funding. With OIL out there on the loose, it's more important than ever to bring RGT to fruition. Am I clear?"

"Yes, sir."

"And by the way, you look terrible. Take some time off. Rest up. Blow off some steam. Maybe the nightmares will stop."

"But, sir, I don't think—"

"That's an order, Captain. I am going to be granting Sergeant Birdsall a pass for one week. We'll be watching him. Take some time off."

"Yes, sir. Thank you, sir."

Chapter 7

Fort Bliss
Debriefing Room
11:15 HRS

"I would like to congratulate you on a successful mission," said Betancourt officiously to Peter, Nolan, and Carl. "Not only did you discover this weapons smuggling operation, but you interceded and neutralized the operation without any American casualties or collateral damage.

"The President is very pleased with the news. It appears that the program now has found its role in keeping our borders safe."

"Thank you, sir, for saying so," said Peter.

"You and your men earned it, Captain. Sergeant..."

"Yes, sir."

"How were you able to detect the activity going on in that house?"

Carl took a brief moment to consider the question. "I can reach out and sense living things, sir. People, animals. On patrol, I picked up on all of those pulses."

"Pulses?"

"Yes, sir. I can feel them like drum beats and together in rhythms."

"Remarkable. And while on patrol, you were...reaching over the fence?"

"Yes, sir. It's kind of like radar. I was able to do this without crossing the fence." Carl noticed Peter's drum beat accelerate next to him.

"Yes, but in a way you were 'reaching' over the fence."

"Not corporally, sir."

Betancourt paused, frowning. "Well, that's good enough for me. That detail doesn't leave this room, and the Mexican government can never prove it anyway."

"Yes, sir," they all confirmed in unison.

"Sergeant."

"Yes, sir."

"I need not remind you that when on leave, you are to refrain from using any of your...abilities."

"Yes, sir. I understand."

"I know some of them have become second nature to you at this point. When you are out in public, you are to keep them under wraps. There's no telling how the public would react if they found out *the*

Automaton was walking in their midst. It could be dangerous, for them and for you."

"Yes, sir."

"Did you hear?" Betancourt said shaking his head and changing the topic. "They are making action figures of you guys." He chortled at the thought. "Don't let it go to your heads. Sergeant, I want you to submit for some follow-up neurological testing. Then you all get one week's leave. You earned it."

"Thank you, sir," Peter responded for the group.

"Dismissed."

Carl waited until they were far enough from the debriefing room and Betancourt. He nodded to Nolan, who then promptly excused himself.

"Well, he sure seemed pleased," said Peter without realizing why Nolan had made himself scarce.

"He didn't seem all that pleased to me," Carl replied.

"What are you talking about? That was him practically jumping for joy," Peter jested. "Hey, at least we weren't getting chewed out for once."

"A pat on the back and then straight to the lab."

"Oh, Carl, you're being too sensitive."

"Pete, when are they going to stop treating me like their science project?"

"He just wants follow-up tests. Carl, we've been through this. This has nothing to do with treating you like the enemy. Your skills are unprecedented, and they're developing. They just want to try to figure out why and make sure you are okay in the process."

"I feel like a dog on a leash."

Peter didn't know quite what to make of that statement. "Carl, we've been through this already. We are all the property of the U.S. Army."

"No, I mean I feel like they are holding me back."

"What do you mean? You just exposed and stopped a major weapons smuggling ring. You're not still harping on your demotion, are you?"

"No, rank means nothing to me at this point."

"Then what *are* you talking about, Carl?"

Carl started to finger the scar on his head.

Peter saw it. "It's just for now. I'm sure that if you keep up the good work and don't give any sass, they'll eventually remove it. It's just a precaution."

"They don't trust me."

"They will."

"Do you trust me, Pete?"

"Of course I do."

Carl noticed a brief quickening in his big brother's pulse. "Could you do it?"

"Do what, Carl?"

"Push the button. Pull the trigger. End me."

"Carl, I never asked for—"

"Answer me, Pete. Can you do it?"

"If I had to, yes."

"Just like that?"

"Why are you asking me this? You have no intention of defecting or murdering your own team, do you?"

"No, of course not."

"So you're the same old Carl that I know and love. You are a good person. There would be no reason for me to press the button…unless there's something you're not telling me."

Carl noticed his own pulse momentarily quicken. "No, there isn't. What would I have to tell you?"

"You tell me, Carl."

"This is turning into an inquisition."

"I'm just trying to tell you that everything's going to be okay. Go get your tests like a good lab rat and then we can go see Dad."

"He's probably having a cow watching the news."

"Hey," Peter elbowed Carl playfully, "do you think my action figure is going to be bigger than yours? I think so."

"I don't know. I *am* the Automaton, you know. Maybe mine will glow or something."

"Yeah, but I think the Captain Peter Birdsall figure will sell more."

"No way. The Automaton may not be the leader, but he is mysterious. He has powers."

"Yeah, the power to piss me off in a single bound. Just remember, bro, every super hero has his kryptonite."

Carl felt his scar itch. "Now you sound like a super villain, *bro*. Picture this: the all-American older brother, the popular athlete, Captain…yet it's not enough. You see, secretly he has been harboring resentment of his once wimpy little brother who now, due to a freak accident, is faster and stronger."

"Really, now," replied Peter sardonically.

"And he waits, biding his time, until he can find the one weakness of this great patriot. Then the government hands him one…"

"Carl…"

"A kill switch for a chip implanted in his brain, because the government doesn't trust him."

"Oh, so now I'm the bad guy," replied Peter playfully.

"Who do you think they'll get to play us in the movie?"

"Oh, so now there's going to be a movie?"

"Why not? Action figures, video games, a movie. You know it's going to happen. 'I Am Automaton,' the movie," said Carl in an announcer's voice.

Peter rolled his eyes, "Oh, brother. Spare me."

Carl put his hands up in front of his face as if framing a scene. He spoke in a deep, grave voice. "In a world where terrorists run free and cartels are threatening our borders..."

"Jesus, Carl..."

"...in a world of economic and civil unrest, one man stands alone..."

"Here it comes..."

"...to stand up for truth, justice, and the American way...THE AUTOMATON."

"Sounds like a throwback to one of those cheesy Arnold Schwarzenegger action flicks from our grandparents' day."

"What, I think it would be great. Maybe we could play ourselves," Carl mused.

"Now you're really dreaming."

"Why? In the twenty-tens, Navy Seals were starring in movies."

"I'm glad your mood seems to have improved. Get your ass to radiology so we can blow this place. I want to see Dad."

Carl nodded and started towards radiology.

Peter was still worried about his brother. Although things seemed to be getting better, he sensed that there was something Carl wasn't telling him. Something that was frightening Carl, himself.

Carl was still a little resentful and bitter, but who wouldn't be after the Major Lewis fiasco. He was still green, and that was his first experience in the army. Betancourt appeared to be an honest man. Strict, but honest. Hopefully, Carl would see that and adjust his attitude.

***

Carl had submitted to a physical examination and had given blood. It was still red. Now he lay on the MRI table, ready to be inserted into the long tube. Carl had done it so many times it didn't even faze him anymore.

"Are you ready?" asked the technician from her booth.

96

"Yes," Carl said.

The table slid slowly into the tube, the top and sides of which were only centimeters from his body.

"Okay, you know the drill. No moving."

"Yes, I know," said Carl.

"Here we go."

The rhythmic tapping began, which turned into rhythmic clanging as the powerful magnet did its work of reorienting his body's atoms. He closed his eyes and let the rhythm of the clanging sooth him.

It wasn't like the beat of a human pulse or like the humming of their brains inside their skulls, but it was a mechanical beat. It spoke to something deep within him, a visceral connection.

He tried to synch it with the beat of the girl in the booth, which was calm and even. How he wanted to quicken it, to taste the fear, to savor the terror...

He quickly changed gears in his mind.

He closed his eyes again, letting his mind wander to other places. After some time, the clanging of the electromagnet and the closed space of the tube gave him the sensation of hurtling through space at a great velocity.

The tube became a vessel containing only him. There was the comfort of impending purpose. When he reached his destination, he would leave the vessel and take to his dark craft.

His own internal rhythm began to quicken, and his body was electric. He emanated power in concentric waves. It warmed his body, like a car engine warmed up, preparing for high performance.

"Whoa. That's interesting." The voice of the technician from the booth woke him from his reverie. The sensation of a vessel travelling through space abruptly ceased.

"Is everything okay?" he asked.

"Please don't talk, Sergeant. We are almost finished."

The table slid out from the tube, and Carl sat up. "So what was that all about?"

"There was some unusual activity in your brain," the technician answered. "I am sending the file to your neurologist for analysis."

Carl stood up and stretched. "What sort of activity?"

"Not *what*, but *where*," she corrected him. "Your medulla and limbic system lit up like a Christmas tree."

Carl thought for a moment. "Aren't those parts of the reptilian brain?"

"I'm just a technician. You'll have to discuss this further with your neurologist, Sergeant."

"Yes, of course." Shit, a Christmas tree. He and Peter had to pick something up on his way home for their father. Christmas was two weeks ago, but this was their opportunity to celebrate with him.

***

"Are you sure alcohol is a good idea for Dad?" Carl asked his brother, following him around the small liquor store. It was one of the few businesses that kept storefronts and hadn't shifted entirely to the internet. This was probably because liquor was often purchased impulsively, often last minute for social engagements or holidays.

"Last I saw him, he was doing much better, Carl."

Carl looked uneasy. He was never a drinker. "Well, what do we get him?"

"Dad loves his tequila. We'll get him a bottle of good blue agave tequila."

"Blue what?"

"It's a rare plant that only grows in one area, but all the best tequila is made with it." He saw Carl's perplexed look. "Hey, while your nose was in the books, I was conducting some very important research of my own."

"Yes, you're quite the scientist, Pete."

"It wouldn't kill you to loosen up every once in a while, Carl."

Holo-ads floated in the air in front of the racks for various alcoholic products. Christmas music blared from a speaker overhead. The music reminded Carl of that day at the mall.

He remembered driving his father's car and turning on the radio to be bombarded with endless Christmas music. He remembered his mother waiting inside the mall, unaware that he had just pulled up. She had just gotten her traditional haircut and styling for Christmas.

He remembered the man in the car revving his engine in the driving rain. He remembered pulling out of the way as the man careened past him and into the mall entrance. He remembered the flash of light, and his car being thrown.

"Do you think of Mom often?"

Peter was holding a bottle of tequila, appraising it. "All the time, especially this time of year."

"When she was...died," Carl said, "everything changed. For all of us."

"The world is changing, Carl, whether we like it or not. We have to do our best to keep up. And *we*, you and I, are doing our best to make sure the world doesn't go down the shitter."

"I knew that someday we would be dealing with this," Carl said.

"You mean Mom and Dad dying?"

"Yeah. But not this soon and not so suddenly."

"Carl, I've been thinking about this myself. Mom was murdered, snuffed out of our lives. But at least she never got to experience being an old lady. You know, watching her mind and body fall apart like some people."

"I always thought Dad would go first," said Carl.

"I think Dad thought so too," Peter said, "which is why we have to do our best to support him. I am sure he's been thinking about Mom too. It's just past the one year anniversary of her death."

"Yeah. He must be hurting."

"She's gone, Carl. There's nothing we can do to change that, but we have to pull together as a family. He's all we have left besides each other, and we're all he has left. I think we owe it to him to have a good visit. He'll be glad to see us."

"Yeah, he will," Carl smiled.

"Plus," Peter added, "it's not every year he gets to spend Christmas with THE AUTOMATON."

"Shush," said Carl, shoving Peter. The cashier looked up from his digi-newspaper over his reading glasses.

"Shush, CAPTAIN," corrected Peter. "Even the almighty Automaton has a boss."

"You wish."

They walked up to the register at the front of the store with the bottle that Peter was holding.

"That'll be one hundred fifty," said the old man at the register.

"Can you gift-wrap it?" Peter asked.

"Sure thing, young man."

As Peter produced his mini-com to scan payment, Carl took notice of the article the old man was reading. It was about him.

THE AUTOMATON UNCOVERS WEAPONS SMUGGLING RING

"So," Carl said addressing the cashier, "what do you think about this Automaton?"

The old man looked up from his transaction with Peter, surprised at the question. "I think he's doing a lot of good, despite what some folks say. A credit to the army. It's about time the government did something to make this country safer."

Peter was glaring at Carl. "Well, thank you, sir. Happy New Year."

"Happy New Year," the man replied without much sentiment and returned to his paper.

"You're a real wise ass," Peter said as they left the store.

Carl smirked. "Hey, I have to keep in touch with my adoring fans."

***

Blueberry Hill
Texas
09:58 HRS

Peter drank in his hometown as he and his brother sat in the back of the cab. The golden fields, Veterans Memorial Park, the Blueberry Hill Water works. They passed the 1950's style burger joint, the one his grandfather used to go to, and thought Fats Domino was wrong—one had to leave Blueberry Hill to find any kind of a thrill.

They pulled up to their childhood home. Peter paid with his mini-com and the cab pulled away. He was clutching the gift-wrapped bottle of tequila as they mounted the front path leading to the front door.

Carl rang the doorbell. Their father answered.

"Guys! You're here. It's so great to see you. Come on in."

He held the door open for them to enter, and each son got a hug as they stepped inside. Peter was happy to see that his father was fully dressed, fully shaved, and the house looked in order.

"Let me look at you guys." They stood in the middle of the living room awkwardly as their father appraised them. "Well, you look good, considering."

"Merry Christmas, Dad," said Peter, holding out the bottle. Carl detected a slight acceleration in his brother's pulse, which probably meant he was changing the topic before their father could elaborate on the "considering."

"Oh, this looks interesting," their father said, holding the bottle. He gestured with a hand for them to enter the kitchen. Most families met in the living room or a den. The Birdsall's always met in the kitchen from time immemorial.

Carl took a seat with his father at the kitchen table. Peter took his customary place leaning against the counter. Their father unwrapped the bottle gingerly and smiled at the result.

"Ah, very good boys. What time is it?"

Carl consulted his mini-com. "It's just after ten."

"Hell, it must be noon somewhere in the world. Pete, get us three glasses, won't you."

Carl shot Peter a disapproving look, but Peter shot him back a "shut up" look. He turned around, opened up a cabinet, and grabbed three tumblers together with his thumb, fore, and middle fingers. He placed them down on the table.

"Dad," Carl started, "it's a bit early—"

"Carl, there's nothing wrong with wanting to have a drink with my boys. I haven't seen you guys in quite some time."

Peter smirked at Carl as their father opened the bottle and poured three generous servings of tequila. Peter and his father took up their glasses in their hands, while Carl looked at his as if it was going to jump up and bite him on the ass.

Peter smiled at this. He was pleased to see some remnant of the old Carl. Good old nerdy Carl. He was in there after all.

"A toast," their father announced. He waited expectantly for Carl to raise his glass. Carl caved into the peer pressure and raised his glass. "To my two boys, real American heroes."

"To us," Peter seconded jovially.

Peter and his father downed their tequila while Carl stared at his. Carl took a sip, was only able to down half of it, and coughed loudly.

Peter and his father laughed.

"I remember the day you were born, Carl. You were a little runt of a baby, scrawny. Your mother was being sewn up in the recovery room and I was holding you. Your brother, here, was begging me to let him hold you…"

"Oh, Dad. I wasn't *begging*," Peter blushed. "Honestly, I thought he was a new pet chicken."

"Anyway," their father continued, "I sat him on the chair, showed him how to position his arms, and I lowered you ever so carefully into his lap. He held you, and I remember his eyes were as wide as platters."

"I must've been startled when I realized that he was a baby and not a chicken," Peter snickered.

"What about when Pete was born, Dad?" Carl interjected, sensing his own pulse quickening.

"Ah, your brother. I remember when they pulled him out of your mother, he looked like a bunch of her intestines, all grey and dimpled. But then he began to cry…"

"Oh, so macho man was a little sissy after all," Carl huffed.

"They brought him over to the examination table to do the APGAR, and the doctor called me over. As they were hosing your brother off, he began to look like an actual human being. The doctor told me to talk to you."

"What did you say?" Peter asked.

"I introduced myself to you, and the damnedest thing happened…you immediately stopped crying. You looked up at me with these big eyes. So I just kept talking. I told you about our house, our back yard, and the toys we bought for you. I was rambling on like an idiot, but it didn't matter to you. You just stared up at me like I was imparting the most profound wisdom."

He looked at his boys. At that kitchen table, they didn't look like soldiers. They looked like his boys, smiling at the story as they did when they were children.

This wasn't the first time they heard this story, but every time they heard it, there was something new—a new detail, a new feeling, a greater understanding of the importance of their births to their father.

They all paused, savoring the reverie. Barry remembered it like it was yesterday, the experience having been gleefully etched into his soul. It was almost like old times, only their mother was missing. Things changed, and there was no going back, but he was thankful for his boys.

Carl sensed a slight acceleration in his father's pulse.

"So, what's this business of tunnels by the border?" Barry asked.

Without the preview of detecting accelerated pulses, Peter was taken off guard by the sudden change in direction of the conversation.

Carl answered. "Nothing we couldn't handle."

"CARL," Peter reprimanded. "Dad, we really can't discuss it."

"Oh, I know something about it. Did you use the zombies?"

"Dad," Peter warned, "Carl shouldn't have told you about what he did in the program. Isn't that right, Carl?"

Carl shrugged his shoulders. "There's no harm, Pete."

"Carl, this is classified information. CLASSIFIED. Did it ever occur to you that you put Dad in danger by telling him?"

Carl hadn't considered this. "Danger? What do you mean?"

"Carl, the government added something to *you* to protect the program. What makes you think they aren't taking precautions to make sure that things don't leak out?"

Barry looked confused. "What do you mean they *added* something to Carl, Pete? Carl, what is he talking about?"

Carl put up a hand dismissively. "Nothing, Dad. Nothing you need to worry about."

"Oh, so now you boys are getting all tight lipped on me. It isn't fair. It isn't fair that I know as much as I do and have to stay up nights worrying about you."

Peter scowled at Carl.

"It's my fault, Dad. I'm sorry. I shouldn't have ever told you about what we did."

"Now there's all of this talk in the news about you having superpowers," Barry said to Carl. "What am I supposed to make of all this?"

Peter frowned. "We can't discuss this with you, Dad. It's for our safety as well as yours. You have us here now, we are okay, and we just want to visit with you. Can't we just leave it at that?"

Barry considered this for a moment. His expression lightened. "I suppose you're right. I have my two boys here with me now, and that's all that matters. You boys want to go out to eat?"

"I was hoping for some good ol' Texas barbecue," Peter said.

"I can fire up the grill," Carl added. "You have any meat in the fridge?"

Barry looked at Carl with faux seriousness. "Son, I am a widowed man living all alone, and barbecue is the only cooking I know. You're damned right I got meat in the fridge."

"Great, I'll get everything ready," said Carl.

"Should I do a beer run?" Peter asked.

"Yeah, I'm running a little low," said Barry.

"Good. We'll have ourselves a barbecue, some suds, and a decent game of Texas Hold 'Em," Peter declared.

"Sounds like a bit of heaven to me," Barry said.

"I'll take your car," Peter said. Barry reached into his pocket and pulled out his mini-com. He handed it to Peter. "A case of Becks?" Peter asked.

"That sounds about right," Barry said. "Use my mini-com to pay."

"I got it, Dad," Peter insisted.

"Yeah, now that he's a captain he can afford it," Carl said sardonically.

Peter flashed him a "screw you" look and left the kitchen. As he stepped out the front door and heard the digi-lock engage behind him, he noticed a cable company worker hanging off of a pole in front of his father's house. Below him was a cable company truck.

Peter nodded up at the man, who reciprocated with a small nod of his own. Blueberry Hill was a small town in the middle of nowhere, and Peter remembered always having problems with the cable service growing up.

He unlocked his father's car and slipped in. He had a few choices for a beer run. He remembered there was one gas station on Main Street that had the cheapest beer. Although his pay grade as a captain was pretty adequate, he wanted to make the most of his peanuts.

He got in the car and turned on the ignition. Immediately, his father's preset oldies station began to belt out some crusty old Kelly Clarkston song. He reached over and turned the radio to the AM dial. He was only half-listening to the Brandon Plato show as he pulled away.

He thought of Carl. He hoped that while he was gone, Carl wouldn't spill any more classified information to their father. He was annoyed at how much his father seemed to know already. However, Carl had been different lately. He wasn't so reckless anymore. Maybe he was finally maturing.

Carl was pulling the meat out of the freezer—steaks, hamburger patties, hot dogs. He put the meat on the countertop and opened the door to the large microwave hanging above the stove.

"So what was all that mess with the border?" Barry asked standing behind him.

"You know I can't discuss that, Dad," Carl said with gentle reproach. He ripped open the packages of meat and placed the meat in the microwave.

"I just worry about you," Barry explained. "I mean, it's pretty weird having the Man From Tora Bora as a son. I think your life would have been quieter as an engineer."

When the microwave was full, Carl closed the door and punched the defrost button. The inside of the microwave lit up as the circular glass tray rotated the meat. Carl was startled…the microwaves were visible to him.

His father mistook his reaction as a reaction to his comment. "Not that I'm not proud of what you're doing now."

"Dad, that life is long gone and never was," Carl said absentmindedly as he gawked at the microwaves in astonishment.

"I blame myself for that, Carl. I should've worked harder, made more money."

"It's not your fault, Dad. There was nothing you could've done. There was nothing many parents could've done. The unemployment rate is at 27%. I was in good company."

"A lot of young men and women are dropping out of college and enlisting," Barry said pensively. "Sometimes I think the government doesn't want to do anything about the economy so it can prey on our youth."

"Boy, that's a cynical view of government," Carl remarked.

"The government doesn't always do what's best for its people, particularly when it gets too big," Barry preached.

"Politics was never my strong suit. I'm a scientist, remember?"

"You said it yourself, Carl—that life is long gone. You're an instrument of government now. You need to consider the political climate. It directly affects you."

"Pete says that a good soldier is a blunt instrument. We enforce policy. It's not our place to question it."

Barry stepped closer to Carl and looked him in the eye. "Son, that approach has always worked for your brother. He always did as I told him, as his football coach told him, and now as the army tells him. But that's not you, Carl."

"What am I supposed to do? I can't go around questioning every order I receive."

"No, but don't turn off your brain, Carl. Never stop thinking. You are not a…"

"Automaton?" Carl asked. "That's what the press calls me. I am a machine, remember."

"I didn't raise a machine," Barry said softly. "I raised two bright, capable young men."

"Do you really think the government wants high unemployment?"

"Well," Barry said, leaning against the kitchen table, "look at what they are doing. They are taxing us into oblivion, crippling small businesses. They are making affording a college education an impossibility."

"But the government has tried to subsidize college tuition," Carl said.

"Which only resulted in universities raising the tuition further," Barry corrected. "They increase the amount of entitlements—welfare, food stamps, entertainment credits…so the only options left to young people are welfare or enlisting."

"But with all of the enlistment, our military is stronger," Carl added.

"And who's going to pay for all of this?" asked Barry. "With the private sector shrinking, China, Japan, and Germany have been methodically buying up our country. We have become indentured servants to foreign nations. We are no longer free. The government can't take care of us, Carl."

Between the microwaves streaming inside the microwave and his father's point, Carl was getting a headache. "So what are you saying, Dad? We're all screwed?"

"I'm saying that while you and your brother think you are out there protecting our borders, I'm telling you that they've already been breached, and it's our government that opened the door."

"Jesus, Dad. Is this what you think about?"

"Well, I've had to close the hardware store more often, so I guess you can say I've had more time to think. And without your mother…" His eyes welled up with tears.

Carl didn't know what to do. He looked down at his sneakers. He had thought his father was doing better. Apparently, it wasn't going to be that easy. "I think about Mom every day…it's what drives me."

Barry stood there looking off into space somewhere above Carl's right shoulder. The microwave beeped, signaling that the meat was defrosted. A tear trickled down Barry's cheek.

"You've got to have hope, Dad."

"It's hard for me to have hope, Carl. It just seems like things are getting worse every day. I lost your mother, and now I'm afraid I'm going to lose you boys."

"Do you have any idea what Pete and I have been through?"

"You told me—"

"Well, then you should know that Pete and I don't go down that easy."

"You've both been lucky," said Barry as he wiped the tears from his eyes. "I'm not saying that your training didn't have anything to do with it, but you've both definitely been very lucky. One day luck will run out."

Carl wanted to tell his father about the changes. If only he could explain to his father that he could sense enemies before they even knew he was there, or that he had extraordinary strength and speed.

Peter came bounding through the front door and into the kitchen bearing a case of Becks. He held it up like a hunter held up a trophy quail and grinned. His face fell as he registered the scene he had just wandered into.

"Is everything okay?" he asked cautiously.

"I'll be outside firing up the grill," Carl said, and he left the kitchen.

"Jesus, what happened while I was gone?"

Barry wiped his eyes one last time and plastered a brave smile on his face. "Oh, nothing. Your brother and I were just having a heart-to-heart."

"Dad, did he—"

"Carl didn't do anything. I just became a little morbid."

Peter gave him a sympathetic look.

"Oh, don't look at me that way, Pete. We're going to have a nice barbecue. I'm just overwhelmed to see you guys, that's all. Help me finish defrosting this meat."

Peter opened up the case and put the bottles of beer in the refrigerator. Then he helped his father open the rest of the packages of meat. He looked out the sliding glass door at his little brother on the deck fiddling with the grill. He was turning the valve on the propane tank.

"You know..." his father said putting more steaks into the microwave, "I am grateful for every chance I get to spend with you boys."

"I know, Dad."

"I don't want you to worry about me. Times are tough, but I'm going to be just fine."

"Glad to hear it," Peter said grinning uncertainly at his father. "Why don't you go watch some TV while I get this meat out to Carl?"

Barry looked at his son and nodded. He washed his hands at the sink and shuffled off into the living room.

Peter punched the button for the defrost mode, and the microwave lit up again. He heard the television turn on and blurt out dialogue from some old movie in the living room. He was glad it was lighter fare and not the news or a talk show.

"SHIT," Peter heard from outside. It was Carl. Peter saw him clutching his left hand.

Peter ran to the sliding door, flung it open, and stepped onto the deck. "What happened, Carl?"

"I-I wasn't paying attention, and I let too much propane build up. I burned my hand."

"Jesus, Carl. Are you okay?"

"What happened?" called Barry as he ran into the kitchen. "Carl, are you all right?"

Carl looked Peter directly in the eye. "Keep Dad inside, Pete."

"But, Carl—"

"JUST DO IT, PETE."

Peter turned around. "He's okay, Dad. There was a big flame and he just got scared."

Barry was peering around Peter. "Why is he holding his hand?"

"I'm okay, Dad. I just burned the hair off my arm," Carl called to his father.

"See," Peter said, "he's okay. Just relax and watch some TV. We'll have the meat cooked in no time."

Barry looked at his son tentatively. Then he reluctantly walked back into the living room. "For Christ's sake," he shouted back over his shoulder, "make sure your brother doesn't cook himself."

Peter sighed and walked back out onto the deck. He saw Carl rubbing his hand. It looked all right, if not just a little red.

"Jesus, Carl, what's wrong with you?"

"I just got startled," Carl said doing his best to look sheepish. What he really wanted to say was that, when he tried to start the grill, he sensed something from inside the house, something like the microwave. Maybe it was the microwave. This was all so new to him.

Peter looked at him incredulously.

"Really, Pete, I'm okay."

"Still the klutz. The mighty Automaton defeated by a propane grill."

"Just get me the meat, Pete."

When Peter walked back into the kitchen, Carl rubbed his left hand, deep in thought. Apparently, he could recover quickly from injury now, even burns, but something didn't feel right.

Hell, nothing felt right anymore.

Chapter 8

"Carl, you really outdid yourself," Peter said sitting back in his kitchen chair holding his cold beer. His belly was full of red meat and he was feeling a little drowsy.

"You said it," chimed in Barry, who was picking his teeth with a toothpick. "Where'd you learn to barbecue like that?"

"You, Dad."

"Oh, yeah, that's right."

They all drank leisurely from their beers, basking in sweet satiety. Carl felt better about things. Maybe it was the good meal. He no longer sensed the odd signal he was picking up before.

"You boys heading off to Frisky's tonight?"

"We're keeping you company, Dad," Peter said.

"Oh, I had a wonderful dinner. Why don't you boys go out for a little and stretch your wings?"

Peter looked at Carl, who shrugged his shoulders indifferently. "Sure, that'd be fun, right, Carl? You could take pointers on mingling with the lady folk."

"I might surprise you," said Carl wryly.

"I hear a wager coming," Peter goaded playfully.

"Two hundred bucks says I get a woman before you."

Peter stroked his chin. "What do you mean by *get*?"

"Phone number."

"Oh, how 1980's."

"What did you have in mind?" Carl asked.

"Home run."

"On the premises?" said Carl in disbelief. "No way. Third base."

"Oh, boy," Barry said, blushing. "I don't think I want to hear any of this. I'm going to take a hot shower. Best of luck to you both."

As he rose from his chair, neither brother broke eye contact. It was on. Barry left the kitchen and climbed the stairs.

"Third base?" Peter teased. "If you can get to third base you can get a home run."

"That's a little more difficult."

"Okay, third base it is. But we each get to choose the woman for the other."

"Oh, I see where this is going," Carl said, sitting back in his chair. "You're going to pick the hottest girl in the place."

"Well," Peter said, "if you prefer, I could choose the ugliest."

"No, no. The hottest is fine."

"Call us a cab, little bro. I'm looking forward to schooling you on male-female relations. Yup, I'm putting on a clinic tonight."

"Brave last words," Carl jested. He pulled out his mini-com. "Taxi cab." It called up four numbers. Carl pressed one.

"Can you come to 21 Arbor Ave.? Going to Frisky's in town…"

***

Peter and Carl strolled into the townie bar like cowboys in a corny western. They paused by the entrance, sized up the joint and its patrons, and moseyed their way over to the bar.

"Two Heinekens," Peter instructed the middle-aged and well-inked barmaid.

Carl was leaning casually with his elbow on the bar watching the small dance floor. Peter smiled at his little brother. He was normally ill at ease in these types of places, but Carl looked very relaxed.

"You see anything you like?" Peter asked as the barmaid placed two green bottles in front of them.

"That'll be eighty dollars," she said over the bad rock music as she blew smoke into Peter's face, possibly by accident.

"Jesus," Peter spat, "this goddamned economy needs to pick up and quick or I'll have to be promoted to major just to afford a couple of suds."

"A lot of ladies in here tonight," Carl said, ignoring his brother's gloating about rank.

"You find one for me yet?"

"I'm sizing up my options," Carl said coolly.

"Don't you mean *my* options, bro?"

"Whatever."

Peter handed Carl his beer, and they clanked bottles.

"Blueberry Hill, lock up your daughters. The Birdsall boys are in town," Peter offered as the toast. They each took a healthy gulp.

"What is *that*?" Carl asked pointing over to a strange contraption in the corner surrounded by a copious amount of what appeared to be orange padding.

"That, little brother, is a mechanical bull."

"That's different."

"Yeah, they must've put it in since the last time we were here," Peter speculated.

"No one's going near it," Carl observed. "Hey," he called to the barmaid, "does that thing work?"

"Hay is for horses," she said sardonically, "and it better work. It's brand new." She pointed to Carl's groin, "Hey, does that thing work?"

"He doesn't know," Peter interjected, "he hasn't taken it out of its wrapping yet." She rolled her eyes and moved on to the next customer.

"I see from your way with women that I'm going to have some competition tonight," Peter said sarcastically.

The bar was electric with pulses and heartbeats, the sound waves of the jukebox twirling through the air like ribbons. Carl noticed that the barmaid's pulse did not change when she spoke to him, but he wouldn't gratify Peter's teasing by telling him she was a lesbian.

He sensed the ones that weren't, as their energy swelled around them when they spoke to local men folk doing their darndest to get laid. The whole scene, which he once found uncomfortable, was now a playground of stimulation.

Before long, he noticed a few of the ladies glancing over at him and Peter. At first, they were furtive glances, easily missed if one wasn't looking. Inevitably, their eyes would drift over to where Peter and he stood at the bar.

"I got one for you," Peter announced, looking across the room.

"Where?"

"Right there. Standing at the end of the bar."

"The brunette?" Carl asked. He knew damned well which woman Peter had in mind. She was gorgeous. Tall, stacked, the longest legs you ever saw, and her eyes, sultry pools that would swallow up the bravest of suitors.

"The one surrounded by all of those cowboys," Peter added with sadistic glee.

"Okay," Carl said, and he began to walk over.

Peter grabbed him by the arm. "Wait a minute."

"What's the problem?"

"You're going to go over just like that? I was kidding. She's out of your league. I'll find you another one."

"That one'll do just fine," Carl reassured Peter.

"I was only joking," Peter pleaded, "there's too many sharks around that tuna."

"It's no problem," Carl insisted. He shrugged off Peter's grasp and began to stroll over.

"We're going to need a bigger boat," Peter quipped as he took one last draught of his beer. He placed the bottle down firmly on the bar and got ready to bail his little brother out. This was going to get messy.

Carl strolled along the side of the bar, women turning from their drinks and meeting his eyes as he walked. He tasted their interest like sugar on his tongue, and their escalating lust fueled his excitement.

Peter cocked his head sideways as he watched his brother. Could it be…his little egghead brother suddenly had…swagger?

Carl traded smiles and flirtations as he crossed the room, sex in motion. It was a new sensation for him, but it felt like second nature. The pheromones wafted in the air in front of him, and he drank them in. They quenched his thirst better than the cold beer he left behind and stoked it at the same time.

He made it up to the throng of men around the beautiful woman. One looked back at him like a predator looks over its shoulder at a rival while stalking coveted prey. Carl felt the man's annoyance at his proximity, but it didn't concern him.

"Excuse me," Carl said casually as he gently brushed the man aside. The others turned around to see who was working his way into the group.

As they parted one by one with obvious animosity emanating in waves off them, Carl saw that the woman wasn't alone. She was flanked by two less attractive but delectable friends who displayed growing annoyance at the realization that the cowboys were there for their friend.

"Excuse me," Carl addressed the group. He reached out a hand to each of the friends, "but you ladies are coming with me."

They looked at each other with surprise, but smiles of vindication spread across their lips as they each took the offered hand. Carl pulled them gently out of the feeding frenzy and towards the dance floor. The two women allowed themselves to be taken, their eyes gazing expectantly into his, their skin electric with the excitement of possibility.

Carl turned around, guiding them through the bar gracefully behind him. Peter gawked at his brother, completely dumbfounded.

"I told you the brunette," Peter shouted as Carl passed in front of him.

"Wait for it," Carl offered back as he slunk his way to the middle of the dance floor with his entourage of two. Peter leaned back on the bar in astonishment, absentmindedly spilling the second beer he ordered.

Carl pulled the ladies close to him and they began to dance. He twirled them around him to the country rock song blaring across the bar, giving even attention to each. They moved around him like satellites orbiting a planet, moving and swaying, a seduction on display.

Peter looked down the bar at the throng of cowboys and the brunette. The guys were half-looking at Carl and the girls on the dance floor, and the brunette—who probably wasn't used to being out of the center of attention—looked pissed.

"Clever boy," Peter said to himself under the music and din of the bar.

On the dance floor, Carl danced with his girls as if he had done this every night. Peter marveled at it because he had never seen Carl dance before. He didn't even know he knew how.

The girls swung their hips almost in unison around Carl, dipping and sliding up and down. Before long, everyone in the bar was gawking at the sultry triad.

Peter looked back across the bar and saw the brunette stalking over, her heels pounding the floor in outrage, making her way to the dance floor. When she reached the edge, her steps slowed and she slunk onto the floor, gyrating to the music.

It was like watching a car merge into traffic on a highway. The brunette danced her way over to the other three and then, ever so gracefully, insinuated herself into the mix. She, too, swung her hips, dipped, and slid herself up and down Carl.

For Carl, the room spun as the girls' three pulses blended with the music and the rhythm of their beating hearts. He felt their energy rise like heat off of their skin. He became one with them, mimicking their moves. His motion was both mechanical and fluid simultaneously.

After dancing for what seemed to Carl like a long time, he led his train off the dance floor and over to the bar. They were all dripping with sweat, and Carl promised them all a round of drinks.

They walked over to where Peter was standing, watching them quite obviously.

"Hey, Pete. I'd like you to meet my new friends…" Carl suddenly realized that he didn't know their names.

"Larissa," interjected one.

"Pam," said another.

"Yvette," said the brunette bombshell.

"This is my brother, Pete. Say hi, Pete. Yes, well now that we've gotten introductions out of the way…"

"I need to talk to you," said Yvette to Carl, "…alone."

Carl shot a knowing glance at Peter and a playful smile at the other two ladies who looked annoyed at Yvette.

"Uh, he danced with *us*," said Pam. "Maybe *you* can play with his brother."

Yvette didn't even give Peter a look. "Forget about these tramps. I want to get to know you better." Her accent was intoxicating. Carl couldn't place it.

Peter was incredulous. Three attractive women fighting over his geeky brother. The whole scene was unbelievable, but most entertaining. He just sipped his beer, quietly taking it all in.

"Ladies," Carl beseeched with no small amount of pleasure, "I'd like to get to know all of you."

Yvette leaned in close and whispered in his ear, "I know who you are."

At first, Carl had no idea what she was referring too, but as it dawned on him his skin went cold. He sensed her heart rate was stable; she was cool as a cucumber.

"Okay," he said. "Why don't we step into my office?" He gestured towards the men's room.

Peter's eyes went wide. "Carl, are you sure that's such a good idea?"

"You can get to know Pam and Larissa here. We'll be right back."

The other two girls looked at Carl and Yvette with disgust as they walked across the bar and disappeared into the men's room.

"Hi, I'm Peter."

Carl closed the door behind him and latched it shut. It was a small bathroom with barely enough space to hold two people. It was designed for single occupancy.

Yvette leaned with her back up against the sink. He was directly in front of her, only inches away, with his back against the door.

"All right, Yvette. What's this all about?"

"I've been watching you since you came in."

Now Carl was confused. Maybe all she wanted was a little boom boom in the men's room after all.

"Oh, well, I'm a little unprepared," he said sheepishly, wishing that he had grabbed some condoms on the way.

"I know you are the Man From Tora Bora, the Automaton."

Shit. "That guy," Carl said nervously. "They say he's not even human."

"That's right," Yvette said smiling.

"Who are you?" asked Carl.

"Let's just say I work for an organization that has been following your work from the beginning."

"What organization? Government?"

"No, not government," replied Yvette.

"How did you know who I was?"

"*How* is not important," she answered cryptically. "*Why* is."

"Okay, then why do you know who I am?"

"Because you are a very significant person, Carl. More than you even know."

"Significant? Significant how?"

"We know about your…gifts."

He heard them referred to as abilities or powers, but never as gifts. "And how could you possibly know—"

"Carl, you are in danger," she said urgently. "The government is using you, and RGT—"

"R-G what?"

"Retinal Gateway Technology."

He thought for a moment. Then he remembered Gitmo and Camp X-ray. Fiona's little toy.

"Yes," Yvette continued, "they've used it on you to look into your memories. They don't trust you, Carl."

"Okay, so?"

"You, what's happening to you, the undead drones, RGT—it's all connected."

"Connected? How?"

"Carl, the government plans to use RGT to spy on its citizenry as part of the Second Patriot Act."

"What? How is that possible?"

"Through television and computer screens, using the screens as the interface, like a touch screen. Only they will tap into your retinal nerve pathways. Like the way they are watching your father."

"My father? What are you talking about?"

"His television is one of the pilot applications. It's been part of how they've been keeping tabs on you. You haven't said anything sensitive to him, I hope."

It dawned on Carl. That weird sensation he felt when he burned himself with the grill. It was coming from his father's television in the living room, not the microwave.

"Shit, I have to go." Carl turned around and unlatched the door, flinging it open.

"Wait, Carl. It's not safe—" Then he was gone.

He stalked back across the bar to where Peter was seated. The girls weren't there. "Carl, back so soon?"

"Pete, we've got to get home."

"Home? Why? What happened in there?"

"Pete, Dad's in danger."

"What? Why?"

"I'll explain on the way," said Carl as he produced his mini-com and quickly toggled through cab companies. He selected the company they used to get to Frisky's and then selected *Return Trip*.

"Hey, asshole."

Carl turned around. It was one of the cowboys that were vying for Yvette's attention earlier...and his whole posse.

"We were just leaving," Carl said and tried to walk past the group. The cowboy put his hand on Carl's shoulder, preventing his exit.

"Here we go," Peter said, standing up from his bar stool.

"What seems to be the problem, gentlemen?" Carl asked as cordially as possible, given the situation.

"You are," said the cowboy.

"I don't understand."

"Well, let me explain it to you. You don't just come waltzing in and get between a cowboy and his girl."

"She wasn't exactly *your girl*, partner, but you can have her."

"Well, you see, it's not just me. My friends were hoping to get with her friends, and you can imagine their disappointment."

"They really weren't that interesting," Peter chimed in. "I couldn't wait to get rid of them. We did you guys a favor, believe me."

"I wasn't talking to you, dipshit," said the cowboy without breaking eye contact with Carl.

"I didn't mean to crash your rodeo," Carl reassured. "You have my deepest apology. We are leaving, and you can have all the rest of the ladies in this place to yourselves. Isn't that right, Pete?"

"Absolutely," said Pete staring down the cowboy insulter.

The cowboy looked around at his friends, each one bigger than the next. Five of them in total, a regular Stetson commercial. "That just isn't good enough." He began to crack his knuckles.

Carl saw Yvette saunter up behind the group. "Don't waste your time with that boy," she said, "he couldn't even get it up. I want to dance with a real cowboy." She grabbed the cowboy's arm and gently tugged it in the direction of the dance floor, looking at him imploringly.

The cowboy shrugged her hand off his arm. "When I'm done with limp dick over here."

Carl looked at Peter. "I guess he wants to dance with us, then."

"I reckon you might be right," Peter answered.

Peter took advantage of the cowboy's distraction with Yvette, and he threw the first punch at one of the posse. Another stepped in and punched Peter in the face.

The cowboy, startled but ready, grabbed Carl by the throat. Carl head-butted the man and grabbed his wrists and squeezed. The massive man yelped in pain and let go of Carl's throat. Carl shoved him back and then front kicked the man so hard that he went flying back into a waitress, sending her drinks flying.

Another of the posse rushed Carl, swinging wildly, but Carl dodged him, sending him off balance. He then grabbed the man and threw him into another who was coming at him, sending them both crashing into a table with patrons.

The patrons stood up in outrage and rushed Carl. Peter was ducking and throwing punches, handling his two cowboys just fine. Carl stood his ground as the two patrons cursed him out. The cowboy came rushing back, this time with a rather large fold-up knife. He shoved his way past the cursing patrons and tried to stick Carl.

Carl was too fast. He dodged the lunge and smashed the cowboy in the face. Nose bloody, the man dropped to his knees and held his face and newly dislocated teeth while screaming.

One of the posse broke a stool over Carl's back, sending him flying against the bar. Peter punched a cowboy in the throat and then shoved him into the one that hit Carl.

"We gotta get outa here," he shouted at Carl.

"Out the front door," Carl shouted back looking at his vibrating mini-com. "Cab's here."

Peter ran for the front door. Carl body punched a cowboy as he ran past and flipped over the back of another who was trying to tackle him.

Carl looked momentarily over his shoulder for Yvette, but she wasn't anywhere to be found. What he saw made him do a double take. Across the dance floor, he thought he saw…himself. Or a man that looked an awful lot like him. He was grinning wickedly at Carl.

A man bumped into him and, when he looked again, his doppelgänger had vanished in the crowd. He saw his brother disappear out the front door. He followed suit and made his exit as the bouncers came running over to the melee. One grabbed his wrist, but Carl turned it and flipped him in one deft motion.

"Sorry," Carl called back and he ran out the front door.

Peter was already in the cab. "C'mon, Carl!"

Carl jumped in. "Let's go," he shouted to the driver, who wasted no time and pulled away as five bloodied cowboys ran out the front door of the bar waving bruised fists in the air.

"Next time," Peter said panting, "you pick your own girl."

***

As the cab pulled up to the house, Peter and Carl saw government vehicles parked all over their father's front lawn, the twirling lights reflecting off of the front of the house. Neighbors were out on their front porches looking on in disapproval. There goes the neighborhood.

Carl jumped out of the cab as Peter swiped his mini-com in payment. Men in suits were taking his father away in cuffs—FBI.

"Now wait just a minute," Carl hollered at the suits. They halted and drew their guns.

"Stand down, Sergeant," an agent ordered him.

"What the hell is going on here?" Peter demanded.

The agent walked up to them holding out his badge. "Agent Holliswood, FBI. We're taking your father into protective custody, Captain."

"Protective custody…to protect him from what?" Carl asked.

"It appears your identity, Sergeant Birdsall, has been compromised."

Peter looked at Carl. Yvette.

"Really," Carl spat, "and this wouldn't have anything to do with the RGT installed into my father's television."

Holliswood gestured for the other suits to place Barry into one of the cars. "I have no idea what you're talking about, Sergeant."

"What's RGT, Carl?" Peter asked.

"Pete, this was what Yvette was telling me about. What Fiona used on me. They've been spying on us through Dad's television set."

"Is this true?" Peter asked Holliswood. He remembered the cable man and wondered if it was just a coincidence.

"I'd take care of your brother, Captain. He seems a bit paranoid."

"You can't take him," Carl declared. "He didn't do anything."

"Stand down, Sergeant Birdsall," Holliswood warned.

"Where are you taking him?" Peter asked.

"If I told you, then it wouldn't be protective custody, Captain," stated Holliswood coolly.

"If he's in protective custody, then why is he handcuffed?" Carl asked.

"I'm getting Colonel Betancourt on the horn," Peter announced, pulling out his mini-com. He stepped to the side to make the call.

"You can't do this," Carl shouted.

"We can and are," Holliswood answered. "Take your brother's lead and stand down. Your father will be just fine."

"Who is he being protected from? Did anyone make any threats?"

"I suggest you return to base and question your superiors. I am afraid I can't tell you anything else."

"Let me talk to him."

"I'm afraid that's out of the question."

Holliswood got into his car and pulled away. The other cars followed. Just like that, the circus on their front lawn packed up and left, only leaving tire grooves in his father's grass as evidence that anything had transpired. The block was quiet again.

"Colonel Betancourt is ordering us to return back to base immediately," Peter told Carl.

"None of this makes sense, Pete. If they were spying on me, why would they take Dad away? We need to go back to Frisky's and find Yvette."

"Wait a minute, Carl. The reason why they took Dad was because you told him too damned much. They must've sensed it with that..."

"RGT," Carl finished Peter's thought. "That's illegal, Pete."

"Not under the Second Patriot Act," Peter said. "And forget about this Yvette."

"We have to go back, Pete. How did she know?"

"Yes, exactly. That's the question Carl. How did she know? She must be some kind of spy."

"Which is why we have to find her."

"Which is why we need to leave her alone," advised Peter urgently. "And besides, we just got thrown out of Frisky's. We can't go back."

"No one threw us out, Pete. We walked out on our own. And we didn't start it."

"We can't go back, Carl. Those cowboys might still be there. If they see us again, they'll kill us this time."

"They were thrown out too. I'm sure they're long gone by now."

A cab pulled up.

"Goddammit, Carl. You called another cab."

"I'm going with or without you, Pete. This Yvette knows what's going on and, friend or foe, I need to find her. If she's right, the government's up to something..."

"Did it ever occur to you that *she* may be the one up to something?"

"Or," Carl continued, "she may know who is threatening Dad."

"Carl, maybe she's the one threatening Dad. And if she knows who you are, then chances are she's not the only one. You're in danger. We need to return to base."

"With or without you, Pete."

"Dammit, Carl..."

Carl looked into Peter's eyes and got into the cab.

"Carl, I'm your commanding officer. WE HAVE TO HEAD BACK TO BASE."

Carl closed the door and the cab pulled away.

Peter stood there dumbfounded. He knew he had to return to base, but his brother was headed back towards the bar and probably into trouble. He had no idea where they were taking his father. Carl had been right about the RGT being implanted in their father's television set. Everything was happening all at once and none of it made any sense.

Chapter 9

Carl's mind was racing. How long had the government been using RGT surveillance on his father? Where were they taking him? Why wasn't Peter doing anything about it?

He was hoping to get some answers from Yvette. Within fifteen minutes, he was back at Frisky's. He paid the cab driver and rushed through the front door.

"Hey, we don't want any more trouble," shouted the bartender, clearly unhappy to see Carl again so soon. The bouncer was approaching him quickly from the right.

"I'm not going to cause any trouble. Is that woman still here? The brunette? Her name was Yvette."

The bouncer grabbed him firmly by the shoulder and began to push him out. "You heard the man. You have to leave."

Carl spun around, throwing the bouncer off balance, and quickly crossed the dance floor looking around the bar for Yvette. The nervous patrons parted as he approached.

"I'm calling the police," the bartender announced, snatching up his mini-com.

Carl thought of identifying himself as a soldier, but after the show he put on he was afraid someone would put two and two together as to who he was. Then his problems would double.

He stalked to the ladies room, the bouncer only steps behind him, and flung the door open. There was no one in there. The bouncer slipped behind him and put him in a sleeper hold. Carl felt his oxygen slowly being cut off as the bouncer's pulse raced and his grip tightened like a python.

Carl had enough, and he had no time to screw around with this goon. He put his right foot behind the bouncer's right foot and lurched backward. The bouncer tripped over Carl's foot and released his grip as he began to fall off balance. Carl accented his move with a solid shove that sent the large man sliding onto the dance floor.

Carl stalked back across the dance floor, past the bouncer who laid there stunned on his back, and began to make his way towards the door.

The bartender reached below the bar and pulled a shotgun, aiming it at Carl. "Hold it right there."

Carl kept walking until he hit the cool night air. Dammit. Yvette was nowhere to be found, and he needed some answers. Maybe Peter was right and he should just return to base. He and Peter could appeal to Colonel Betancourt for their father's release.

He pulled out his mini-com and called for another cab. Unfortunately, the wait time for an available cab was a half an hour. Blueberry Hill was a one-horse town, and there were only two local cab companies.

So Carl began to hoof it back to his father's house. He dialed Peter.

"Carl?"

"Yeah, Pete, she wasn't there."

"I told you as much. Where are you now?"

"There are no cabs, so I'm walking back."

"We gotta return to base. We can talk to Colonel Betancourt."

"That's what I figured. We can—"

There was a loud thump, and Carl felt like his soul had been yanked out of his body. He felt himself hit the ground and slide across blacktop taking some skin off his arms.

"Carl...Carl? What happened?"

Pain shot through his body as he heard doors open and slam shut and then a howl of triumph.

"Well, lookie here," said a familiar voice, "it's that little shit from the bar, all by his lonesome." It was the cowboy and his posse. "You don't look so tough now, do you?"

Carl looked around for his mini-com. It was knocked out of his hand from the impact of the rusted blue pickup truck. Jesus, was everything in this town a cliché?

"Throw him in the back of the truck," the cowboy ordered, "he's going for a little ride."

Carl felt strong hands reach under his armpits and pull him up. He was half carried, half dragged to the back of the pickup, lifted up, and tossed into the back. Two of the posse hopped in the back with him. He heard the doors open and close again and the truck began to move.

He slipped in and out of consciousness, the sound of tires on pavement, the pistons of the engine, the rhythm of the heartbeats of the two men with him, and the other three in the cabin forming an odd harmony.

After some time, the truck came to a stop, the doors opened and closed again, and the tailgate clanged open. They dragged his sorry carcass out of the truck bed and onto the dirt.

Carl looked around in the dark and saw silhouettes jutting up out of the ground. "Look, guys, I'm a soldier. U.S. army." He had nothing to lose at this point. He was in deep shit.

"Shut up, soldier boy."

"C'mon guys. You made your point. What are you going to do?"

"Hey, man. What if he is army? Maybe we should check his ID."

"Check him," said the cowboy.

Carl felt hands rummaging in his shirt.

"He's got dog tags, Bart."

"I can get those anywhere," said Bart the cowboy. Check his wallet.

More hands rummaged in his pockets. He felt his wallet being pulled out.

"He's got an army ID card."

Bart took the card. "So you're a soldier boy after all. Hey, boys. Sarge thinks he's better than us townies. Don't you, boy?"

Carl couldn't believe it. He survived a category four hurricane, rogue zombie drones, traitors, cartels, terrorists, and now these shit kickers were going to clean his clock good.

"Hold him up."

Carl was hoisted up to a half standing position. Pain shot through his back and his legs were wobbly. Bart punched him hard in the stomach. Carl doubled over gasping for air, but the two men holding him pulled him back up. Bart punched him again.

"You don't just waltz in on another cowboy's rodeo, Sarge. Where's your friend? Is he army too?"

"He's a captain," Carl gasped.

There were sarcastic ooh's from the group.

"A captain? Wow. Fancy. You boys must think we're just a bunch of hayseeds."

"Now what would give anyone that impression?" Carl asked sarcastically, coughing up what felt like a lung.

Bart punched him in the face. Pain now radiated across his jaw.

"He's not so tough now," chimed in one of the posse.

"Well, to be fair, you did hit me with your truck."

"Still a wise ass," Bart said. "You won't be crackin' jokes after I mess you up."

This was who Carl was fighting to protect, risking life and limb. These were the noble citizenry of their great democracy. Carl tasted copper in his mouth and was disgusted with the world.

There wasn't any honor anymore. The degenerates were reproducing faster than decent folks were. Townies like this spent their welfare money pickling themselves silly while living off the taxpayers' dime, and do you think they watched the news? Do you think they knew that the army was fighting terrorists and cartels across the world, keeping the borders safe so that they can cash their government checks to go out drinking?

Were they grateful? How could they thank him if they had no idea what he had done for them? The whole country was turned inside out.

"C'mon…please…"

Bart laughed in his face. "I thought sergeants were supposed to bark orders, not beg." The posse laughed heartily. Carl felt some heartbeats accelerate. They were nervous. Maybe one of them thought this was about to go too far.

"C'mon, Bart. I think he's had enough."

"I'll tell you when he's had enough. Let him go."

The two holding Carl let him go and he dropped to his knees clutching his ribs. It hurt to breathe.

"Now drop and give me fifty, soldier."

Carl looked up at his tormentor to assess if he was serious.

"Do it, boy."

Carl put his palms in the dirt and lowered himself, his lips touching the dirt. As he pushed back up, the sting in his side nearly made him pass out. To make things worse, Bart put his foot on his back and pressed until Carl was face first in the dirt. There was a heartbeat faster than all the others.

"Bart, that's enough. Let's get out of here."

"I still don't think he learned his lesson."

"Bart, we're going to be in deep shit. Let's get out of here."

"Pull his pants off," Bart barked.

The situation had just gone from bad to worse.

"He wanted some action, I'll give soldier boy here some action."

Two of the posse pulled on Carl's pants. Now Carl felt his own heart rate thunder in his head. Even the cartels didn't sink this low.

"Bart, what the hell are you doing?" The posse member gave him a shove. Carl felt the cool breeze on the backs of his legs.

"I'm not down for this shit," said another. The posse had reached its limit.

They all became quiet, as there was the sound of a car approaching. Headlights shined in their direction.

"Quick, pull him up," said Bart, "and for Chrissake, pull his pants up."

They scrambled to pull Carl to his feet. He felt his pants pull up and hastily buttoned in front.

"Who is it? The sheriff?"

The car pulled closer. It was a van.

"Nah. Cemetery caretaker maybe."

The van pulled to a stop next to the pickup. Two people got out of the driver and passenger sides.

"Can I help you?" Bart asked defiantly.

Carl struggled to make out who the two people were, but the headlights behind them made distinguishing their features impossible.

There was a flash of lights and loud pops as the two figures gunned the posse down. As the grips were loosened around his arms, Carl again dropped to the dirt. Other than the pain in his side and the weakness in his legs, he did not think he was shot.

"Get him in the van...carefully."

He knew the voice, the pulse...the fragrance.

"Yvette?"

He felt more hands pulling him up. As something hard slid over his head blocking out the sounds of the world, he slipped out of consciousness.

***

"Drive slowly," Peter told the cab driver. He was looking for Carl, tracking the signal of Carl's mini-com. "Okay, stop."

He got out of the car and looked around the side of the road. "CARL!...CARL!" No answer.

He searched the ground as the screen of his multi-tasker blinked faster. He saw it on the ground. He reached down and picked up Carl's mini-com. Its screen was cracked.

"Dammit," he muttered to himself. He cursed himself for letting Carl go alone. He dialed Colonel Betancourt. "Colonel, Carl is gone."

"What do you mean he's gone?"

"I found his multi-tasker on the side of the road. The screen is cracked."

"Return to base immediately. I'll send out the MP's to look for him. We'll collaborate with local law enforcement. Road blocks, checkpoints—no one gets in or out of Blueberry Hill without us knowing about it."

"Yes, sir." He terminated the call.

He gave one last look around, but he knew something had happened to Carl. He thought that maybe he was hit by a car, and maybe he was taken to the hospital. He called up Christus Spohn Hospital on his multi-tasker and dialed the emergency room.

"Christus Spohn ER."

"Hello, this is Captain Peter Birdsall of the U.S. Army. I was wondering if there was a Sergeant Carl Birdsall taken to your ER."

"Hold on, let me check."

He was placed on hold as a song from 2014 blared on his mini-com. Great, oldies.

"No, there's no one here by the name of Sergeant Carl Birdsall, Captain."

"He's missing, and he may have been involved in an automobile accident. Can you contact me if he's brought in?"

"I sure can, sir."

Peter sent his number to the person on the other end. "Thank you."

He walked back over to the cab and got in.

"Take me to Fort Bliss."

***

Carl woke up in a dark room. After a moment, he felt his own warm breath on his face and realized that he was wearing something over his head that was blocking the light. He reached up to feel what it was. It was some kind of helmet, like for a motorcycle. He gripped it on both sides and was about to pull. He felt the rhythm of a pulse in the room...

"I wouldn't do that if I were you."

He turned and saw Yvette sitting in an old armchair, the moonlight barely illuminating her shape. He was on a couch. She reached over and turned on a lamp.

"Yvette? Where am I?" His voice sounded strange to him. There was a kind of strange reverberation.

She leaned forward and looked right at him. "You are safe now, Carl."

"You killed those guys."

"They were going to kill you...or worse."

Carl remembered his pants being pulled down.

"What's this on my head?"

There was another pulse in the room. "We've taken the liberty of designing a helmet that would block any transmissions to that chip you have implanted in your brain stem." It was a man's voice. Carl saw a small, but well-muscled man standing to the side of him dressed in black. Apparently, they were in some kind of apartment.

"And who the hell are you?"

"You can call me Night Stalker."

Carl chortled. "What, did your parents read too many comic books? How do you know about the chip in my head?"

"We know everything about you, Carl," said Yvette. "We also know that you are being used by your government. But they don't fully understand your condition. The authorities have found the dead bodies of those cowboys by now and you are missing. I wouldn't remove that helmet if I were you."

"*My* government," Carl emphasized. "So now I know you aren't American. Who are you? And why would you know any more about my condition than the army or my doctors?"

"Who we are, at this moment, is unimportant," said Yvette. "As to how we know about your condition…you are not the first."

Carl sat up. His body ached, but the pain was gone. He felt…stronger. "How long was I out?"

"You were unconscious for two hours," Yvette answered. "Let me guess. You feel almost as good as knew. Better even."

Carl rubbed the back of his stiff neck. "How did you know that?"

"Carl, we have records indicating that throughout history, there have been others like you."

"How is that possible? I don't even know why this is happening to me."

"All throughout history, scientific and cultural advancement has always gone hand-in-hand with superstition, fear, and hysteria. The Dark Ages, the Renaissance, the Enlightenment…even in times of great progress and growth, society has subscribed to the darkest of superstitions, outlandish old wives tales of witches, vampires, and boogiemen in the night."

"This is a great history lesson and all, but I don't see how—"

"Why don't you let her finish," threatened the man who called himself Night Stalker.

"You must forgive him, Carl," Yvette implored. She shot the man in black an admonishing look. "Night Stalker's talent is not diplomacy."

"With a name like Night Stalker, I'm not surprised."

"Retinal Gateway Technology is one of those advancements," she continued, "but concomitant with that advancement are the undead drones and, well, you."

"You're saying I'm the boogieman?" His modified voice was unnerving and made his question ironic.

"Where do you think this technology came from, Carl? Do you think your government created it?"

"Are you suggesting they stole it? From who?"

"Not exactly stole," Yvette said, "found is more like it. And believe me when I tell you it is not of this earth. As you now know, they plan to install it into televisions and monitors all over the country to spy on the populace. That was why they took your father."

"So what you are telling me," said Carl, "is that the United States military is using, what, *alien* technology that they just found?"

"There was a crash site in the Congo during the Tutsi-Hutu conflict in 1994. It was reported as the plane crash of the Hutu leader, but there was something else. An unidentified craft of unknown origin."

"A spaceship?" Carl asked incredulously.

"Villagers in the area became infected by a mysterious virus…"

"THV," Carl interjected.

Yvette nodded. "They became cannibalistic, attacking the other villagers. Those who were infected through bites turned into cannibals themselves…the undead. The problem was neutralized and your military salvaged the craft. During analysis of the technology found on the craft, they found RGT."

"So that's the connection."

"Your military developed the infantry drone program, weaponizing the THV, and received funding in a time when terrorists were hiding in caves in the Middle East, where conventional armies and weapons couldn't reach them. The approval for the program was immediate."

"And the RGT?" Carl asked.

"The First Patriot Act enacted under President George W. Bush had been repealed. America was not ready for Retinal Gateway technology. The climate for it had been poisoned. But as long as they had funding for the Infantry Drone Project, they had the resources to develop RGT."

"Then the Second Patriot Act is about to be enacted thanks to the Order for International Liberation," Carl added.

"Correct," said Yvette. "Now the climate is conducive to RGT. The military has developed it to the point where it is ready for application. Under the Second Patriot Act, your government can observe the populace—reading their thoughts, their memories—all without having to disclose how they are doing it."

"All in the name of national security," Carl concluded. "How do you know all of this? Who do you work for?"

"We work for your government," Yvette answered simply.

"But how…what do you mean…son of a bitch!"

Carl leapt to his feet and across the room to where Yvette was sitting and he had his hands around her throat in seconds. "YOU ARE OIL."

Suddenly his skull thundered with pain. Electricity erupted in his helmet and he staggered backwards. Night Stalker took his hand off a button and delivered a front kick into Carl's solar plexus, sending him falling over and behind the couch. He stood up gasping for breath, the sounds coming from the helmet sounding inhuman and monstrous.

Yvette was rubbing her neck. "So now you see Night Stalker's talent. I wouldn't do that again."

Carl spat the words out, still catching his breath, "So what is this…I've traded one leash for another? You bastards killed my mother…I'll take my chances…with the kill chip."

"We don't want you dead, Carl. If we did, Night Stalker would have killed you already."

"So, what is it you *do* want?"

"We, too, were used by your government, Carl. They used us as a salient enough threat to justify the Second Patriot Act. They've used us to destabilize dictatorships in the Middle East so that radical groups fill the gaps, and now that they are on the cusp of passing the law, they are hunting us down with the Infantry Drones. They used *you* too, Carl, and now they'll perceive you as a threat. You went AWOL, as far as they are concerned. You are dangerous and at-large. With RGT ready for application, they no longer need the Infantry Drone Program. You have become a loose end that needs to be tied. What happened with your mother was regrettable…"

Carl hissed at them through the helmet.

"But maybe we can help you save your father."

"How?"

"I want to introduce you to Simon Belmont. After meeting him, I think you'll see that we are no al-Qaeda. We fight for freedom. With RGT, your country's people are in danger of losing it without even knowing it."

"And what if I don't want to meet this Simon Belmont," Carl said spitefully.

"You are free to go at any time. You can take your chances with the army, but you won't last very long and it won't help your father."

"Why should I trust you? You killed my mother."

"*I* didn't kill your mother, Carl, but I can take you to the man who can help your father. You also swore to protect the citizenry when you enlisted in the army. Right now, the government is trying to take away their freedom. Big government at its worst, poking its dirty fingers into everyone's business."

"Now you sound like my father."

"Carl, you were the victim of treachery in your own military."

"Peter."

"Excuse me?" Yvette looked confused.

"My brother, Peter. I have to tell him what's going on. He needs to be involved."

"Where was your brother during the operation in Xcaret when everything went wrong? He was missing when you needed him most and then, just like that," she snapped her fingers, "he reappeared…*convenient.*"

How did she know all of this? "My brother is a good man."

"Where was he when they were taking your father away like an enemy of the state? Did he lift a finger to help?"

"You don't know my brother."

"No, Carl, it is you who doesn't know your brother."

"This is bullshit."

"Time is wasting, and I can't guarantee your father's safety," Yvette said urgently.

"How do I know this Simon Belmont didn't mastermind the mall attack that killed my mother?"

"I assure you that he didn't. There are factions in OIL that are unruly and extreme. We are not a part of that faction. But if we don't help your father and do something about RGT, I don't know if we'll be able to control them."

Carl's head was swimming. Here he was, talking to OIL operatives, and they're not only accusing the U.S. government of using them, but now they're saying that they are on his side. It wasn't all that far-fetched. The government used the Taliban against the Soviet Union in Afghanistan, but the Taliban then turned on the United States.

In this case, Yvette was saying the U.S. turned on OIL. Maybe the government learned from its past mistakes…or maybe it didn't. Then there was the RGT installed on his father's television. No one had notified him of the surveillance, and now his father was in custody like a terrorist.

None of this added up. He didn't trust these two OIL operatives, but he didn't trust the army or the government either. He knew his father was in danger.

"Okay. Take me to your leader."

Night Stalker chuckled at the statement uttered in the helmet's other-worldly voice.

"Screw you, *Night Crawler*."

"Come," gestured Yvette, "we have no time to waste."

"One day you won't have that button," Carl said to Night Stalker as he passed him.

"One day I won't need it," retorted Night Stalker.

Carl left the apartment. Yvette glared at Night Stalker. "You aren't threatened by this kid, are you? Don't push him. We need him."

"I'll back off for now," assured Night Stalker, "but he won't always be in the dark and one day I'll have to deal with him."

"Are you frightened?" she taunted him.

"Just trying to be practical," he said coolly.

"Be practical and pull the car around," she ordered.

His eyes met hers, there was an unspoken understanding, and he left the apartment brushing Carl's shoulder as he passed.

"What's his problem? He is in desperate need of some people skills." Carl quipped.

"He's a killer, plain and simple, and the best," said Yvette. "He doesn't need to be nice."

"Well maybe he just met his match," Carl said with a hint of menace, as he followed behind Night Stalker.

'*That's what I'm counting on*,' Yvette thought to herself.

***

"You are sending Barry Birdsall *here*?" asked Fiona incredulously.

"He will be detained at Camp X-Ray until we take his son into custody. The MP's found five dead bodies in a graveyard in Blueberry Hill, and they match the description of the men Sergeant Birdsall and his brother tussled with at a local bar."

"Are you suggesting that he murdered these men, sir?"

"It doesn't look good, Captain. He's missing and potentially very dangerous. We are considering utilizing precautions—"

"The kill switch."

"We may have no choice. Captain Birdsall mentioned a woman his brother met at the bar who seemed to know who he was. She told him about the RGT in his father's television. If he's been abducted, he's a security risk."

"If he hasn't been abducted, he knows about the RGT. He'll be pissed off and looking for his father and you're leading him straight to Camp X-Ray. He knows I'm directing the RGT research. He'll be coming for me."

"Even with his enhanced abilities, he's quite alone, Captain. No drones. If he comes looking for his father, GITMO is completely equipped to handle him."

"I pray you're right, sir."

"Keep me posted on any developments. In the meantime, keep Barry Birdsall comfortable. Give him the Club Fed treatment. This situation will resolve."

"Yes, sir."

Colonel Betancourt terminated the call on the other end.

She couldn't believe how short-sighted he was being. Carl was teetering on the edge as is. Now they pushed him over, and he'd be coming for revenge. With his knowledge of the RGT in his father's television, her fingerprints were all over the ketchup bottle.

Betancourt had no idea how dangerous Carl really was, and Fiona had no evidence to support her instincts. It was in her dreams. He was a clinical, ruthless killer. The ultimate hunter and, worst of all, he may not be under his own volition.

By spying on his father and taking him into custody like a criminal, Betancourt may have just set off a doomsday machine...

...and he was going to start his Armageddon with Camp X-Ray.

***

"With all due respect, sir, what do you mean we may have to flip the kill switch?" Peter asked dubiously.

Colonel Betancourt stroked his chin thoughtfully. "Let's play out every scenario. Sergeant Birdsall is missing. He may have made contact with someone who somehow knew who he was, probably an OIL operative. He's either been abducted, in which case he's a potential security leak, or he's gone rogue and he's going to retaliate for your father being taken into custody."

"Or he's wandering around injured somewhere trying to turn himself in," added Peter.

"The authorities found the bodies of the men you and he had an altercation with," countered Betancourt. "Shot to death, all five of 'em."

"Carl wasn't carrying a gun, sir, and I found his mini-com on the side of the road with its screen cracked. I think he's in danger, and while we're on the topic, sir, what was RGT doing in my father's television?"

"I'm not at liberty to say, Captain. But I can say that it was for your father's own protection. Your brother's knowledge of RGT makes him even more of a security risk. No one knows about it. Did you think you were the only ones? It's highly classified and well above your pay grades."

"And now I know about it. So are you going to off me too, sir?"

"Watch your tone, Captain. There's been a lot of heat on this Infantry Drone Program. With everything that's happened, we will likely just shut it down. If you're not careful, you may be reassigned to Afghanistan or some equally unpleasant hellhole."

Peter sat forward in his chair. "Are you threatening me, sir?"

"I'm saying that the army needs to do what it needs to do in the name of national security. In the meantime, I am suspending all operations of the program. Your priority right now should be to reach out to your brother and get him to come in peacefully, so I won't have to seriously consider using the kill chip in his head. Am I clear?"

"Yes, sir."

"Dismissed."

Peter stood, saluted, replaced his headgear, and left the office. He met Nolan Kettle in the hallway.

"What are they going to do about Carl?" Kettle asked.

"We've been disbanded. If we can't bring Carl in quietly, they're going to activate the kill chip."

"Jesus. Do you think he murdered those men?"

"What do you think, Nolan?"

"No, that's not him."

"Damned right it ain't him. Any ideas?"

"Well, sir, he doesn't have his mini-com. We know that."

"There was someone at Frisky's, a woman he met."

"A woman? Carl?" Nolan asked.

"I know. Stay with me for a moment. She seemed to know who he was, Nolan. She knew our father was being taken into custody. He went back to look for her."

"Do you think he found her?"

"I don't know. Last I heard from him, she wasn't at the bar. Maybe she found him."

"Well, if he's being held captive, then we're going to have to find him. If he went willingly, I think he would've contacted us by now. He knows he's expected back at the base."

"Right," Peter said, "but we don't know who took him."

"What did this woman look like? Did she have any distinguishing feature? A tattoo, anything like that?"

"She was smoking hot," Peter quipped.

"Are you sure this was the woman Carl was talking to? You really have to take me next time you guys go out."

"I didn't really hear her speak, so I don't know if she had an accent. Then they danced for a little bit, and then she took him into the bathroom."

"Holy shit," Nolan exclaimed. "My little Carl's all grown up. Big Pete Birdsall showed up by his egghead little brother."

"You're not helping, Nolan."

"Right. Sorry. Was she with anyone else?"

"Two other women, but I don't think they really knew each other."

"Did you see who she left with?"

"No, we were thrown out of the bar for brawling with some townies."

"Holy smokes!"

"Nolan…"

"Right. Sorry. Does the bar have any security cams?"

"That shithole?"

"Just asking. What about the bodies of your cowboys? If there's a connection, she may have left something about her behind."

"Local authorities said the bullet wounds were consistent with a professional hit. Double taps in the foreheads all around. Ballistics is running the bullets and casings."

"Shoe prints? Tire treads?"

"Nolan, you watch too much bad television. This is Blueberry Hill. They don't have sophisticated CSI."

"How did this woman know Carl and his new friends were going to be at the graveyard? They must've been tailing them from the bar."

"I find it hard to believe that Carl would've gone to a cemetery with those guys," said Peter.

"Who said he went willingly?" Nolan pointed out.

"Great, so Carl was abducted by one group and then rescued by a second abductor." Peter rubbed his eyes in exasperation.

"Yeah, but the first abductors are dead and they had the bullets of the second abductor in them."

"Well, until we hear from ballistics, we have nothing there. Besides, if we do find out what type of gun fired those bullets, how would that help us?"

"It might tell us something about our mystery guest," Nolan said arching his eyebrow.

"You really love this shit, don't you?"

"I just want to find my friend," Nolan said gravely.

Peter's multi-tasker went off. He looked at the screen. "Speak of the devil…ballistics got back to me. The bullets were fired from a Zigana M16 pistol."

"That's Turkish," said Nolan authoritatively.

"How do you know that?"

"Sir, I'm a Texan. It's my business to know my guns."

Peter smiled at Nolan. "Kettle, you're not as dumb as you look."

"Thanks, sir."

"If you're right, then these were likely OIL operatives."

"So where would OIL operatives be hiding in Texas?" Nolan thought out loud, stroking his chin.

"The JTTF," answered Peter.

"The what?" Nolan asked as if Peter was speaking in tongues.

"The Joint Terrorism Task Force," Peter said. "It's a joint effort between the FBI and local law enforcement. They gather intelligence and move in on local terrorist cells. It's been around since 9-11."

"So how do we contact them?"

Peter put up a finger telling Nolan to wait. He dialed Colonel Betancourt. "Hello, Colonel. Ballistics came back saying the bullets in the bodies were from a Turkish handgun…yes, sir, they think it was a professional hit…yes, OIL…I need you to call ahead to the FBI. We need to talk to someone working in the JTTF…Yes, sir. We think they may have an idea where they took Carl…thank you, sir."

"So, what did he say?"

"He's going to call ahead to Dallas and get them to arrange a rendezvous with the right local law enforcement. If they have any hunches about local OIL dens, maybe we can check them out and see if Carl is there or left us a clue that he was there."

"How many hunches do you think they have?"

"Doesn't matter. We'll split up into squads and check out each one if we have to."

"Right. I'm already on it," said Nolan as he got on his mini-com to raise the men.

***

Carl was led inside by Night Stalker and followed by Yvette. He had a sack over his helmet, but he could sense everyone in the structure by their heartbeat. Yvette's was accelerating; she was nervous. Night Stalker stayed cool as a cucumber, heartbeat like a metronome.

He was guided into a room with two sentries on either side of the door and three men across the room. When Carl entered the room, the one in the middle became a little more aroused than the men on either side.

"Simon Belmont, I presume," said Carl in a reptilian voice.

"The Automaton, in the flesh," Belmont responded. "I am honored."

Carl felt Night Stalker stir a little, his vitals fluttering. He likely had his finger poised over the button that administers painful shocks within his helmet. Someone pulled the sack off of the helmet. Belmont was a tall, older black gentleman sitting behind a desk with two bodyguards on either side of him.

"Forgive the helmet," Belmont said, "but it is the only thing protecting you from the government's signal to that kill chip in your skull."

"I suppose I have you to thank for that," Carl croaked.

"No thanks are necessary. Please, have a seat." Belmont gestured to a wooden chair in front of the desk.

Carl looked around him and sat. Yvette nodded at Belmont and backed into a seat behind Carl. Night Stalker remained standing, but also behind Carl. Carl sensed that everyone in the room was nervous…except Belmont. He was anticipating.

"So, I'm told you can help my father," Carl started.

"I think that I am one who can sympathize with your situation, Sergeant Birdsall."

"Oh yeah? How's that?"

"I, too, was used by my government and then discarded. I am sure you are familiar with Darfur?"

"Yes. I am. Quite the genocide you guys had there years ago."

"Yes," Belmont looked down at his shoes. "There is great confusion over what happened there."

"Not from our perspective," Carl said.

"No, of course not. Let me tell you my perspective, Sergeant."

"Please, all my friends call me Carl," he said sarcastically.

"Yes…Carl. Have you ever heard of the Janjaweed?"

"Yeah, they were the Muslim fanatics who raped and massacred villages of non-Muslims."

"Fanatics, no. I was Janjaweed when I was much younger. The Sudanese government employed us to deal with the rebellion, which was much like the South's in your American Civil War. The rebellion was tearing the country apart. Animals not fit to live in the country. Pigs."

"Non-Muslims," Carl challenged.

"Trouble-makers," Belmont countered.

"Oh, yeah, those Christians and animists are a brutal bunch," Carl mocked.

"We were charged with keeping law and order," Belmont continued, ignoring the sarcasm, "and we did so rather unapologetically, I'm afraid. That is, until the formation of the Popular Forces Group that subsequently denounced us as mercenaries who didn't represent their cause. The Terejem, once our brothers, turned on us like we were enemies."

"Well, you know what they say: no honor amongst thieves," Carl taunted.

"I was driven out of my home," Belmont continued, ignoring the remark. "Exiled."

"You were murderers and rapists. I don't see how any of that relates to me."

"Carl, you use the undead to hunt enemies of the United States. They are eaten alive. Some in your own country would call you a monster. And now that they've found the bodies of those men you had a problem with at the bar, you, too, are now a murderer."

Carl felt his own pulse liven. "I don't murder innocent people for religious fanaticism."

"No, you do it for freedom, democracy, the American Dream. You are a killer, now more than ever. You are changing, Carl."

"Call me Sergeant Birdsall."

"Whatever. You lust for carnage. I can see it now. You want to kill me."

"I am not the same as you."

"You're right, Sergeant. I've never used the living dead to eat my enemies alive. I'm not saying that I'm an angel, by any means, but we both did what our government required us to do. Now we are both pariahs, just for performing our sworn duties."

"No one was killed who didn't deserve it," Carl said. "All terrorists. No civilians."

"Sergeant, in a civil war, there are no civilians. I regret what I did for the Sudanese government. That is why I am doing what I am doing now."

"OIL."

"Yes."

"Terrorism," Carl pushed.

"To the oppressors in power, I suppose so. To those who are oppressed, disenfranchised, exploited, we are liberators. Hence the name, 'The Order for International Liberation.'"

"That's kind of vague for a mission statement, don't you think, Mr. Belmont? That probably isn't even your real name."

"It is who I am now, Sergeant. A reinvention, if you will. Just like you."

"You don't know the first thing about me, pal."

"On the contrary, Sergeant. As I am sure Yvette has explained to you, you are not the first of your kind."

"Oh, yeah. She told me about the aliens. So what are you guys, some kind of homicidal Scientologists or something?"

Belmont chuckled at the reference. "All throughout history there have been leaps in cultural advancement."

"Yeah, yeah, I heard this already," Carl said impatiently, "and with those jumps, superstition. Boogiemen, monsters, yadda yadda yadda."

Belmont smiled almost sympathetically. "During those times, there were singular individuals such as yourself who emerged with developing, extraordinary abilities. They became incredibly fast and strong, developing the ability to heal quickly, and they were the ultimate predators. Sound familiar?"

This got Carl's attention. "Go on."

***

Peter was stationed with a squad and local law enforcement just outside of an old farm in Blueberry Hill. The local sheriff was ornery. A federal agent, Grant, was en route.

"We've been gathering intel on this farm for almost a month. How the hell is it that you guys got wind of it and are horning in on our operation?" asked the sheriff testily.

"I'm not at liberty to say," answered Peter. "Are your men in position?"

"Yeah, they're ready. We were waiting for someone big to be linked to this site, a higher-up in OIL. This whole thing is damned premature. They're going to pack up shop and run their operations elsewhere."

If this townie asshole only knew the stakes, Peter thought. The reason why the U.S Army was now involved in such short notice, the reason why the FBI cooperated with Colonel Betancourt, was because OIL had kidnapped the Automaton himself. But this yahoo didn't need to know that.

"Captain, we're in position."

It was Kettle. He was stationed outside an old house on the outskirts of Beeville.

"Copy that, Lieutenant. Stand by."

"Copy."

There was some movement on the farm. Sentries posted in strategic locations. Farms didn't post lookouts. Something was about to go down. Maybe Carl was inside.

"When is this Agent Grant getting here?" Peter asked. Time was of the essence. Every minute Carl was with OIL, he was in danger. Not just from OIL, but from the army. They were nervous, and their fingers were poised over the button activating the kill chip in Carl's brain.

"He'll get here," insisted the sheriff. "We can't move until then."

"We don't have much time," said Peter.

"We'll wait for Grant," reiterated the sheriff. "This ain't your dog-and-pony show, Captain. You can't just waltz in here and take over. Just what is it you expect to find anyway?"

"We may have a man in there," revealed Peter reluctantly. "He may be in danger."

"What do you mean a man? A soldier? Army?"

Peter nodded.

"Jesus," hissed the sheriff. "What the hell is army doing in an OIL den? You guys doin' undercover work now?"

"Not exactly."

The truth was that Peter didn't really know that this was an OIL den. Furthermore, he didn't know that Carl was going to be here. He didn't even know for sure that Carl was taken by OIL. All he had to go on was that those cowboys from the bar were shot with a Turkish handgun. Here he was, sitting outside a farm, hoping that his brother was inside and safe.

"So, do you know anything about those zombies the army's using on the border?"

Great. Now the sheriff was making small talk.

"I heard something about it. A different unit."

"I'll say it's *different* all right. Ain't that the damndest thing you ever heard? Zombies patrolling the border. It makes sense though."

"I guess." Peter was counting the minutes to when this Agent Grant was arriving.

"Lieutenant," Peter said into his mini-com, "any sign of your agent?"

"He's en route."

"Yeah, copy that. Same here. Over."

Damned bureaucratic red tape. If they didn't move soon, Carl was either going to be killed by OIL or by the army. Either way, dead was dead.

"You believe all that shit about the Automaton?" The sheriff was probing under the dubious guise of small talk.

"Don't know anything about it, really."

"Well, I think he's a freakin' hero, if you ask me."

"I suppose."

"You suppose? He's out there risking his ass to save all of us, and all you can say is you suppose?"

"Like I said, I don't really know anything about it."

The sheriff scratched the stubble on his face thoughtfully. "Who do you suppose watches *his* back?"

***

"At first, these singular individuals were heralded as heroes, saints even," Belmont continued, "but then they were feared, and eventually persecuted. This happened in Native American villages in the New World, in villages in Africa, the witch hysteria in Europe. These poor people were killed, their bodies desecrated in their graves for fear they'd return to prey on the living. What they failed to realize, Sergeant, was that these individuals were also gifts."

"So now I'm a gift."

"You can be, but only if you use your given talents for good. However, your government would have you use it to their ends."

"I don't see stopping terrorists and drug traffickers as a bad thing."

"Then what's next? Toppling dictatorships that the United States deems intolerable."

"I thought that's what OIL was for, according to you and Yvette," said Carl.

"Yes, and now they've conveniently discarded us. So they use you and your drones to eradicate us...and ultimately take our place."

"You've got to be kidding."

"It makes sense, Sergeant. We've served our purpose. We created an outside threat in ourselves so that your government could justify emergency powers: the Second Patriot Act. It is all but passed. Liberties will be lost, but for the sake of national security. Now, so that America's hands aren't dirty, it commissions a special unit of infantry drones to hunt us down and wipe us out. You, Sergeant, are America's new saber, and you are being rattled. Your unit is the biggest thing since the nuke."

Carl was unsure of himself and the whole situation. Of course, the whole scenario made sense, but it sounded like paranoia, the fodder of whack-a-doo conspiracy theories. Then there was Major Lewis and his corruption. Until that all came to light, he would've never have believed that anything like that could have happened.

"Sergeant, you do realize that you can never go back. Either way, you have been compromised. By now they will have figured out that you are with us. You now know the truth about our original purpose, about how we were used."

"It's just OIL propaganda," Carl said. "I don't believe a word of it."

"But you murdered those poor men."

"I was unarmed. They know that."

"You could have taken the gun off of one of them," Belmont said, "and then used it to kill them."

"Why would I do that?"

"Because you are unstable, Sergeant. Because the army fears you. Now that they will have the green light to use RGT, you are no longer necessary."

"I thought you said I was going to be used to dethrone dictators and destabilize regimes," Carl said.

"That was before the UN Security Council's resolution that your unit be used strictly for defense, and before you went AWOL."

Carl knew that Belmont wanted him to feel trapped, like joining them was his only option. It was at this point that Carl knew he had to kill Simon Belmont. It was only a matter of when.

"So tell me about how you can help me…"

Chapter 10

Peter was losing patience.

"Colonel."

"Yes, Captain."

"We're running out of time. I can't wait for this agent. We have to move now."

"Negative, Captain. You and Lieutenant Kettle must wait for an agent to arrive at each of your locations. It was one of the conditions under which the FBI even agreed to cooperate with us, even given the...special circumstance."

"Sir, with all due respect, every second that we wait, the objective is in danger."

"Hold your positions until the agents arrive at both scenes. Am I clear?"

"Yes, sir. I still think we'd do better with some drones."

"Negative, Captain. Too risky, and the situation doesn't call for them. The FBI is well equipped to handle this type of scenario."

The Waco siege from Peter's high school history class popped into his head. "Even if Kettle and I each had one drone, maybe ...the objective could communicate with us. Maybe they could track him down."

"That's a negative, Captain. They're not bloodhounds. We can't have drones wandering the backyards of Texas sniffing out the objective. If the objective is compromised, those drones could turn on us. You, of all people, should be mindful of that."

"Yes, sir."

"Over and out."

The sheriff walked over to where Peter was standing off to the side for privacy. "This man of yours, Captain Birdsall, he must've been kidnapped from the sound of the urgency in your voice."

"I can't discuss it," said Peter crossly.

"You must be involved with the border if OIL took one of your men right here on our own soil."

Great. This yahoo wasn't that dense after all.

"From all of this urgency and immediate cooperation from the Feds," he continued, "this soldier must be pretty damned important."

Just then, a Chrysler Intrigue with tinted windows pulled up. The clichés just kept on coming.

"Looks like the FBI is on the scene," Peter announced, happy to change the subject.

Agent Grant stepped out of the car. Peter strode over, meeting him halfway. "You must be Agent Grant."

"And you must be Captain Birdsall."

"Our agent has arrived, Captain," said Kettle from his location.

"Copy that. Same here. Stand by."

"Roger."

The sheriff scampered over.

"Sheriff Brody," said Grant.

"Agent Grant," said Brody in return.

"So you think the broken arrow is in one of these two locations we've been scouting, Captain?"

Broken arrow? Carl wasn't a missing weapon. He was a soldier. "We have reason to believe that he might, Agent Grant."

"Enough to jeopardize two different operations, Captain?"

"You know the stakes, Agent Grant."

Grant looked at the sheriff, who was in turn watching him expectantly for some indication of what all of this hoopla was about.

"You'd better be right about this, Captain. I don't like to waste 'hard to come by' intel on hunches."

"I understand," said Peter gravely.

"Okay," said Grant. "I have two teams in place flanking the farm. Sheriff, your men will take the front. Captain, your squad will bring up the rear and take the barn on my signal. My teams will converge on the house. Brody, you'll back us up."

Peter and Brody both nodded. Peter walked over to Sergeant Vassar.

"Vassar."

"Yes, sir."

"We're taking the squad around back, quietly. On Agent Grant's signal, we take the barn."

"Yes, sir. Men, formation."

The squad got into a two-by-two column formation. Vassar gestured and they crept quietly behind him. Peter was beside Vassar. They silently snaked their way around the farm, passing one of Grant's teams, using the trees and bushes as cover. It was dark and the moon was just a sliver of light in the sky covered by clouds.

When they reached the rear of the farm, the barn was in clear view. Monochromatic in the night's illumination, it loomed over a few bales of hay next to a wooden fence with wooden cross-beams forming an x underneath. It looked like a painting.

Peter spotted two sentries walking a path around the barn and he signaled to Vassar. The farmhouse sat silently beyond the barn, towards the front of the property. Only a dim light was shining out of the kitchen window in the back.

"Captain, are your men in position?" It was Grant.

"Copy that."

This was it. The moment of truth. Peter prayed that his brother was in this house.

"Hold position."

***

"I can provide you with the means to take your father back safely," Belmont said.

"Take him back," Carl repeated. "You realize he's at Guantanamo Bay."

"Yes, I know."

"That's a heavily fortified position. We can't just waltz right in there and ask for my father back," Carl snickered.

"I never said anything about breaking in," answered Belmont. "And who says we're asking?"

"Enough with the kung fu bullshit. If we're not breaking in, then how are we getting my father out?"

"You, Sergeant, were at Camp X-Ray. You know what is there."

"Holding cells and RGT, but I don't see what that—"

"You forgot something else," Belmont said. "That is where your government creates and stores the drones."

"What are you suggesting?" Carl asked, already knowing the answer.

"You will break your father out from the inside using the undead." Belmont said it as if the answer was so obvious. "We will lend support from the outside."

Belmont was right. Major Lewis had told Carl before the Tora Bora mission where the drones were made. Camp X-Ray at Gitmo. Jesus, he was being held right next to them in a cell after his extraction from Pakistan, and he didn't even realize it.

"They may anticipate that move," Carl said. "As you said, by now they know I'm with you. I've killed some locals...if they really believe I've gone rogue, it would follow that I'd make a move on Gitmo. They'd destroy the drones in Camp X-Ray or move them."

"Oh, I'm counting on them anticipating that move, but there is a more parsimonious move they can make instead of moving or destroying drones."

A chill went down Carl's spine. "They'd never use the kill chip. It's too premature."

"Once again, Sergeant, you overestimate your usefulness to them and underestimate your liability. With you out of the way, there would be no urgency to address the several hundred drones they have housed on the premises."

Carl thought of Peter. Of Fiona. Betancourt was a good man, just like Peter said. "Nice try, Belmont, but you don't know the politics involved. It's not that simple."

"And you're not that expendable, is that it?"

Carl steadied his heartbeat as he took stock of his surroundings. The time to make a move was coming. Belmont was going to lose patience or motivation at some point. Carl was going to have to find his opening and end this man. What better way to prove his loyalty to the brass and prove he hadn't gone rogue?

"I expect that you're not going to do me the favor of helping return my father for free."

Belmont smiled collegially. "You know human nature well, Sergeant. We will want the RGT. It is dangerous in the hands of your government."

"They installed it in my father's television. There are other prototypes. You would only be getting the original. Besides, you expect me to believe that it's safe in your hands? Now, whenever you'd capture American operatives, you'd have something to interrogate them with. You could learn about future operations."

"We would use it to survive," responded Belmont. "Evading capture or worse would certainly help our cause."

"And what is that again?" Carl asked.

"To free the oppressed from their oppressors."

"Kind of like you did in Darfur," Carl sneered. "I'm sure all of those women and children feel *liberated*."

"The RGT is a small price to pay for your father's safety." Belmont was trying to hit Carl where he lived. Make him forget about the bigger issues and focus on the ones close to his heart. This man was some piece of work.

"How would we get the RGT out? The apparatus isn't exactly portable," Carl said, "it takes up half a room."

"Where do you think they're taking your father's television?" Belmont pointed out. "We just need the television and the main unit's hard drive for interpretation of the retinal scanner in the television. We can fill in the rest."

"In order to accomplish that, someone *will* have to be going in," Carl said.

"They don't just keep me around for my good looks," quipped Night Stalker.

"He is a specialist in infiltration, espionage, and sabotage," Belmont stated with sinister pride. "Besides being a world class assassin."

"You're just a jack-of-all-trades, aren't you, Night Crawler," Carl jeered.

"You just worry about your daddy," responded Night Stalker. "Leave the rest to the professional."

"How do we get my father out anyway?"

"We'll have a cigarette boat waiting," Belmont said. "They won't know what hit them. They'll be too busy dealing with the drones to track you and your father."

Carl thought of Fiona. She was in there, too. She was involved in planting the RGT in his father's television. She was in charge of monitoring him. She was partly to blame.

He thought back to the therapy sessions with Fiona in her office at Fort Bliss. All of the personal conversations, things shared in confidence, their conspiring to kill the traitorous Major Lewis...Was Carl now being dealt with as a traitor?

He thought about the night they met at Frisky's, before he was in the Infantry Drone Program, when he was still an egghead college student—nerdy, weak, and shy with women. Now look at what the army made him—a monster, a damned freak.

He was supposed to be out hunting those responsible for his mother's death, and instead, he was becoming a killer. Now the army was afraid of him. Afraid enough to put a kill chip in his skull. Afraid enough to plant borderline illegal technology into his father's house to spy on him. Then they took his father.

Carl put his helmeted head in his hands.

"When does all of this go down?"

***

"Okay, move in."

It was time. Peter signaled to Vassar, who in turn signaled to the rest of the squad. He said a little prayer that his brother was somewhere on this farm. Law enforcement had cast their net. If Carl wasn't here or in Beeville, he was lost. They'd be out of leads.

They began to move in on the barn...the old fashioned way. No drones, just men. Live flesh, blood, and bone. They crept low across the field towards the wooden fence. The two sentries were walking away from them, their backs turned on the approaching squad.

In the distance, gunshots came from the farmhouse. It was going down. The sentries peered in the direction of the farmhouse but then turned and ran back towards the barn.

Two privates intercepted them. The sentries were placed in plastic restraint strips and gagged. Peter signaled and they moved in on the barn. Peter held up two fingers and pointed up.

Vassar selected two men and they stepped forward. One gave the other a boost up onto the roof. That soldier then pulled the other up. They crept over to a window, slid it open, slipped in silently, and positioned themselves on the loft above.

Peter positioned the squad on either side of the large barn doors. He signaled for his men to hold their position as the night popped in the distance with volleys traded between sides.

"It appears to be some kind of lab," one of the privates whispered over his mini-com from his position on the loft.

"Give 'em gas," Peter whispered into his mini-com.

They heard the thump of two tear gas grenades and yelling from inside the barn. There was thrashing around and shouts and the doors flew open. Peter's squad plucked the men as they ran out covering their faces, ten in total.

They were thrown to the ground and bound. There was what could only be cursing in another language, something between Arabic and French. Maybe both.

"Any sign of the objective inside?"

"Negative, sir."

"Sergeant Vassar, clear the barn."

"Yes, sir. MASKS."

Vassar and the squad put on their gas masks and then entered the barn, rifles raised. There were folding tables in the center of the barn with various parts lying on them. Bomb parts. Several minutes passed as Peter covered the prisoners and checked his watch. The popping in the distance had stopped.

"All clear, sir. The objective isn't in the barn."

Dammit.

"This is Grant. We've cleared the farmhouse. No sign of your man."

Apparently, they had moved in on a bomb-making cell. A good move, but not their primary objective. He had to call it in to Betancourt.

"Colonel. Captain Birdsall reporting."

"Yes, Captain."

"The objective was not at the farm. Repeat. The objective was not at the farm."

"Lieutenant Kettle reported in a few moments ago. The objective wasn't at his location either. Return to base immediately."

"Yes, sir."

Peter pulled off his helmet and ran his hands through his thinning crew cut. That was it. They were back at square one. These were their two biggest leads, and neither produced Carl. If OIL had him, they had him in a location unknown to the intelligence community and local law enforcement.

With the net in place, there was little chance that Carl was getting out of this alive. At this point, whoever was holding him, their best bet was to kill him and dump the body. It was their only way out of it. There was no way they were slipping him past any of the checkpoints undetected.

Statistically, they had 48 hours from Carl's abduction. After that, the chances of finding him shrank from slim to none.

"I'm sorry, sir," Vassar offered.

"We have our orders," Peter said harshly. "Back to base."

***

"We would have to move quickly," Belmont stated, "to take them off guard."

Suddenly Night Stalker's mini-com was buzzing. He looked down at it and read the screen.

"What is it?" Belmont asked.

Night Stalker walked over to Belmont and whispered into his left ear. When he was finished, he backed away and continued to read the screen.

Belmont smiled. "It appears that the army's attempts to find you have failed."

Carl wanted to wipe the smile off the smug bastard's face. Night Stalker was distracted. It would only take a second.

Carl leapt from his seat as he heard a tone go off in his helmet, but there was no pain. It wasn't from Night Stalker's button.

Before anyone knew what happened, Carl had hurdled the desk and was on top of Belmont with his hand wrapped around his throat. There was a message flashing across the inside of the visor of his helmet.

The bodyguards in the room had laser sights trained on Carl, red dots gliding up and down his body. Night Stalker fumbled for the button to induce electrical charges in Carl's helmet, but Belmont put out a hand to halt him.

"What the hell is this in my helmet?" Carl asked without loosening the grip on Belmont's throat. The man's eyes looked like they were going to pop.

"You hear the tone?" Night Stalker asked smirking.

"There's a message inside my helmet: transmission successfully blocked." It dawned on him what had almost just happened, and he slowly released his grip on Belmont's throat.

"I told you," Belmont wheezed, "you were a loose end. That helmet that we took the liberty of providing you just saved your life."

Carl crouched on top of Belmont's desk dumbfounded. The pulses of everyone in the room thundered in his head like a cacophony. They did it. They really did it. Peter, Fiona, Betancourt...they had all betrayed him. A couple of failed attempts to find him and they gave up on him just like that.

If they were going to write him off so easily, what were they going to do to his poor father? If Peter had allowed the army to harm his little brother, could he...would he protect his own father?

He put his left palm on the desk and quickly shifted his weight, sliding gracefully off the desk. Every time he moved, everyone's pulses accelerated in the room...even Night Stalker's.

"Will I ever be able to take this helmet off?"

"Not as long as the signal is being transmitted to your kill chip," Belmont said softly, almost sympathetically. "I would imagine that they will transmit for a while to make sure it is done."

Icy thoughts filled Carl's head and then, just like that, they cleared. Something had taken over him. A switch had flipped. No rage, no betrayal, no sadness. Rather, a clinical detachment washed over him, like in Xcaret when he was surrounded by hordes of rogue undead drones...but more profound.

"You would like this helmet to stay on, wouldn't you?"

"Actually," Belmont said, standing up and leaning forward, resting both of his palms on his desk, "I would like you to join us of your own free will. We have done nothing to harm you."

"I will take my father back."

"Yes, and we will help you. By helping us obtain the RGT, you will be helping your people. You see, now, how your government operates. They are not to be trusted."

"Where do we start?"

"First, we must make you stronger."

"I am strong enough. I could've killed every one in this room before any of your men could've gotten a shot off."

"Be it as it may," Belmont said, "you can be stronger. If you are going to get your father back and punish those who have betrayed you, you will need to be as strong as you can be."

"Who's to say that once you get your RGT, you won't try to dispose of me like the army?"

"Number one," said Belmont, "if I had wanted you dead, you'd be in the ground already." Carl chortled at the bold remark. "Number two, I have just offered to make you stronger. If I were planning to discard you, why would I do that? I'm not one of the oppressors now, Carl. I, like you, have been awakened. Join us. Help us punish the corrupt. Help your father."

"So how do we make me stronger?"

"It won't be pleasant," Belmont said candidly. "You will gain power every time you sustain trauma. You will lose a little more of your old self each time."

His old self. What a joke. Was Belmont referring to the wimpy science geek living with his parents or the duped soldier who was fool enough to think that he was doing something good for his country?

No, he wanted to fully embrace his inner hunter. He was a perfect killing machine. Mercenaries like this Night Stalker had nothing on him, and now the army was going to pay for what they did to him.

"Nice office. Is it yours?"

Belmont smiled. "What better place for a man in my position than to be liberating young minds?"

Carl reached across the desk and righted the toppled desk sign that read PRINCIPAL.

"A long way from raping and pillaging," Carl remarked.

"I, too, have come a long way, Carl. Let me guide you there."

"So what is Night Creepy, the gym teacher or something?"

"Go with him," Belmont instructed. "He will take you to one of our safe houses. With you presumed dead, they will soon call off the searches and checkpoints and we'll be able to get you out and ready."

Carl nodded. Night Stalker gestured towards the door and one of the bodyguards opened it. Carl started to walk out, but he stopped in the doorway.

"What is it?" Belmont asked.

Carl chuckled bitterly. "This is the first time I've ever been in the principal's office."

Part III
Retribution

Chapter 11

Fort Bliss
Texas
08:21 HRS

"Permission to speak freely, sir." Peter was trembling with anger, barely keeping his composure.

Colonel Betancourt was stoic as ever. He anticipated this reaction the moment he pressed the button. "Go ahead, Captain Birdsall. But before you do, for the record, I was following orders from General Ramses."

"There were other options," Peter launched right into it. "We could've used the drones to find him."

"We have been monitoring the drones from the moment you reported him missing," Betancourt said. "Just in case he was going to send a message through them. There was nothing. No movement, no signals."

"Why wouldn't he have sent out a signal?"

"Maybe he didn't have the chance."

"But, sir, I don't understand why the button had to be pushed."

"It wasn't my call, Captain."

"Well then, I'd like to speak to General Ramses."

"Not a good idea," stated Betancourt frankly. "Do you want to end up in the brig? He gave an order, and I followed it. We both know what the General's rationale was."

"But it was wrong."

"Careful, Captain. I can appreciate that this was your brother and all, but to question a General's order is unacceptable."

Unacceptable. The fact that his whole family had been snatched from him in one way or another, and being powerless to do anything about it, was unacceptable. The fact that he was somehow supposed to soldier on alone, yet again, and take his licks was unacceptable.

"Yes, sir."

"I am sorry for your loss, Captain."

"Does my father know?"

"Not yet. He will be informed."

"Great. He gets to hear the news and suffer with it all alone."

"There's a full complement of medical and psychiatric staff where your father is," Betancourt added, but it was no consolation to Peter.

"What is going to happen to my father?"

"He is going to be held in protective custody."

"But Carl is dead—"

"Captain, as far as the public is concerned, your brother is still alive. As long as the public thinks he is still alive, your father is in danger."

"What about the program?"

"We will suspend all missions. You and the drones will continue to train here at the airfield."

"Oh, I see," Peter said. "So now we're the weapon the U.S. has ready to be deployed at any moment but never is. Like the stealth bomber or the nuke."

"For all anyone will know, you are standing ready."

"So all of the funding, the research, the training…"

"We are about to be given the green light to develop another technology," Betancourt said.

"RGT," Peter said.

"The hope is that with this new technology, we won't need the Infantry Drone Program."

"I don't understand," Peter said. "So the government is going to spy on every household in America looking for terrorists?"

"I cannot discuss this with you any further," Betancourt said curtly. "You will continue training exercises on the base."

"Can I talk to my father?"

"Not at this time." Betancourt saw the look on Peter's face. "You will at some point but, given where he is at the moment, it is impossible."

"Yes, sir."

"Once his body is found, we will hold funeral proceedings for your brother."

"Thank you, sir," Peter tried to conceal his bitterness, "but what if we never find his body?"

"If OIL has him, I'm counting on them giving us back the body and taking credit. That would be a major blow to our morale. Your brother became a symbol of sorts."

"So, you are counting on the media knowing eventually."

"I'm counting on nothing, Captain. If OIL gives his body up, we'll use it as a rallying cry to double our efforts."

"You mean make my brother a martyr to push RGT," Peter needled.

"Or," Betancourt continued, ignoring the remark, "they never come forward and we find the body. Your brother will again become a rallying cry for RGT."

"Either way my brother is a martyr and you win."

"Win, Captain? How exactly do we win? We just lost the key to the Infantry Drone Program's success after all of the hurdles to keep this program running."

"My brother is a martyr, sir, but he wasn't killed by OIL."

"He would've been...or worse. We spared him that."

"With all due respect, sir, we really don't know what the outcome would've been."

Betancourt shook his head. "The outcome would've been inevitable. Your brother is a hero."

"Hearing you say it cheapens it, *sir*."

Betancourt frowned at Peter. "Easy, Captain," he said menacingly. "Remember, it wasn't my call. I happen to agree with you that perhaps more could have been done before hitting the kill switch."

Peter was surprised by the admission. To do so would be to question General Ramsey. Betancourt could burn for it.

"Thank you, sir."

"Now get back to your unit. I expect training to commence within the hour."

"Yes, sir."

"Dismissed."

"So what did he say?" Nolan looked concerned.

"He said that he was only following orders from General Ramses," Peter replied.

"What about using the drones—"

"Negative. We've been enough trouble."

"What about the program?"

"We're to continue conducting training exercises. But we're off the border, or any other mission for that matter."

Nolan stroked his chin thoughtfully. "RGT."

Peter sighed deeply, "Yeah."

"So what, we're chopped liver now?"

"And Carl is going to be a martyr."

Nolan became incensed at this. "They kill him, and then they're going to call him a martyr. Let me guess, to push the RGT."

"Exactomundo. They're going to say OIL did it."

"That's bullshit, sir. Carl deserved better."

"Thanks, Nolan."

Nolan leaned against the wall and looked up at the ceiling. "I remember this one time during Basic; we were doing Ground Fighting Technique. It was the final session."

"Ah, yes," Peter recalled. "Each platoon selects a man for combat in front of the drill sergeant."

Nolan smiled. "Yeah, we had this real hard-ass, Maddox."

"They're all hard-asses, Nolan."

"Anyway, we had so many big guys in the platoon. Fromm was one of them."

"Yeah, I can see he'd be an obvious choice. Carl told me you went around the platoon and convinced them to choose him. Why?"

"He wasn't the obvious choice, which made him a profitable bet," replied Nolan. "He had this fire in him…" His eyes welled up. "An intensity. I really believed he could do it. He fought Cronos."

"Jesus!" Peter laughed. "That sasquatch? No wonder he was pissed at you."

"He did okay at first, but Cronos caught him and put a choke on him. He should've tapped out. Anyone would've…but Carl didn't. He held on until he blacked out."

Peter smiled to himself. "That's my little brother. Stubborn as a mule."

"I visited him in the hospital. Snuck him Playboy mags even. He held a grudge for a while."

"He was lucky to have a friend like you, Nolan."

"Shit," Nolan chortled, "I was lucky to have a friend like him. You should've seen him in Tora Bora, man, with the drones around him and all. He marched into that cave with no other living being and tore the ass out of it. He killed terrorists like it was free. Then there was his transmission from inside—"

"I know," Peter said, "it was foolish."

Nolan huffed. "It was the ballsiest damned thing I ever heard of."

"Yeah," Peter said reconsidering, "I guess it was."

"He may've been your little brother, sir, but he was one tough bastard."

***

Two Weeks Later
22:04 HRS

Carl knelt on a concrete floor in a large, unfinished basement in an OIL safe house, his jaw broken and his mouth dripping blood onto a large crack in the floor. He had sprouted an extra eye above each of his original eyes, which added to his depth perception—all four of them red and stinging from mace.

Night Stalker delivered another well-placed kick to Carl's ribs with his black combat boot, and this time Carl felt something crack. He struggled to catch his breath, his chest cavity shuddering with pain each time he inhaled.

Night Stalker walked over to a folding table and picked up a flame thrower, strapping it on slowly. "I would be lying if I said all this didn't bring me some amount of pleasure."

Carl looked up with fierce eyes and spoke through gritted teeth, "Bring it on, asshole."

Night Stalker waved around the tip of the flamethrower as if he were conducting an orchestra. "As you wish."

He shot a stream of flames across the room and engulfed Carl, who screamed in rage and pain. Night Stalker cut off the stream quickly, careful not to put Carl out of his misery. The whole point was to maim Carl, not kill him, which of course appealed to Night Stalker's sadistic nature.

Carl crouched on the concrete smoking, parts of his skin charred black. He shuddered, and Night Stalker laughed as Carl was going into shock.

"It's days like this that I realize that I really love my job," Night Stalker taunted. "Ready for more?"

Carl looked up, his body quaking madly, and nodded deliberately. Night Stalker smiled and gave him another burst of fire.

Yvette walked down the simple wooden staircase and stood next to Night Stalker. "He's had enough."

"Oh, c'mon. He's a tough guy. He can handle more."

She glared at him. "Any more and you'll kill him. I said he's had enough."

The two stared each other down for a few heartbeats, and then Night Stalker put his hands up in feigned surrender. "All right, all right. Hell hath no fury like a woman's scorn."

"You have no idea," she replied icily.

Carl was now squirming on the floor, grunting and coughing. His body was a roadmap of trauma. Yvette considered him clinically.

"Place him in his cell," she said. Then she walked back up the staircase.

"Yes, ma'am," Night Stalker said sarcastically to himself. He reached down, grabbed Carl by one of his ankles, and dragged him across the floor, leaving a smear of blood and fluid trailing behind. Carl screamed at the friction.

Night Stalker opened up a door to a small room and dragged Carl in. He then stepped over Carl and looked down at him.

Carl looked up, shivering violently, giving little yelps. Night Stalker smirked and delivered one final boot into Carl's side, and the scream that resulted was deafening.

"Nighty night, Mr. Automaton. Get nice and strong because one day soon, you and I are going to have it out." Night Stalker slammed the door behind him as he left the room.

Carl lay there on the floor in the dark. No light, no bed, no window. All of that was unnecessary. He just needed a space the size of a closet to spend the night in agony as his body healed itself and changed. This was the seventh day of a nightly treatment of trauma and torture. The more damage that was done, the stronger he became. After the healing, he was never the same as before.

His skin had become obsidian, the trauma (especially the heat) resulting in increased polymerization. His form had become elongated, lithe but powerful. His eyes glowed red. He had become a walking nightmare, a killing machine with a singular purpose—to end lives.

He found the strength to sit up against the wall. He felt his body restructuring itself. His skin tingled as it reorganized its molecular structure. His organs shifted, accommodating his thin frame. His muscled stretched painfully on his limbs and his fingers elongated.

He sensed the heartbeats of the OIL operatives upstairs. He knew they were discussing him, but he didn't care. He was getting stronger. For his father. For the retribution that the army had coming to it.

"He should be ready after tonight," Yvette declared.

"Then I will make preparations," Belmont said.

"And what if we pull this off?" asked Night Stalker. "Then what?"

"Then we move on to the operation in Italy," answered Belmont.

"What about his father?" Night Stalker was picking his fingernails with a very long hunting knife.

"What about him?" Yvette asked reproachfully.

"We're really not going to drag him around with us, are we? I'm not a babysitter, you know."

"He'll be none of your concern," Yvette snapped. "Just do your job."

"She's right," said Belmont. "We made a promise to Carl and we're going to keep it. It's none of your concern, Night Stalker."

"Okay, just asking," snapped Night Stalker petulantly.

"Just focus on getting the RGT. That is your concern," said Belmont.

"I'll start making the preparations," said Night Stalker. He eyed them both significantly before leaving the room. They heard the front door slam.

"He gives me the creeps," Yvette told Belmont.

"Yes, well, he's a necessary evil. All mercenaries have a rotten disposition. It comes with the territory, but he's the best at what he does."

"I can't wait to be done with him," Yvette sneered.

"Now, now. He's part of our dysfunctional little family, mercenary or not," Belmont said. "A man with his talents always comes in handy."

"Where did you find him anyway?"

Belmont smiled. "Actually, he found me."

"You have an annoying habit of collecting strays," said Yvette sardonically.

"You, too, were once a stray, my dear."

Yvette blushed a little.

"If it weren't for my…intercession," Belmont mused, "your life would be very different."

Yvette remembered it as if it was yesterday; only it was twelve years ago. The busy streets of Florence. The orange rooftops. The covered bridge over the Arno River. The Piazza della Signoria.

"I remember," she said…

She and her sisters fanned out in the crowd, filthy and ragged, with eager fingers searching for unsuspecting pockets while her father waited on the outskirts of town. If they were unproductive, they would be beaten.

She saw this one American tourist talking rather loudly to a local asking for directions, as if speaking louder would make him easier to understand. His wife stood apart from him, looking awkward, her large purse jutting off to one side.

Yvette approached quickly, building enough momentum for a nice 'accidental' bump. She collided with the woman's large purse, sending the distracted woman reeling around.

"Oh, pardon me, young lady." When she saw Yvette's ragged appearance, her demeanor soured.

Yvette had already tucked her hand with the wad of Euros into her shawl, but the woman was checking her bag.

"Wait…come back." The woman tugged on her husband's sleeve. "That girl took my Euros."

The husband turned and saw Yvette already backing away. "Get over here!" The angry husband began to advance. Yvette turned to run, but someone grabbed her arm tight.

It was a man in dark blue pants, a light blue shirt, and a dark blue cap. Polizia. The cop told her to give the Euros back, tugging on her arm with a tight grip.

Yvette looked across the plaza and saw her one younger sister watching her from behind the statue of Neptune. There was nothing she could do. She was on her own.

She reached into her shawl and produced the colorful wad of Euros. The cop snatched it from her hand and handed it back to the wife. The wife took it graciously and placed it back into her purse.

As the cop pulled her away, the husband of the woman shot Yvette a reproachful look. His wife, however, looked rather uneasy watching Yvette being taken away. Was it pity? Guilt?

Yvette prepared herself for the fallout that was to come. Her father was going to be displeased that she was caught, and she would be beaten. Her sisters would then be beaten for allowing Yvette to be caught, even though there was nothing they could've possibly done about it.

Then there was Djordji, her father's friend to whom she was promised. He, too, would be displeased. He was fifteen years her senior.

The cop took her under the covered bridge, where she was passed off to someone else. The second man was not a cop. He was older, perhaps in his fifties, well dressed, but his grip was equally as strong on her arm.

She found herself in a small town in Tuscany called Montecatini. She was placed in a small hotel across the street from the police station.

"What is your name?" the older man asked her.

She did not respond.

He pulled a wedge of nougat covered in chocolate and almond slices. "What is your name?"

She did not take it. "Dooriya."

"Romanian?"

She nodded.

"You will now be called Yvette."

She was taken by an older girl wearing too much makeup into a bath where she was scrubbed thoroughly. She sat sheepishly in the cast iron tub looking at the faded tile in the bathroom, avoiding eye contact with the older girl. She studied the square molding along the edge of the ceiling. By the time it was done, she had never been so clean in all her life. Her skin actually shined.

The older girl then silently took her into a small bedroom and sat her in front of a large mirror. The room contained a small bed with a thick cream-colored spread. The wallpaper was old and yellowed, and the maroon carpet felt plush under her feet.

The older girl began to open a container of foundation, but Yvette put her hand up. "No. No, thank you."

The older girl smiled warmly at her. Obviously not comprehending Yvette's decline, she reached to apply some foundation on her face.

Yvette stood up and backed away from the mirror. "I said no, thank you."

"No?" Asked the older girl.

"No," repeated Yvette.

The older girl looked nervously at the door to the bedroom. Yvette wheeled around to find the older Italian man standing in the doorway.

He waved the older girl off casually. She nodded reverently and put the foundation back on the small table in front of the mirror. She shot Yvette a nervous glance and then excused herself from the room.

The older man entered and said something in Italian that she didn't understand. He closed the door behind him and locked it from the inside. Yvette didn't need to speak Italian to know what was going to happen next.

The older man slowly pulled off his shirt exposing a chest prolific with gray hair. He reached at his waist and unbuckled the belt of his pants.

She backed nervously into the chair in front of the little table, banging the table against the wall. He tittered in delight that she was so frightened, as if it was going to heighten the experience for him.

He doubled up the belt deliberately in his hands and pulled it taut, snapping the two parallel straps of leather. She had to do something fast because, by all appearances, he meant to beat her.

The beating didn't scare her in the least, as her father beat her and her sisters frequently. Her father beat her when she was unproductive or disobedient, but he was her father. It was his household.

This old pervert was not her father and therefore had no right to beat her for being unproductive or disobedient. He had taken her and cleaned her up for her indentured servitude. Yvette was a traveler of Romany. She had been to many towns and seen houses such as this...from the outside.

She stepped forward, pleading with her hands pressed together as if in prayer. The older man stopped and considered her for a moment.

He smiled the smile of a favored uncle and she, for a moment, thought she had a chance.

He swung wildly, clapping her on the side of her face with his belt. The blow sent her reeling backward, and her hand reached up to feel the sting of a welt forming on her tender face.

The older man clenched his teeth and advanced, bringing down blow after blow onto her. All she could do was crouch and cover her face, her arms taking the brunt of the leather strap, but she did not yelp or cry out. No, she wouldn't give this son of a bitch the same courtesy she would her own father.

As suddenly as the assault came on, the blows stopped. Yvette kept her hands up in case the old bastard was taking a breather, but the man was listening to something. She heard it, too. She put her hands down and stared at the door as she heard the screams of other girls and furniture thrashing about outside.

The older man appeared equally confused as he was wondering what the hell was going on outside. There were heavy footsteps just outside the door, and then someone began to turn the doorknob from the other side.

The older man looked frantically around the room. He decided to wait on the left side of the door. He put a finger up to his lips telling Yvette to hush, telling her that they were in this together.

The door was kicked open with a heavy boot strike, sending it swinging inward. It covered the older man with the belt, and a young Simon Belmont came storming in clutching a rather large serrated knife in his right hand.

He looked down at the young girl staring at him in an off-white terrycloth robe. There was a brief expression that Yvette had never seen prior to that day, except from the tourist wife that she tried to pickpocket. It looked like pity, no remorse, but what was it that this man had to be remorseful about? He was not responsible for her state in life or her grim situation.

As this unspoken understanding passed between young Yvette and this man, the door was flung back shut and the older Italian reached over Belmont's head with the belt. He quickly pulled back, tightening the belt around Belmont's throat.

Belmont lurched backward, stabbing wildly with the knife, but he never found his target. He gurgled and growled as his face began to turn from red to a shade of purple, a vein popping out of his forehead and the chords of his neck jutting out in shocking relief.

Yvette stood there in her robe watching the scene unfold before her. She and this older Italian man had succeeded in their ruse. Soon it would all be over and things would go back the way they were before this interruption.

She reached down and picked up the knife in her small hands. It appeared to be like a machete or small sword in her little hands, like she was a Roman soldier from ancient days. The Italian man shouted something in Italian at her, but she didn't understand.

She nodded.

Belmont had dropped to the floor on his knees, now clawing at the strap around his neck, his eyes bloodshot and bulging out of his head. The Italian man wrapped the slack of the strap around his right wrist and flexed his biceps, tightening the strap around Belmont's neck. The older Italian man reached out with his right hand, palm up and gesturing wildly.

He wanted the knife.

Yvette walked up to him, towards the beckoning right hand. She grabbed the large knife firmly by the handle and stared at it for a moment in her hands.

Just like that, she drove it into Belmont with all her might. He leaned forward and clutched the handle tightly, his eyes wide with horror, and he began to go limp.

Surprised, the Italian man dropped his hands and Belmont fell to the ground. He just stared at the girl in astonishment, and then a smile crept across his face. He stood there sweating, with his hair disheveled like a crow's nest, looking proud. This girl was going to fit in after all.

He stepped over the body of Belmont and reached out for Yvette, but she backed away. For a moment, the Italian man looked confused, but he stepped forward to hold her. Again, she retreated.

Finally, he became irate, yelling at her in Italian, pounding his fist into his hand mightily. He was the king of his castle, and he demanded respect. At least that's what she thought he was trying to say.

Suddenly, the crumpled form of Belmont pushed itself up, and he sliced into the right Achilles tendon of the Italian man. The Italian dropped like a stone onto the lush red carpeting. He yelled, clutching his ankle, blood streaming between his fingers.

Belmont stood up, rubbing his neck and wiping the saliva from the side of his mouth with the back of his hand. He walked around the Italian man squirming on the floor so that he could look into his face. The Italian man spit at him. "Tutsun."

Belmont took the knife and drove it through the top of the Italian man's head. "Yeah, but I'm the one with the knife." He pulled back and the large blade slid out of the man's head, coated in his blood. The body dropped to the floor and blood began to pool, making the maroon carpet appear darker.

Belmont reached out his hand to Yvette, who looked at it. She reached out hers and took it...

"Your intervention did not come without a cost," Yvette told Belmont, back in the here and now. "You weren't just rescuing. You were recruiting."

"You were free to go at any time," said Belmont softly. "We had interests in Montecatini. The local bosses didn't like our presence in Italy. We were foreigners who didn't pay them their tribute. We had to send a message. Besides, you were the only girl from that house who became a true believer."

"And here I am now," said Yvette thoughtfully.

"We have another rescued soul in our basement," said Belmont. "He is no less vulnerable than you were. No less vulnerable than I was when I had been betrayed by my government. When I had realized I had been used."

Yvette understood what she had to do. "I'll go talk to him."

Carl was shuddering on the floor in his cell when he heard someone fiddling with the digi-lock. It disengaged, and Yvette stood there in silhouette.

"I thought you could use some company," she said. He said nothing in reply.

She stepped over him and sat on the bench. "Jesus," she said. "It's just like a prison cell."

"It's...only temporary," Carl croaked through the helmet.

"You know, when Belmont found me as a young girl, my whole life was a prison. My name was Dooriya."

"Why...did you...change it?"

"When he found me, I was reborn. I was supposed to be someone else, but then I realized I had a greater purpose than wandering from town to town pilfering money and bread from the pockets of the rich."

"And...what higher purpose...is that?"

"To liberate others just as I was liberated. To free those who had been held down and used for the greed and ambition of others. I, too, was involved in all kinds of corruption. As a child of Romany—"

"You...were a...gypsy?"

"Why are you so shocked?"

"You appear...too..."

"What? Beautiful? Civilized? When Belmont found me, I was drafted into another type of corruption. I was to be a plaything, purchased by rich men at their whimsy while their wives tended to their children at home."

"I'm sorry."

"Why? I'm not. If my life hadn't taken that ugly turn, Belmont wouldn't have found me. I would be dressed in rags, married to some terrible man, sending my children out to beg and steal."

"I guess you dodged a bullet." Carl's breathing had become more regular.

"You know, you, too, are being reborn, Carl."

"Into a monster."

"No. You are becoming something greater than yourself. Something beautiful."

"Beautiful. Look at me. I look like a walking horror. A monster who controls other monsters."

"You are meant for something extraordinary. You are no longer Carl Birdsall."

"I was thinking about this," Carl said. "What if I am becoming what created the THV virus and RGT? I have these memories that aren't mine, feelings that aren't mine."

"They are yours now."

"And what if my new purpose is to destroy humanity?"

"What do you mean?" she asked.

"I have dreams that I am on other worlds leading attacks. I am the perfect killer leading legions of undead to either consume or convert all who stand against me. What if that is my purpose?

"You said so yourself. There have been others throughout history, others that have shared my experience, and each had been killed by their own people. Maybe their own people figured out the poor bastards' purpose. Maybe I should be killed, not encouraged. I'm too dangerous, Yvette."

"Or," she added, "maybe your purpose is to use your gifts to fight oppression in the world. Maybe you can use your undead drones to fight against the powerful so that countless lives of the innocent can be spared."

"You don't get it, Yvette. Maybe *I* am to be an oppressor, working for distant would-be overlords."

"I hardly think so," she said dismissively.

He sat up with great pain. "Why not? It makes sense."

"The Outworlders have been an influence throughout the ages," she said, "planting ideas and technologies along with superstition to keep us humble. Why would they now want to come and destroy humanity?"

"Because modern society no longer subscribes to superstition. The world has lost faith in the great religions. Environmentalism, cloning, smaller and smaller computers, electric cars. These are our idols.

There's no fear of fire and brimstone guiding society. Religion is used as an excuse to commit atrocities."

"I'm hardly talking about religion," Yvette said. "I do not think they are connected to Christianity, Buddhism, or Islam."

"No," Carl said, "but vampires, devils, and boogiemen. What makes you think these 'Outworlders' are beneficent at all? You and Belmont talk about the oppressed and justice. Maybe there's something bigger happening than politics or wars."

"And what is that?"

"I don't know. Armageddon. Extinction."

"We all choose our paths in life," Yvette said. "Do you want to use your gifts to destroy humanity or help it?"

"Yvette, from everything you've told me, we are shaped by circumstances. You wouldn't be who you are today unless Belmont found you, right?"

"Yes."

"Well, maybe something found me and now my future circumstances will dictate what I will be."

"You've been exposed to something," she said, "and you are now changing. But I believe your exposure was an accident."

"You don't know that," Carl said.

"If the Outworlders wanted to destroy us, they'd come and do it themselves," she said. "They wouldn't need you to go through all of this. If they are advanced enough to create Retinal Gateway Technology, then they'd be able to do their own dirty work."

Carl thought about this. She had a point. Maybe his imagination was running wild. "None of this makes any sense to me."

"That is because you are going to have to redefine yourself. You are no longer Carl. You choose what you are to become. Circumstances insinuated themselves into your life, but now you decide what to do with it."

"You want me to change my name..."

"Belmont did it. I did it. It's a new beginning."

"What about Night Crawler?"

"He's an ass," she said. "He's not one of us. He's a mercenary. You are special."

Carl thought about this. He really wasn't the biggest fan of Carl Birdsall, the geeky student who lived in his parents' house, or the Sergeant demoted below his big brother despite unbelievable acts of heroism.

"Kafka," he said sardonically.

"I see you haven't lost your sense of humor," she said.

"When do we go for my father?"

"In a few days. We have to strike while they are still looking for your body."

"You mean before they realize that I'm not dead."

"Exactly."

Yvette got up and stepped over him to the door. "Good night, Kafka."

"One more thing…"

"Yes?"

"Were you really attracted to me at the bar, or was that all part of the act?"

She smiled. "You mean you cannot tell?" He felt her heartbeat accelerate.

He knew.

Chapter 12

Guantanamo Bay Detention Facility
Two Days Later
22:09 HRS

"Increase patrol along the perimeter," Captain Fiona London ordered. "I want an inspection of all motion detectors and security cameras."

"With all due respect, ma'am, we've inspected them already."

"Well do it again, Lieutenant McCall."

"Don't you think we need to run this past Major Lyons?"

"Are you questioning a direct order, Lieutenant?"

"No, ma'am. I'll have it done."

Fiona hadn't slept in days. She was saddened by the news of Carl's termination. She understood the decision, but something inside of her made her feel uneasy. The nightmares intensified, but she ascribed it to her exposure to what she saw when using the RGT on Carl. Poor Carl.

She remembered how goofy he looked at Frisky's the night she went to meet Peter. He went from awkward and bookish to strong and brave...and then something else entirely. Poor bastard.

Then there was Peter. The poor guy was one hundred percent hero. He had to witness losing two units, his mother and brother—hell, they didn't even find Carl's body yet—and his father was rotting in a cell in this place like a terrorist.

Then there was the RGT. Betancourt relayed orders from General Ramses to green light RGT for expanded use in anticipation of the passage of the Second Patriot Act. This meant that every television, mini-com, and computer screen was going to be connected to RGT. No civilians were going to know about it, and it was all going to be legal.

"Ma'am."

"What is it now, McCall?" She saw the look on her face. "What's wrong, Lieutenant?"

"It's the drones in Camp X-Ray, ma'am."

Her skin went cold. "What about the drones, Lieutenant?"

"They're...restless ma'am."

"Restless? What do you mean—?"

"They're struggling against the restraints, ma'am. If we don't do something, they're going to get loose."

"What about the Amygdala Inhibitor Kill Switches?"

"They aren't working," the Lieutenant said in horror. "They're all on, but they're not immobilizing the drones."

"We're going to have to put them down. Has Major Lyons been informed?"

"Yes, ma'am. He has. He wants you to report to his office immediately."

"I have to get Betancourt on the horn."

"He's already working on that, ma'am."

"How many drones?"

"Five hundred, ma'am."

Jesus. She had no idea there were that many.

"I'm off," she said. "Place a heavy security detail outside the drone containment facility."

"Yes, ma'am. The Major already ordered it."

The shit was about to hit the fan. After they had flipped the kill switch on Carl and put the Infantry Drone Program on hiatus, there hadn't been enough time to determine what to do with all the leftover drones.

Did they sense that Carl was gone? Did they somehow know? Her mind raced, but she forced herself to focus on the situation at hand. Speculation was a luxury she couldn't afford.

As she stalked down the hallway towards Major Lyons' office, passing through locked security checkpoints, she heard the alarm sound outside. She reached his office and stood in front of the retinal scan. There was a tone and the door opened.

She entered, removed her headgear, and saluted the Major, who was behind his desk on a call with Colonel Betancourt.

"We need permission to put them down, sir," he said with urgency. "If they breach the perimeter of Camp X-ray, we're going to have a real problem."

Camp X-Ray was mostly a containment facility. There were a few squat bungalows, one containing the RGT, and a series of fenced-in cages with flat roofs and barbed wire. The perimeter was a tall fence with barbed wire and four guard towers, one at each corner.

"I don't know how this happened, sir…no the Amydala Inhibitor master kill switch isn't working…yes, sir…I understand." He hung up the phone.

"Captain London reporting, sir."

Major Lyons nodded in acknowledgement. "We can dispense with the formalities, Captain. We're on the verge of a full-scale undead riot."

"Did the Colonel grant permission to put them down?" she asked.

"Affirmative. But we have to move fast. They're already at the perimeter."

"That was fast," she said aghast.

"They're moving with a purpose," Major Lyons confirmed.

It was only an expression, but perhaps Lyons was right. "You know, they only mobilized like this when Carl Birdsall was directing them."

"But he's dead now, Captain."

"They haven't yet found a body, sir."

"It's inevitable," Lyons said. "There was no way he could have survived the kill chip in his head."

"Yes, sir."

"I want you to take a small security detail around the perimeter of Camp X-Ray to the back, to the bungalow housing the RGT."

"Sir?"

"If we're going to have a bunch of zombies running loose on the grounds, we need to secure the RGT. I want it moved into the prison facility. In here, we can withstand an onslaught for some time while we put the drones down."

"Yes, sir."

"Get moving, Captain. We don't have much time."

Fiona barged into her office with Lieutenant McCall and ten fully armed soldiers. She opened her armory cabinet and grabbed two automatic assault rifles, handing one to McCall.

"We need a truck and some tools," she ordered McCall.

"I'm on it," she replied and called downstairs on her mini-com.

"All right," she said to the small detail, "we have to creep around the perimeter while avoiding drawing the attention of the drones. Watch the friendly fire once we're on foot. The guard towers will be shooting anything moving on the ground. I need to remove the RGT motherboard and the retinal interface."

They all nodded in confirmation.

"McCall, do we have the truck and tools?"

"Yes, ma'am."

"Let's move."

They drove out of one of the vehicle bays of the prison, and the security door lowered behind them and locked into place. McCall was driving, Fiona was riding shotgun, and the security detail was in the back.

"Kill the headlights," Fiona ordered.

McCall killed the headlights and slowly crept around the perimeter of Camp X-Ray, giving it a wide berth. In the dark, the camp had an eerie look. There were orange jumpsuits staggering around in the moonlight, faces hidden in the shadows, but eyes glowing like cats eyes by the light of the moon and the occasional spotlight. There were squads of soldiers along the perimeter opening fire on the drones. The drones were at the external fence, rocking it back and forth.

"They all seem to be heading out the front of the camp towards the prison," said Fiona.

As they crept towards the rear of Camp X-Ray, the drones' numbers appeared to thin out. Fiona saw the dark outlines of the bungalows.

"Pull around the back," she instructed McCall.

McCall stopped the truck behind the back end of the fence. She was going to turn off the ignition, but Fiona touched her hand. "Keep the engine running." McCall nodded.

Fiona exited the truck with toolbox in hand. The small security detail piled out of the back of the truck.

"Okay, Obermeyer, breach the fence with the cutters. The rest of you, two-by-two column formation. We need to get to the third bungalow. Keep your eyes peeled for drones. Let's move."

They crossed the dirt and low brush to the fence, and Obermeyer used the cutter to cut a vertical line through the chain links. She pulled it apart and they filed in. On the other side, they went into formation and began to sneak around the first bungalow.

Fiona was at the rear of the formation. She strained her eyes and ears for drones. All appeared quiet. They were passing around the second bungalow. Still quiet. Fiona hoped that maybe this was going to be easy. They reached the third bungalow.

She came to the front of the formation and produced her mini-com. She disengaged the digi-lock and she went to open the door. Obermeyer stopped her. "We need to clear it, ma'am."

Fiona nodded. The detail breached the bungalow in column formation. "All clear," said Obermeyer from inside. Fiona entered and saw the large RGT apparatus. She flicked on the lights, crossed the room quickly, and put her toolbox down in front of the RGT. She put down her rifle and knelt to open the toolbox.

"I need one of you to help me with the retinal interface. It's delicate."

Fowler stepped forward. "I'll do it."

"Okay," Fiona said, "grab the interface here and hold it while I separate it from the rest of the apparatus. Don't let it fall."

Fowler nodded and grabbed the apparatus where Fiona indicated. Fiona took out a socket wrench and got to work.

"No windows here. Beal and Cleary, I want eyes outside. One on the roof and one on the ground," Obermeyer ordered. They nodded and stepped outside. "The rest of you, cover the front and back doors." They all moved into position.

Fiona disengaged the retinal interface, and Fowler held it gingerly in her hands.

"Now I have to separate the motherboard and we're home free," said Fiona. Fowler stepped back to allow Fiona some room to work.

Fiona took out a screwdriver and unscrewed the side panel, placing it on the ground next to the machine. Then she took a mini flashlight out of the toolbox and shined it into the unit. She reached in with her right hand and disengaged the motherboard, sliding it out.

She backed away from the machine. "Okay, we're good to go."

Just then, they heard a thump on the roof and a body sliding off.

"I'll check it out," Obermeyer volunteered. She went to open the door and there were orange jumpsuits everywhere. She slammed the door shut and activated the digi-lock.

"What is it?" asked Fiona.

"Jesus, we got drones!"

***

"At approximately 22:00 HRS, Guantanamo Bay reported activity from the drones held in Camp X-Ray," announced Betancourt. "We are now receiving reports from Major Lyons that they have escaped the confines of the camp and are surrounding the prison facility."

"How is this possible?" Peter asked.

"The drones are no longer responding to the Amygdala Inhibitor master kill switch. We don't know why. We need to mobilize your unit to lend support in putting the drones down."

"With all due respect, Colonel, we don't have the best record in combating the drones."

"If you are referring to the botched mission in Xcaret, there were special circumstances."

"Actually, sir, the Navajas cartel fried the AI inhibitors with an EMP. We were overrun."

"So you can sympathize with our men at the facility. This time you'll be flanking the drones, trapping them between you and the facility. Your primary objective will be to secure the RGT housed in a bungalow in Camp X-Ray. Your secondary objective will be to protect the prison facility."

Peter thought of his father being held there. "Shouldn't it be the reverse, sir?"

"These are orders from General Ramsey, Captain. He's made protecting the RGT a priority."

"We'll need something better than assault rifles," Peter said.

"Grenade launchers, flamethrowers, the works," Betancourt said. "Your unit will mobilize in fifteen minutes. You should be at GITMO within three hours."

"Yes, sir."

"Dismissed."

***

"What do you mean we got drones?" Fiona asked.

"We're surrounded, ma'am," said Obermeyer. "They're everywhere."

"Check the back."

Obermeyer nodded and ran to the back door. She cracked it open and saw more orange jumpsuits. She closed it quickly and re-engaged the digi-lock. "More drones, ma'am!"

"Why didn't our spotters warn us?" Fiona asked.

"They were neutralized quickly, ma'am," Obermeyer answered.

Fiona knew what she was getting at. There was no way the drones could've gotten the spotter on the roof. "Then the drones aren't alone. There's someone coordinating this attack, and they knew we'd come for the RGT."

"Which means that they knew that we had the RGT here," added Obermeyer.

"It's Carl Birdsall," Fiona said.

"Ma'am?"

"He knew it was here. Only he could coordinate the drones like this. But he was terminated."

Obermeyer looked at her confused. Fiona forgot that she wasn't cleared for any of that information.

"I think I know who's behind this. If I'm right, he's come for the RGT, and he's really pissed off at me."

Major Lyons' mini-com flashed with an incoming call. It was from one of the sergeants outside. He took the call. "Yes, Sergeant."

"We have taken the bungalow housing the RGT," said a crackling, inhuman voice on the other end.

Major Lyons was startled by the voice. He was expecting Sergeant Saragosa. "Who is this?"

"This is Kafka from the Order for International Liberation."

"What do you want?"

"I do not want the RGT. I am willing to make a trade."

"I don't know about any RGT."

"Don't be stupid, Major."

"A trade? For what?"

"For one of your detainees."

"I'm not authorized to make such an exchange," explained Major Lyons. He then muted his mini-com. "Lieutenant Gauger, get confirmation that the RGT is surrounded."

"Yes, sir."

Major Lyons unmuted the mini-com.

"We can wait a moment while you obtain confirmation that the RGT is in fact in our custody."

"I have to obtain authorization. It's going to take some time."

Lieutenant Gauger came back into Lyons' office and nodded confirmation.

"Time is a luxury you don't have, Major."

"How are you doing this?"

"You have fifteen minutes to give me your answer. If you don't, we will breach the prison walls and flood it with the undead. They are very eager, Major. They hunger for your flesh."

"Listen, I don't know—"

Kafka ended the transmission.

"Gauger, pull the men into the facility. I want snipers on the rooftops and at every window. I need to get Betancourt on the line."

"Yes, sir."

Lyons' mini-com flashed an incoming call.

"Captain London, are you all right?"

"Yes, sir."

"What is your status?"

Another voice came on the line. It sounded cold, but human. "We have the RGT in our possession. If you don't want it taken and your soldiers here executed, you best be working on an answer to Kafka's trade." The man on the other end terminated the call.

Major Lyons contacted Colonel Betancourt and explained the situation in a nutshell.

"Under no circumstances are you to hand the RGT over to this Kafka. Make the trade. I don't care who it is. We have a specialized unit with experience in dealing with these drones en route."

"He only gave me fifteen minutes," said Lyons. "Your men won't be here for—"

"Another two hours," said Betancourt. *"Stall him. Take your time in setting up the trade. Make him jump through some hoops."*

"Yes, sir."

The fifteen minutes were up. Lyons' mini-com was flashing an incoming message.

"It's him, sir. I have to go."

He terminated the call with Betancourt and answered the incoming call. "Kafka."

"Do you have an answer for me, Major?"

"We'll make the trade. But I find it hard to believe that you are going to just give up the RGT just like that."

"The detainee I want is much more valuable to me."

"How do I know you will actually deliver the RGT?"

"You will have to trust me."

"Forgive my hesitation. I want Captain London and her detail to deliver it so she can confirm that it is in fact the RGT."

"That is acceptable."

"I want to make the exchange in the prison yard."

"So you can lock my messengers in, seize the RGT, and your snipers can take them out? I think not."

"I'm trying to play ball with you, Kafka, but I need certain reassurances."

"We will make the exchange just outside the front wall of the prison. Neutral ground."

"That's hardly neutral ground, Kafka. You have control of the outside."

"You can cover the exchange with your snipers on the wall."

"I want Captain London and her detail unescorted. When I get the nod from her, I will send out your detainee."

"What is to prevent you from taking Captain London and keeping the detainee, Major? How about I send in an escort, promise they will not harm anyone—your snipers can see to that—and my escort takes custody of the detainee."

"I have a better idea, Kafka. Send Captain London and her detail forward with the RGT and, given her nod of confirmation, I will send out your detainee to walk right past her as she walks inside."

"Fine. And don't think, Major, that I don't have snipers of my own."

"You haven't told me who the detainee is."

"Bartholomew Birdsall."

"Bartholomew Birdsall? What in God's name do you want with him?"

"No questions, Major. You have fifteen minutes."

"Kafka, I need more time. We have to locate him and then prep him."

"Twenty minutes. If you are a minute late, I eviscerate Captain London and her detail and take off with the RGT. Their blood will be on your hands."

"No need to make threats. We'll have him out in twenty minutes."

Kafka ended the transmission.

"Jesus," said Gauger, "is that detainee even a terrorist?"

"No," said Lyons. "It's Peter and Carl Birdsall's father. He must want Barry Birdsall for leverage. But for what?"

"Giving up the RGT wasn't in the plan," said Night Stalker to Kafka.

"Shut up and bring me Captain London," croaked Kafka through his helmet.

Night Stalker walked over to where Captain London was being held at gunpoint by a few other OIL operatives. "Captain, Kafka wishes to speak with you."

The OIL operatives parted to allow her to pass through. Night Stalker grabbed her by the arm and yanked her over to where Kafka was standing.

"Watch it, asshole," she snapped.

"Night Stalker, no need to be impolite," Kafka said in his tinny voice.

"What is this, Halloween?" chided Fiona.

"Captain London," said Kafka with some amusement, cocking his head sideways, "you have served your country well."

"Oh yeah? And what the hell are you supposed to be?"

"An admirer, Captain. You have sacrificed much for your country. I've seen it in your dreams."

Fiona's skin went cold. How could he possibly know her dreams? Nightmares were more like it.

"How is your Nana?" Kafka asked with feigned sincerity.

Fiona's eyes went wide. It was impossible. "How could you possibly know?" she gasped.

"Why Fiona, I'm that thing scratching on the other side of the door. I'm the creeping inevitability that you cannot escape."

She looked at him horrified. None of this made any sense. "How were you able to coordinate the drones?"

"That's my little secret, Captain," teased Kafka, "but I do have good news for you. You and the RGT are being traded for a detainee."

"Which one?" she asked.

"Does it really matter?" he responded.

She just looked at him.

"Bartholomew Birdsall," he said.

"Holy shit," she said. "Carl? Is that you?"

Kafka gestured for one of the OIL operatives to approach. He was holding the RGT components, the interface and the motherboard, and a knapsack. Kafka snatched the knapsack and handed it to Fiona. "Put this on."

Fiona took the knapsack tentatively and slid into the shoulder straps. Kafka held up the RGT components. "You will be taking these back into the prison." He spun her around so she was facing away from him. She felt him unzip the knapsack and place the components inside. He then zipped it back up and spun her back around.

"You know, Carl, I never meant for any of this…"

"Life is filled with disappointments," said Kafka icily.

"Where are you going to take your father? What kind of life is he going to have on the run?"

"He'll make due."

"Do you think he'll want to go with you seeing what you've become? Your brother has been sick over your termination."

Kafka saw something amongst the drones. Or at least he thought he did. He saw his doppelgänger with a toothy, savage grin. He looked less human than the last time he saw him. He blinked and the man was gone.

"You and my brother were both part of what I have become. So I guess I should really be thanking you."

"So you're with OIL now? Really? The ones who murdered your mother?"

"Funny, they were there for me when you, Peter, and Betancourt tried to murder me."

She reached out and grabbed his arm, squeezing imploringly. "Carl, I had nothing to do with that. You have to believe me."

Night Stalker walked up to Kafka. "I hate to break up this reunion, but they are sending Birdsall out."

Kafka nodded. "Fiona, you are going to lead your detail up to the front gate. Their spotters will be watching and will expect confirmation that I've given you the RGT. You will nod the confirmation. When they send out Birdsall, you and your detail will walk past him and into the prison facility."

"It's not too late, Carl. You can turn yourself in, or turn back."

"That horse is out of the barn," he said. "At least you will be safe. I'm sending you back. Are you ready?"

She nodded.

Fiona walked out of the throng of undead orange jumpsuits who parted for her like the Red Sea. She walked up to the front gates of the facility. The door opened to a long chain linked corridor lined with barbed wire at the top. She walked forward slowly, carefully, and stopped at the entrance. She nodded emphatically, as instructed, and gave a thumbs up. Then she waited.

Down the corridor of fencing there was a small dot moving in her direction. It grew in size, and she saw it was a man in an orange jumpsuit. She began to walk forward, her detail following closely behind her.

Barry Birdsall was getting close. She was able to make out his face now. He looked scared. Poor bastard. Thought he was being handed to the wolves.

"Good," said Major Lyons from a tower looking through binoculars. "She's coming. They're about to pass each other."

Barry was now about to pass Fiona. He looked terrified.
"It's Carl, Barry. He's come for you," she said.
"Ma'am," Obermeyer said admonishingly behind her.

"What's she doing?" Lyons asked Gauger. "She's stopped. Why did she stop?"

"What?" Barry asked.
"It's Carl. You're going to be okay." She hoped she was right.
"I don't understand," he said.
"Ma'am, we have to go," said Obermeyer impatiently.
Fiona nodded and kept walking. Barry, confounded, just stood there for a moment. Then he resumed walking to the entrance.

When he reached the entrance, a dark figure whisked up to him and snatched him, carrying him away with great haste. A wall of undead formed behind them, protecting them from behind.

Fiona heard the commotion and double-timed it down the corridor. She had to tell the Major that this Kafka was Carl Birdsall. He wasn't dead. He was part of OIL. He was now the—

An explosion erupted, swallowing Fiona and her detail in bright orange flames. A large fireball wafted into the night sky, illuminating the sea of undead outside the prison walls.

"What the hell!" shouted Lyons. "They rigged her pack with explosives! Tell the men to open fire!"

Gauger nodded and got on his mini-com. "It's a double-cross. Fire at will."

Kafka and Night Stalker fled with Barry Birdsall as gunfire erupted from the prison's perimeter wall behind them. Suddenly there was gunfire from the front. They were Americans.

"Your brother's squad?" Night Stalker shouted.

"No, too soon. They're Camp Blanding, Florida," Kafka shouted back.

As the Camp Blanding forces were inexperienced with the undead drones, they were vastly underprepared and quickly overwhelmed. There were screams of terror as the hungry undead sunk their jagged teeth into army flesh.

Kafka, Night Stalker, and Barry Birdsall ran for the beach where a cigarette boat had pulled up during the commotion and was waiting for them.

"Get in," Kafka ordered Barry, and Barry obeyed.

The boat zoomed off into international waters. After a while, the driver eased off of the throttle and the boat slowed to a stop. There was a disturbance on the water next to the boat. The tower of a small submarine broke the surface next to them.

"Jump," Kafka ordered Barry. Night Stalker jumped into the water and swam to the submarine. Barry jumped rather clumsily in, almost hitting his head on the side of the boat. Kafka tossed a black bag up onto the bridge of the submarine. Belmont was there to catch it.

Then Kafka jumped into the water.

The battle at GITMO outside the prison was brief. The three hundred odd drones that remained walked toward the beach and into the Caribbean Sea. As the heads of the final undead drones disappeared under the surf, Peter's Black Hawks came thundering over the beach.

They set down on the beachhead, and his squad quickly fell into formation.

"Shit, looks like we missed the party," said Peter surveying the bodies. There were a few reanimated soldiers staggering about the carnage.

"What a mess," said Kettle looking at the bodies in the sand. "Three to four dead soldiers for every dead drone."

Peter took aim and fired a shot right through the left eye socket of an approaching reanimated soldier. "All right, men, up we go to the facility. Alpha and Beta Squads, you take Camp X-Ray. Delta and Gamma Squad, you take the prison. Let's move."

"You did it," said Belmont, opening the black bag. "The components are now in our possession."

"Nice submarine," Kafka said.

"I got it from the Russians on sale," Belmont said. It's terribly outdated, but the price was right."

"I have to admit," said Night Stalker begrudgingly to Kafka, "that was some slight-of-hand you did."

"When I turned her around and reached into her bag, she assumed I was putting the RGT components into her knapsack instead of C4 strapped to thermite," said Kafka. "That was why I let her know it was me. So she would trust me."

"That's cold, even for me," said Night Stalker.

"She had it coming," said Kafka, "and the best part is, now the military thinks we blew up the RGT prototype. They have no doubt stashed away the schematics to build others, but they don't know we now possess it."

"Carl? Is that you?" asked Barry.

"Yes, Dad. I came for you."

"You planted explosives on Fiona."

"She was the one who planted the RGT in your house to spy on you."

"RGT. What is all of this?"

"Fiona spied on you to get to me. The army had decided that I was too dangerous, so they tried to kill me. They took you prisoner as leverage."

Barry looked startled. "I was afraid of something like this. They were afraid of you, Carl."

"The way you are looking at me, you seem to be afraid of me, too, Dad."

"What the hell happened to you?"

"More changes."

"Who are these people?"

Belmont stepped forward. "I am Simon Belmont. This is Yvette, and this surly assassin is Night Stalker."

"Are you going to kill me?" Barry asked.

"We went through a heck of a lot of trouble to get you, Mr. Birdsall," said Belmont.

"And, incidentally, the RGT," said Kafka sarcastically.

"We both got what we wanted," said Belmont.

"Who are you guys?" asked Barry.

"We already told you our names," said Belmont. "You mean who do we represent?"

"Yes," said Barry, "that's exactly what I mean."

"The Order for International Liberation," said Yvette.

"Son-of-a-bitch," said Barry emphatically. "So this is who you're running with now, Carl? The bastards who murdered your mother."

"I wasn't behind that," said Belmont. "It was very regrettable."

Barry lunged for Belmont, but Kafka held him back with one arm. "You're goddamned right it was very regrettable," Barry snarled.

"Easy, Dad," said Kafka. "They promised to help me. I'm a dead man back in the states. There's no going home."

"You-you can turn yourself in," said Barry. "They'd protect you."

"They'd try to kill me again. This helmet is the only thing keeping me alive. It blocks the signal to a kill switch in my head. The kill switch that Peter tried to activate."

"Your brother?" said Barry incredulously. "He'd never do such a thing."

"Well, he did it, Dad, and Fiona planted the bug in your house and took you prisoner."

"Bug, what bug? Where?"

"In your television," said Kafka, "and that's not all. You were the pilot. They plan to install this into every television and mini-com across the country without telling anyone, all under the guise of the Second Patriot Act."

"The Second Patriot Act," Barry said, "that's just a rumor."

"It's almost law," said Belmont. "Congress is mulling it over as we speak."

"How do you know all about this, terrorist?" asked Barry.

"I am not a terrorist, Mr. Birdsall. I'm a liberator, as you have just witnessed personally. I know about this because the American government created us as an external threat that would justify the use of emergency powers. Now that they will have the green light to go ahead with this technology, they will use it to spy on its own citizenry."

"You always said the government was getting too big, too powerful," said Kafka to Barry.

"The army used your son as well. This RGT technology is tied to the same technology used in your son's unit," said Belmont.

"You mean the zombies?" asked Barry.

"Yes, Dad. But that's enough for now. There's a whole story behind what's happening to me. We can discuss that another time. The important thing is that you are safe."

"Come with me, Mr. Birdsall," said Yvette. "Let's get you cleaned up."

Barry looked tentatively at his son, but he couldn't make out anything under that motorcycle-style helmet. For some reason, Barry didn't feel safe. Kafka gestured for his father to follow, and Barry let Yvette take him by the hand.

Kafka waited until they were out of the Captain's quarters, the door shut behind them. "So what's next?"

"First we reassemble and refit our new toy," said Belmont. "Then we move onto phase two."

"Italy," said Kafka.

Chapter 13

The Next day
09:00 HRS

"We must've just missed them, sir," said Peter.

"Well, they made minced meat out of the naval base and the men from Camp Blanding. What a mess. The media is eating it all up. Worst of all, they're calling for your brother to help like he's our goddamned secret weapon. At least they didn't get their hands on the RGT."

"Why did they take my father, sir?"

"Leverage. They, too, think your brother is still alive."

"That means OIL didn't take him, because they'd know he's dead," said Peter.

"That also explains why our raid on OIL safe houses turned up zilch regarding your brother. So the real question is: who the hell took him?"

"If he was even taken at all," added Peter, "but his mini-com was smashed."

"Maybe he was hit by a car and he crawled into the wilderness somewhere."

"Number one: why would he crawl away from people?" Peter pointed out. "Two: the searches would've found him."

"Sorry to hear about Captain London," Betancourt said looking down at his desk. "I know she was your therapist in the program."

Peter remembered the night in Frisky's when she came to tell him that he was in the program. She was stunning. "What was she doing at GITMO, sir?"

"She was one of our top intelligence officers, Captain. She was working on RGT, developing it."

"Obviously. Why was she ever stationed at Fort Bliss in the Infantry Drone Program?"

"She was developing the RGT there and using it to monitor the soldiers involved in the program," said Betancourt. "Kill two birds with one stone."

Peter remembered standing outside her office and submitting to the retinal scanner. When he entered, the therapeutic ambience program had conjured up some scene from his memories. He was foolish to believe that the army would use that kind of technology simply for therapeutic milieu.

"Obviously, the RGT was what the brass wanted developed. So why the Infantry Drone Program?" asked Peter.

Betancourt sighed heavily. "Because we didn't have the funding for RGT yet...too controversial, but we did have it for the Infantry Drone Program."

"Kill two birds with one stone," Peter said.

"Exactly, Captain. Congress is going to pass the Second Patriot Act, especially after this fiasco at GITMO. I don't think I need to sketch it all out for you."

"No, sir. I get it. So what now?"

"This is going to be a political shit storm. The drones are all gone, and the program is finished. The surrounding islands as well as the Florida Coast Guard have been on the alert for resurfacing zombies, but there've been none sighted."

"What about my father?"

"We wait. Someone from OIL is going to come forward and demand that we produce your brother."

"What then? Carl's dead and we can't even find the body. Do we announce his death?"

"Not yet," said Betancourt. "It would be a tremendous blow to morale and a moral victory for OIL. The last thing we want to do is embolden the enemy."

"So we just wait?"

"And prepare, Captain."

"For what, sir?"

"I don't know, son. I just don't know."

***

Monterosso al Mare, Italy
10:23 HRS

Yvette was in the sacristy overseeing the project. Three technicians were poring over the makeshift RGT apparatus. They had been at it through the night and were near completion.

Kafka and Belmont were sitting in the pews of the pirate church. Kafka was admiring the stunning reliefs of skulls, crossbones, and skeletons lounging around holding wreaths and scepters. The whole church was white, brown, and beige with striped columns. It looked Egyptian.

"This is odd décor for a church," said Kafka.

"It is rumored to have been built by a pirate," said Belmont. "It's the perfect location for us. Difficult to get to and right off the water."

"Those words above the door, what do they mean?"

"Oratorio Mortis et Orationis," said Belmont. "Those words refer to a secret society that goes back to medieval times that was devoted to liberating souls of loved ones from purgatory, so that they may attain the splendors of heaven."

"That's poetic justice, don't you think," commented Kafka.

"Yes, you might say our mission is similar, in a more earthly sense of course."

Yvette came out of the sacristy. "It's ready."

Belmont and Kafka stood up and followed her back into the sacristy. Night Stalker was on hand watching lazily as he leaned against a rather large wooden cabinet containing vestments.

"Is it operational?" Belmont asked.

"Only one way to find out," said Yvette trading looks with Kafka.

"So we need a volunteer," Kafka hissed. "How about you, Night Crawler?"

Night Stalker huffed at the suggestion. "No thanks."

Yvette pulled out her handgun and trained it on him. He stood up straight with a look of outrage. "You pull it and you better be prepared to use it, little girl."

"I have a better idea," said Kafka. He walked over and grabbed Night Stalker by the back of the neck. Night Stalker tried to shake off Kafka's grip but was unable. "Why don't you have a seat? This won't hurt a bit."

Night Stalker started to panic. He appealed to Belmont. "Aren't you going to do anything?"

Belmont put out his hands and shrugged. "Just a test. I don't see the harm in it."

Kafka led Night Stalker over like a marionette to the metal chair in front of the RGT apparatus and slammed him down into it.

Yvette nodded to one of the technicians, who switched the machine on. An ancillary monitor lit up and the technician adjusted some dials. When he was finished, he gave the thumbs up.

"Now don't you move," said Kafka rather menacingly.

The machine was humming and ready. The technician activated the retinal interface, and images of Night Stalker in Monterosso popped up on the screen. Then there were images of their invasion of Guantanamo Bay. They saw him scale the bungalow in Camp X-Ray and take out the spotter on the roof. Then images of Yvette and Carl in the apartment the night they made contact. Then other operations: assassinations, sabotage.

And there it was…what Kafka was looking for.

The man in the car that drove in through the entrance to the mall in Texas and exploded. The man that would murder his mother. Night Stalker was discussing the attack with the suicide bomber, planning it out. The man was a true believer. Shit, he had to be to be willing to blow himself up for the Cause.

Night Stalker silently slipped his hand into his pocket and pressed the button, sending electricity flooding into Kafka's helmet. Kafka let go of Night Stalker and stumbled backward clutching his head in pain.

Night Stalker stood up out of the chair and snatched Yvette's gun from her hand, turning it on her. Kafka pulled off his helmet. His four red eyes glared with cold-blooded fury as long, black hair fell about his shoulders.

"Leave us," he commanded rather ominously.

Belmont put his hands up and backed out of the room. Night Stalker pulled Yvette around and backed out of the sacristy and into the church. Kafka followed.

"You took a big risk removing your helmet," said Night Stalker.

"Oh, please," said Kafka, "the army thinks I'm dead."

"One step and the girl gets it," threatened Night Stalker. "I know you two are sweet on each other."

"You mercenary shit!" yelled Yvette. "Kill me. You won't make it out that door."

"Come on, Night Crawler," taunted Kafka. "You call yourself a professional? The best? And here you stand shaking in your boots and hiding behind a woman."

"I can take you any time, you freak," snapped Night Stalker.

"Where, to the movies?" jeered Kafka. "Prove it. Show me you're the best."

"I am the best. Your freak powers won't help you at all."

"Good," said Kafka slyly, "then it should be no problem for you."

Night Stalker considered it. He threw Yvette to the ground and pointed the gun at Kafka, pulling the trigger.

But he was too slow.

Kafka ran behind pews and dodged between columns in a blur until Night Stalker emptied his clip. Kafka came dancing back out into the open.

"So I never understood your name. Was it to strike fear into the hearts of those who've heard of you? To intimidate? Should *I* be frightened by your name?"

Night Stalker pulled a rather large hunting knife from his boot. The two men circled around each other, sizing each other up.

"You're not so tough without your drones," taunted Night Stalker.

"Communicating with them is but one of my talents, Night Crawlie. I can't wait to show you my others." Kafka flashed his reptilian eyes and licked his lips.

"You miss your mommy?" goaded Night Stalker. "Don't worry, you'll be seeing her real soon."

"Oh, I see," said Kafka. "You're trying to anger me."

"You're going to have to kill me face-to-face instead of slipping explosives into my pack when I'm not looking," said Night Stalker.

"I liked Fiona, but don't worry. What I have planned for you will be real up close and personal," snarled Kafka.

"Enough talk," said Night Stalker.

"My sentiments exactly," growled Kafka.

They lunged forward at each other and Night Stalker plunged his knife into Kafka's left blocking forearm. Kafka didn't pull away. He grabbed Night Stalker by the throat with the other hand and tossed him backward against the pews.

Night Stalker landed on his back across a hard wooden backrest and rolled off onto the hard floor. Kafka cocked his head sideways, examining the knife in his forearm. He reached out and grabbed the handle, wrapping his long fingers around it emphatically.

"Remember, Night Terror, what doesn't kill me makes me stronger." He pulled out the knife slowly and licked his own blood off the blade. Night Stalker was on his feet, but the throw knocked the wind out of him.

"I'm going to give you a chance to catch your breath," said Kafka, "and then I'm going to kill you with your own knife."

Night Stalker took a moment to catch his breath. Then he stood up straight and gestured for Kafka to come at him.

"Very good," said Kafka, smiling wickedly. He ran at Night Stalker with such speed that Night Stalker almost didn't have time to dodge the lunge. The knife missed the front of his midsection, slicing his black shirt open by his ribs.

He countered with three blows to Kafka's face, and he dodged as Kafka swiped at him and missed. He came back in and delivered a body blow and dodged again as the knife grazed his right cheek. He backed away and wiped the blood off his face.

"You are pretty fast," said Kafka with genuine appreciation, apparently unfazed by Night Stalker's blows. "This will be entertaining."

"If you consider getting your ass kicked fun," retorted Night Stalker. He ran to the front of the church and grabbed the tall metal cross sitting in a rack between two metal candleholders for the altar boys.

He jumped back down in the aisle wielding the cross like a staff. Kafka put his hands up defensively and hissed at the sight of the cross. Startled, Night Stalker looked at the crucifix.

"Just kidding," quipped Kafka, and he ran at Night Stalker. Night Stalker side-stepped him, swinging the cross and just missing the side of Kafka's head. Kafka side kicked him in the solar plexus, sending him flying against the pews again.

Night Stalker never let go of the cross. He pushed back against the pews with his elbows and was on his feet in a heartbeat. He came at Kafka, twirling the metal cross.

Kafka did a split and swung his leg around catching Night Stalker and toppling him over. Night Stalker went down hard on the marble floor, hitting it with a grunt. Kafka kicked the cross out of his hands, and it went sliding down the aisle scraping the marble.

Night Stalker rolled into the pews and scrambled down the row to the other end. Kafka leisurely strolled along the front, following Night Stalker. The reliefs of laughing skeletons looked on in delight from their lofty positions.

"Tell me, Night Gawker, do you think you're going to purgatory?"

Night Stalker was now running down the side aisle towards the front entrance. Kafka leapt across the pews and collided with Night Stalker, sending him crashing into the church candles.

Night Stalker got up on one knee, but Kafka clapped one heavy hand on his shoulder preventing him from rising. "While you're down on one knee, why don't you say a prayer for my mother, you son-of-a-bitch?"

"I thought you don't get angry," mocked Night Stalker. "I thought you were a professional."

Kafka drove the large hunting knife down through the top of Night Stalker's skull. "I lied." The impact of the blow sent a shudder of satiety into Kafka's soul, and he relished the moment.

Night Stalker was grasping wildly at the knife in his head, but his pulse was fading. Kafka twisted the knife and Night Stalker was still.

Kafka dragged him back towards the front of the church and tossed him in front of the altar like a rag doll. The lifeless body lay in a heap like an offering.

"I will say a prayer for you Night Stalker," said Kafka, "because purgatory is too good for you." He walked around the altar and entered the sacristy through the side door. He found his helmet lying on the floor and picked it up. He dusted it off and slid it carefully back into place on his head.

He walked back out into the church and around the altar. Night Stalker's body was still, but Kafka felt another pulse. He knew it was

Yvette. She walked over to him and put her hand gently on his shoulder.

He stood there motionless, staring down at Night Stalker's body. While he could still taste the ecstasy of the kill on his tongue, the significance of avenging his mother left him feeling empty.

"I know how you feel," said Yvette softly. "After Belmont rescued me from that brothel, he took me in, he trained me in martial arts and weapons…he taught me how to read. I tagged along with him. We traveled everywhere, seeing many towns.

"But as I soaked up everything around me, becoming a worldlier person, something ate away at me. I didn't feel it consistently, but it was always there in the background, gnawing.

"So I told Belmont that I had unfinished business. He understood. He took me back to my father. It took some tracking to find him, but we found him not far from here on the outskirts of Viareggio. I wanted to tell him that I was all right. I wanted to see my sisters and how they'd grown.

"But when we found him, he had already sold them to a brothel. He cursed them for being lazy and poor thieves. When he told me he sold them to a brothel in town, he spat on the ground.

"I asked him simply to tell me which brothel they were sold to. He laughed bitterly and told me the place. I told him that I would return. He laughed at me, cursing me. My mother stood quietly in the background looking down at her feet."

"So what did you do?" asked Kafka, breaking the silence.

"Belmont and I found the brothel. When we arrived there, I found out one of my sisters had died. She was brutalized by an overzealous customer. My other sister was there. Belmont and I killed everyone who worked at the house. We took my sister and left the other girls to return back to wherever they came from."

"What about your father?" asked Kafka.

"My father," Yvette said to herself. Then she looked Kafka in the eye. "I butchered him in front of my mother and sister. When Belmont and I left, the entire inside of their RV was covered in his blood. It was justice, but it felt empty. It didn't change anything."

"I know how you feel," said Kafka. "How was Night Stalker allowed to plan the mall bombing?"

"We're a decentralized organization, Kafka. It's one of our greatest strengths, makes us impossible to eradicate. I'm not going to lie to you. While Belmont and I weren't directly involved in that particular attack, we were in countless others. We are killers for our Cause."

"Care to submit to the RGT so I can verify that you weren't involved?" threatened Kafka.

"If you wish. I have nothing to hide, but you may not like what you see."

"You'd be surprised," said Kafka. "Just yesterday, I strapped C4 and thermite to someone I really cared about without her knowledge and blew her to kingdom come."

"What about your brother?"

"Everyone who betrayed me will pay," said Kafka coolly. "Even my brother. I have a feeling our paths will cross again."

"In fact, Belmont's counting on it," said Yvette.

Kafka walked back into the sacristy and eyed the RGT apparatus. Yvette was right behind him. She found him very attractive right now...powerful. Being near him was intoxicating.

"So Belmont is going to be using this on American operatives," said Kafka.

"Americans, NATO, UN," answered Yvette.

"That's a lot of knowledge, a lot of power in the hands of one man."

Yvette walked around to face him. "OIL is more than one man. It's a cause. It's our crusade."

"I can't say it's my cause, Yvette."

"That is how we all felt in the beginning. It is a new feeling to be liberated, truly free."

However, she didn't understand. He was free from his prior two incarnations, but his transformation wasn't yet complete.

"When the operatives are interrogated with the RGT, we will see everything?"

Yvette nodded. "Mission objectives, planning, placements..."

"Training, tactics," finished Kafka.

"Yes. We will have the ultimate in intelligence. We will know everything about our enemies."

Kafka began to step toward Yvette, who slowly retreated with his every step. He reached out for her, but she stayed just out of his grasp, his fingertips grazing her curves.

Never breaking eye contact, she backed into a wooden vestment cabinet, startling herself. He reached out and placed a hand on the cabinet, blocking her exit with his extended arm. She had no desire to run.

"You never answered my question," he asked.

"Was I really attracted to you or was it part of the act?"

"Yes."

She reached up with her hands and touched his helmet. Then she squeezed and lifted it off of his head, tossing it leisurely to the ground.

"We understand each other," said Kafka. "We are both killers. Cause or not, we show strength through our ability to end lives. Like when you butchered your gypsy father."

She nodded, gazing into his four reptilian slits.

"The force," he continued, "the blood, the slow fade of their existence." He reached down to her blouse and pulled it open, snapping her front buttons off.

She allowed him. He was not her father, nor a whorehouse master. He was *her* rescue and, although Kafka was physically superior to her in every way, it gave her some ownership. He was her eager pupil, strong, yet vulnerable.

"You would have me in the back of a church?" she teased.

"I would have you in front of the Pope himself," countered Kafka. He sniffed her neck, sliding the tip of his tongue down the length of it, tasting her mix of fear and lust. He felt her push up against him, her heartbeat thundering against his chest and in his mind.

At that moment, the notion to kill her popped into his head. To murder her, tearing her limb from limb with his bare hands. To spill her blood on the hard tile floor in this holy place.

He looked into the dark hallway to the door that led outside and he saw an extra shadow in the dim light. As it turned sideways, he made out an open mouth with long fangs and claw-like fingernails extending out. He knew what it was.

His doppelgänger had fed him the idea of murdering Yvette where she stood. It wanted it as much as he did, maybe even more. The idea heightened his arousal and he seized her, and they took possession of each other on the sacristy floor.

***

Peter sat hunched over on his bunk with his hands covering his face. His shoulders were shaking and his body was shuddering, but his sobs were silent.

Nolan Kettle entered the barracks and saw his commanding officer. He turned to leave to give Peter his privacy.

"Kettle."

He turned back around and saw Peter wiping his eyes. "Yes, sir."

"Come on over. I was just having a moment."

"Understandable, sir."

"My whole family…taken, and there was nothing I could do about it."

"Carl told me about Xcaret, sir, and how everything went to shit real fast. He told me how you risked yourself to protect him."

"A lot of damned good it did," said Peter bitterly.

"Carl was his own man, sir. A real bad ass in his own right. You couldn't watch over him forever."

"I know, but now he's dead because I let him go back to the bar alone."

"You were only following orders. He was not."

"I should've been there with him."

"Sir, whoever was watching him had been watching him for some time. If you had been with him at that moment, they would've gotten him at a moment you weren't there."

"There isn't even a body, Nolan. Now my father is taken. Did you hear about this Kafka character?"

Nolan nodded. "He sounds creepy."

"He was somehow able to coordinate the drones, like Carl used to," said Peter. "How the hell is that possible?'

"I don't know, sir, but it looks like there's a new player, and I don't think that was the last we'll be hearing from him."

"You think he's going to use my father as leverage, too?"

Nolan nodded. "Why else would he have taken him? He blew up the RGT to get your father."

"I know. It just doesn't make any sense at all."

"These terrorists are savages," said Nolan. "They probably didn't know what they had with the RGT. If they did, they would've taken it and run."

"I suppose so."

"So what now?" asked Nolan.

"There are some three hundred drones missing. Betancourt wants us ready to do clean up. Now we're hunting them, not coordinating them."

"That's a whole different set of tactics," said Nolan.

"You bet. I have some experience going up against these things. I've learned from past mistakes. We need to train the men."

Nolan nodded his understanding. "Airfield."

"Assemble the men. Twenty minutes."

"Yes, sir."

***

Fort Bliss Airfield
13:00 HRS

"We are going to have to engage the drones in a variety of scenarios: open combat, urban warfare, rural combat," said Peter to his unit. "There are a few basic principles in hunting these bastards. The first is visibility. We want to decrease ours and increase theirs because, if they get the drop on you, it's over."

He nodded to Nolan, who pointed to three jeeps. "We will use the portable radar, mounted on the backs of these jeeps, to scan for the drones.

"When engaging the drones, formation is everything. In a squad, we will have five men running point, five on each flank, and two in the rear to lay down cover for a retreat. In open areas, there will be three of these squads, one in the center and two flanking, for extra support.

"The key is to come in heavy, cover each other, and have an exit. You have to remain mobile. If you get bogged down, you're dead. Plain and simple. Get in, get out."

Kettle picked up an assault rifle. "Your weapons will be stocked with hollow points for controlled penetration with maximum tissue damage. When overwhelmed, you will be tempted to go full auto, but you'll only waste ammo and find yourself in a hard spot. Keep it on semi-auto. Short controlled bursts. Go for the head shots, do not waste ammunition."

"If you do find yourself out of ammunition," continued Peter, "your rifles are equipped with bayonets. Quick stabbing motions through the eye socket, a clean kill. You also have your retractable batons for skull crushing.

"When they come at you faster than you can handle, retreat backward under cover fire from your men bringing up the rear. Keep the corridor clear so you don't get tagged by friendly fire. Then the rear will drop back behind the new positions of point and flanks, and so on and so on. Soon your drones will be tripping over the bodies of the slain as they try to get you. That will buy you more time.

"They're slow and clumsy, but make no mistake—they're relentless. They won't stop until you put them down."

Lieutenant Farrow held up one of the black neoprene suits. "These suits will do well to help conceal your body heat signatures. This will initially make you invisible to the undead. They will treat you like a piece of furniture. But make no mistake, once you begin engaging them, they will get wise. If you move quickly and stay in formation, they will have difficulty tracking your movements..." Peter looked at Lieutenant Farrow. "...in theory."

"Shit, sounds good enough for me," said Kettle, slapping Farrow on the back. "What do you say, men?"

"HAROO!" shouted the men in unison.

"There is a psychological element to the drones," Peter added. "Do not think of them as people. Once you do, they start to look like your sister, your best friend, your old college roommate—and then it's all over for you." He thought of the mirrored room in the gym at Xcaret and all the eyes on him. He remembered how some of his men lost it and got eaten because they looked these drones in the eye and saw them as human. "Don't let them get into your head," he said broodingly.

"Good point, sir," said Nolan, recognizing that Peter was having a moment.

"Keep it technical and keep it clean," said Peter. "And for Chrissake, watch the panic. These ain't no insurgents. These are the undead. Zombies wanting your flesh for breakfast. Don't look 'em in the eye. It'll unnerve you. Soon, instead of seeing flesh hungry monsters, you'll be seeing your next door neighbor or cousin or your old girlfriend from high school."

There were grins and smirks in the unit.

"Hell, Lord knows I've dated a few ghouls in my time," said Kettle. "All right men, suit up! It's zombie stompin' time. We're training all day, every day until we're called in to show what we can do."

"HAROO!"

Chapter 14

Siena, Italy
Banca Monte dei Paschi di Siena
One Week Later
09:23 HRS

Yvette strolled across the Palazzo Salimbeni arm-in-arm with Kafka, sans his helmet. They looked like two young lovers out for a walk. She looked up at the mullioned windows of the white building as they approached the statue of Salustio Bandini in his robes holding his book, a stern expression on his face.

They paused in front of the statue, holding hands and staring into each other's eyes. Soon the square filled up with people…lots and lots of people. They milled around the square for a moment, an ordinary scene except for the sheer number that filled the square seemingly all at once. It looked like the moment just before a flash mob broke out.

Kafka reached into his backpack and pulled out his helmet. Yvette gave him a sultry look. He slipped it on and the visor activated.

With a quick, silent command, the flash mob sprang into action. The drones all filed into the bank, followed by Yvette and Kafka, now holding automatic weapons. They entered the bank, dispatching security guards with tooth and nail. They filled the beige atrium and began to mount the spiral staircase. They ascended round and round, offshoots of the undead mob invading each floor, overwhelming the startled clerks and executives, sinking jagged teeth into soft flesh.

Yvette made her way back to the computer center, where all of the financial records, files, and accounts were stored. She shot the guards outside the door and took the technicians inside hostage.

Kafka got off on the floor of the Banca Monte dei Pashi's renowned historical archive. He stormed into the consultation room with its small wooden tables, chairs, and glass encased books, and he began to shoot out the glass.

Undead saturated the golden Galleria Peruzziana, the paintings gallery, meeting hall, and the white walled Salone Strozzi, treading on its classic rugs. Outside, drones roamed the streets grabbing pedestrians, pushing people indoors, snapping their jaws at anyone and everyone.

Kafka produced his mini-com and called the police, switching on the translator application.

"This is Kafka. Terrorists have seized the Banca Monte dei Paschi. American undead infantry drones are being released on the streets of Siena as I speak. We demand that the Americans hand over the Automaton or we will begin killing hostages in the most brutal of fashions."

He terminated the call as he stood outside the doors of the historical archive. Belmont said that the Sienese kept secret historical records dating back to ancient times. The answer to his condition lay somewhere in the archives. He tried to disengage the digi-locks with his multi-tasker, but with no success.

"Yvette."

"Yes, Kafka."

"See what one of your technicians can do about opening the archive. Tell him if he doesn't help, one of the drones will begin to eat him alive, starting from his feet to his head."

***

General Ramses and Colonel Betancourt stood at the front of the debriefing room. Peter and Nolan were seated with their multi-taskers flashing holographic maps of Siena, Italy.

"At approximately 09:30 HRS, terrorists seized the Banca Monte dei Paschi in Siena, Italy," announced General Ramses. "Shortly thereafter, our rogue infantry drones took over the entire city. The local authorities, naturally, were powerless to do anything."

"This Kafka character from the Guantanamo Bay incident called into the local police station threatening to kill civilians if the United States didn't hand over the Automaton," added Colonel Betancourt.

"That's impossible," said Peter. "Carl is dead and his body is missing. Can't we send out a press release to that point?"

"To do so now would be pointless," said Ramses. "They'd never believe us. They'd only think we were protecting the Automaton."

"The Italian government isn't equipped to handle the situation. Siena is a fortified city, and this Kafka is holding an entire city of hostages," said Betancourt.

"There was an emergency meeting of the UN Security Council, and they're calling for us to clean up our mess. They figure it's our drones and we know how to neutralize them," said Ramses.

"This is a trap," said Nolan.

"Yes," agreed Betancourt. "They're trying to make us look bad, as if we've lost control of our own drones."

"Frankly, sir, that's exactly what happened," said Peter.

"Additionally," said Ramses, "the Banca Monte dei Paschi is the oldest bank in the world. It conducts business on a global scale. It is also one of the last economic bastions of the European Union. After Greece, Portugal, and Spain's economies collapsed, only Germany and Italy are keeping the European Union afloat. In fact, the Banca Monte dei Paschi is the only thing keeping the Italian economy afloat. The European Union is blasting us in the media."

"So as you can see, this is a delicate situation on many fronts," said Betancourt.

"But we can't give them what they want, even if we wanted to," said Peter.

"Not necessarily," said Ramses.

"General Ramses," said Betancourt dubiously, "wants you, Captain, to pose as your brother."

"What? So we just hand the Captain over?" asked Nolan in disbelief. "They're going to kill him."

"We don't plan on letting OIL actually have him," said Betancourt. "We have a plan. Kind of like the Trojan Horse."

Holographic images of tunnels popped up from their multi-taskers. "There are a series of ancient subterranean tunnels originating from outside Siena that send water into the city, supplying its fountains. They're called the Bottini," said Betancourt. "While we hand over our faux Automaton, Lieutenant Kettle, you and your unit will be entering the city through these passageways. Fortunately, there is a shaft running right up into the computer center of the bank. There are a couple of problems, however."

"What's that?" asked Peter.

"The tunnels are ancient and, in some sections, in serious disrepair. The Sienese government said that some sections are even caved in, but those sections are unfortunately undocumented."

"What else?" asked Nolan.

"We have no way of knowing if this Kafka or any of his operatives know about the Bottini."

"If they do, it will put quite the damper on our little operation," said Peter.

"It will be important, once you infiltrate the city, to use your recent training tactics to neutralize the drones. Several squads will enter the city through other shafts, but only after you've penetrated the bank. Then you will coordinate the neutralization of the drones around the city.

"Eyes in the sky report that the civilians are being kept indoors with the drones standing guard outside. When you mobilize, you must strike quickly to minimize civilian casualties."

"What about me?" asked Peter.

"You will be gathering intel as you walk through the city. We will equip you with a visor that transmits video and images out to us. We'll gather data on the placements of the drones and relay it to Lieutenant Kettle to help coordinate the strike," said Betancourt. "I will be there personally to do this right outside the city walls."

"Additionally," said Ramses to Peter, "it is imperative that you identify who or what is coordinating these drones and neutralize if possible."

"So I'm walking right into the city, sending back data as I go, and when I reach the bank, I'm supposed to surrender myself, find who's controlling the drones, and kill him," reiterated Peter.

"Exactly," said Ramses.

"I'll be in constant contact for as long as possible," said Betancourt. "We'll be sending in the strike force well before you enter the city. You won't be in the bank long before they strike."

"That's real comforting," cracked Peter.

"We mobilize in twenty minutes," said Betancourt. "Kafka knows it'll take time for us to reach Siena. We'll give the impression that it's taking a little longer than it actually is to buy us time."

"Any questions?" asked Ramses.

"No, sir."

"No, sir."

"Good luck, gentleman. Dismissed."

***

Aboard a NASA X43 Cargo Jet
14:24 HRS

"Something isn't right about this," said Peter.

"Nothing is right about this," said Betancourt.

"No, I mean, we can't find Carl's body. Yet, somehow this Kafka is controlling the drones."

"You think Kafka has your brother?" asked Nolan.

"It follows," said Betancourt. "Maybe Kafka isn't OIL."

"Maybe he knows we don't have Carl because he has him," said Peter. "He knows it would put us between a rock and a hard place to produce him when he had him."

"In the meantime, he's using Carl to control the drones," said Nolan.

"That's assuming that your brother somehow survived the kill chip and could be coerced into controlling the drones for Kafka," pointed out Betancourt. "Don't get distracted looking for your brother in there, Captain."

"I have orders to identify what's controlling the drones," countered Peter.

"Just make sure you focus on your mission," admonished Betancourt.

"That's why Kafka took Mr. Birdsall," said Nolan. "To use as leverage to force Carl to direct the drones."

"That would be treason," stated Betancourt.

"With all due respect, sir, the army put Carl in that position by allowing our father to be traded for the RGT," reminded Peter. "It wouldn't be wise to hang my brother out to dry when it was done to protect a classified technology that doesn't officially exist."

"I don't like your tone, Captain," said Betancourt. "That's something I'd expect out of your brother. I'm no Major Lewis."

"Yes, sir." Peter decided to drop it for now. He made his point. Hope sprang from somewhere in Peter's mind. Maybe Carl was still alive. He was an engineering student. Perhaps he found a way to beat the kill chip.

If he did and he was indeed directing the drones, he was in hot water with the army. Treason. Now Peter wasn't sure if he really wished his brother to be alive.

***

Kafka sat in the archives poring over records using his multi-tasker translation function to decode the Italian. Some of the documents were even in Latin. He found very old documents dating back to the Dark Ages and even before. There were accounts of mysterious objects falling from the sky and found empty. Shortly thereafter, there were outbreaks of cannibalism near the fallen objects followed by reports of vampirism, demonic possession, and lycanthropy.

Individuals displaying unusual characteristics, such as the ability to read minds, were executed as witches. There was mass paranoia and superstition was rampant. When the events were over, the phenomena were frequently attributed to mass hysteria.

Belmont and Yvette were right. The origin of THV and the RGT technology appeared to be extraterrestrial. In all accounts, the fallen vessels were found to be empty. Maybe these aliens…these beings were ghosts or incorporeal in nature. Perhaps that was why they required the physical form of humans to clear a path for them, to engage the locals and wipe them out.

Kafka began to wonder. Was he the harbinger of a war declared on humanity? Was his purpose to lead the first wave of an invasion of some kind that had been tried so many times before?

The periods of cultural growth associated with contact with these 'Outworlders' always followed periods of social upheaval. Perhaps these beings were attempting to exploit the turmoil, using it as a distraction or a backdrop even. None of the singular individuals who were able to communicate with the undead was allowed to live to fulfill his or her purpose...

...until now. Maybe his father was right. Maybe the world had lost its humility and was going to hell in a hand basket. Maybe it deserved a little spring cleaning from other worldly beings.

What Kafka didn't understand was how this all played into Belmont's agenda. He and Yvette didn't seem to put much stock in an imminent threat from Outworlders. They, like the United States government, believed this technology to be found, not planted, and they hoped to exploit it for their cause.

If Kafka's feelings were correct, OIL, the United States, the UN— they were all going to be played for fools. He knew that every time they used the RGT, something else was watching. He could feel it. He felt it the day Fiona used it on him.

Something else was taking note of the planet's superpowers and its defenses. Perhaps this was the plan all along. Plant the technology and count on humanity's ambition and adversarial nature to apply it. They were all pawns in a greater scheme, at least that's what Kafka felt down to his core. He couldn't explain why, but he knew it.

The old Carl would've done something to throw a monkey wrench in the works and save humanity. However, he started to realize that, for quite some time, he no longer felt like a part of it. He never fit in, but now he had his own military trying to kill him despite all that he had done to protect his country.

Because of them, he had become something else. It wouldn't have been his first impulse, but they pushed him into it. They made him, they took away everyone he cared about, and they turned on him. To them, he was a monster, like the characters in the archives. Something to be persecuted and destroyed.

In reality, he felt more than human. He was superior in every way. He was the next stage in evolution. There were new selection pressures in place, and he and his kind were going to survive. The humans were going to go the way of the dinosaur, and Kafka was no longer sympathetic to their continued existence.

***

Somewhere In Between Fontebecci and Siena
15:45 HRS

"Local law enforcement helped us locate an access shaft right outside of Siena," said Lieutenant Kettle into his mini-com. "We are about to enter the Bottini."

"Good," said Betancourt. *"Maintain radio silence from here on. Texting only."*

"Yes, sir."

They dropped rope into the hole in the ground. It was one of those sections in poor repair that partially caved in. They began to repel down into the dark tunnel. They switched on their shoulder lights and Nolan led them into the tunnel.

The tunnel was narrow and tall, the rock hewn smooth. They sloshed around in water and mud as they worked their way into Siena proper. Everyone was silent, save for the splashing of their feet.

Kettle double-timed it because he knew time was of the essence. He had to reach the bank before Peter even stepped into the city. They had to be ready to move out of various ventilation shafts and take down the drones quickly before they harmed any hostages.

***

Peter stood outside the city walls of Siena dressed in Carl's suit. Lieutenant Farrow was outfitting him with the visor that would stream data in the form of pics and videos back to Colonel Betancourt.

"Are you sure this is going to work?" asked Peter dubiously.

"You look just like him, especially with your eyes covered by the visor. I think there's enough of a resemblance," answered Betancourt.

"So, what now, I just walk in and surrender myself?"

"Just walk into town slowly. My guess is that you won't make it very far before you are intercepted."

"But we don't know how they are going to react," said Peter. "They might just kill me where I stand."

"I don't think so," replied Betancourt. "They're terrorists. They're going to want to keep you for a while until they figure out some way they can humiliate and kill you in a grand spectacle."

"They took a whole city hostage," said Peter, "they took control of the oldest bank in the world, and they're going to have me. It doesn't get grander than this."

ATTACK FORCE IN POSITION, flashed Betancourt's mini-com multi-tasker.

"They won't have you for long," said Betancourt. "Kettle's team is in position." Images began to flash back to Betancourt's multi-tasker. "He's transmitting a route back. It appears that there weren't any significant cave-ins that would block travel along that route." Betancourt sent it to Peter's multi-tasker. "If the shit hits the fan, enter the Bottini and follow this route back."

Peter glanced down and saw the route downloading. "So I guess this is it."

"You'll be fine," reassured Betancourt. "Just remember your mission. Don't get caught up in looking for your brother."

"Yes, sir. Don't worry. I'll be busy trying not to get dead."

"Atta boy, Captain. Good luck."

Peter was unarmed, to save Kafka's men the trouble of disarming him or getting spooked and killing hostages. He began to walk through the entrance in the city's massive walls. Siena was truly a marvel, a fully fortified city in the middle of the Tuscan countryside.

He entered the first very narrow gray street. He looked up at the beige and burnt orange buildings towering on either side. The street slanted upward.

He turned a corner and was met by several drones waiting for him. Betancourt was right. It didn't take long. They surrounded him. Peter's heart was in his throat. He'd been in this position before, and it usually didn't end well.

One of the drones reached out and snatched the visor off his face, threw it to the ground, and stomped on it. Great. So much for that part of the plan.

Then one gestured with its arm for Peter to walk forward, its milky eyes cold and expressionless. Peter looked around at the others, who gazed back at him unblinking. They were apparently not going to harm him at the moment, but he was certain that if he made a move to resist, they'd end him quickly.

He began to walk up the narrow street and, as he did so, he felt eyes on him from windows above. Kafka had snipers placed by the entrance to the city. Smart. He must've had military or paramilitary training.

***

An OIL operative entered the archives. "Sorry to bother you, sir, but the drones have intercepted a soldier impersonating you."

"I know," said Kafka not looking up from his documents, "it's my brother."

The operative did a small bow and did not waste time in leaving the archives. Kafka stood up and arranged the documents, shoving them into a file.

So, the prodigal son has returned. Kafka would kill the fatted calf to honor his return, the hostages cowering in the storefronts and cafes. All to honor his brother's return.

First, a little show.

Peter was led to the fan-shaped Piazza del Campo. As he entered the square, he saw people huddled into the center of the square surrounded by undead drones standing watch. Kafka was mocking the Palio, only there wasn't going to be a horse race.

Peter was led to the flat base of the seashell-shaped plaza where one of the drones held out its hand for him to stop. Peter saw the terrified looks on the faces in the crowd. They were gawking at him. Some seemed to recognize him for who he was supposed to be, others just stared at him in wide-eyed anticipation.

"Ladies and gentlemen, your attention, please," crackled a tinny voice over a loudspeaker in the plaza. Kafka. *"I would like to introduce our guest who flew in all the way from America..."*

Peter looked around. The media was present with cameras rolling. Kafka had allowed them in. This was the spectacle that Betancourt said they were waiting for.

"Dammit!" shouted Betancourt. "They destroyed the visor. We're going to have to guesstimate this."

"Sir," said Lieutenant Farrow. "The Italian media is broadcasting from inside the city. It looks like the Piazza del Campo."

"Show me," said Betancourt.

They walked over to a tent with four laptops sitting on a table. They were all streaming broadcasts from various local news stations.

"That's Captain Birdsall," Farrow pointed out.

"What in the hell is Kafka up to?" asked Betancourt, thinking out loud. "He looks like he gathered all of the hostages in the plaza. This makes it easier for our strike force. Relay the positions of the drones to Kettle. Tell him to focus on the Piazza del Campo."

"Yes, sir," said Farrow grabbing his multi-tasker.

"Ladies and gentlemen, I present to you, the Automaton."

There were gasps as the crowd stirred. There were looks of confusion. Was he here to save them? Why did he have the drones corral them into the plaza?

"The Automaton came all of this way to meet the citizens of Siena."

Two drones stepped forward into the crowd and selected four people: two women and two children. The zombies escorted them out of the huge throng and before Peter.

Peter looked at them tentatively. The children, a boy and a girl, were clinging to the women terrified. The women were crying. They pleaded with him desperately in Italian, one woman getting down on her knees and begging.

"Mighty Automaton, here standing before you are women and children of Siena. What is your bidding?"

Oh, shit. Peter suddenly saw where this was going. Kafka meant to execute them in front of all to see. The video would be broadcast all over the world making it look like Peter, appearing as the Automaton, had ordered their execution.

Peter stepped forward and reached out to the children, pulling them away from their mothers. He drew them into himself protectively. The drones surrounding him stepped forward and began to attack the women, biting and clawing at their flesh.

"NO! STOP!" Peter tried to cover the eyes of the children as best he could. They were now screaming and crying into his suit.

Blood pooled on the ground underneath the drones and the screams of pain and terror from the women ceased quickly. Peter was horrified by what happened, but he felt powerless to do anything to stop it.

"Jesus tap-dancing Christ," gasped Betancourt. "Kafka just made it look like Captain Birdsall ordered the execution of those women. I'm sending in the strike force now, before this gets even further out of hand." He texted the following order to Kettle:

ALL FORCES CONVERGE ON THE PIAZZA DEL CAMPO NOW. DRONES SCATTERED ALONG THE PERIMETER OF THE CROWD.

"If Kafka wanted to make us look bad, I think he just succeeded," said Farrow ominously.

The crowd was in a panic. It shifted in waves within the perimeter of the undead drones, but none dared to breach that perimeter.

"Ladies and gentlemen, your attention, please."

The crowd was startled by the voice on the loudspeaker. They began to settle down in horrid anticipation of what was to come next. Peter huddled the two children closely around him with his arms.

"Stay back!" he yelled at the impassive drones. "No more! No more!"

"The Automaton is not pleased with what your city has to offer," crackled the reptilian voice. *"Automaton, what is to become of the crowd?"*

One of the drones, on cue, stepped forward dramatically and stuck out its right arm with its thumb extended out horizontally. Kafka was now mocking the spectacles at the Coliseum where the Emperor determined the fate of a gladiator with a thumb up or down. Only he wasn't asking the crowd. He was targeting the crowd and making it look like Peter's choice.

"Do they live or do they die, mighty Automaton?"

The crowd was stunned into silence as they looked at Peter expectantly, awaiting his answer. There were looks of horror, desperation, and even anger and outrage. The news cameras were broadcasting them all for the world to see.

"Let them live!" shouted Peter desperately. He wasn't going to play along with the charade. "They must live!"

The drone looked at Peter, as if it was listening to his directive, and it slowly began to point its thumb down. The crowd now writhed in terror, shouting and yelling, crying out for justice, but knowing none was coming.

The drones surrounding Peter began to come for the children, and Peter yanked them behind him. The drones surrounding the crowd began to move in when gunfire erupted from somewhere outside the plaza.

Lieutenant Kettle and several soldiers were shooting in the air with their rifles. Instinctively, the crowd ducked and covered their heads. This was what Kettle wanted.

"Headshots!" he commanded. His team surrounded the crowd and took out the drones, aiming high above the crouching hostages and shooting them in the heads.

Peter took the children and ran towards one of the cafes. He threw open the door and shoved them inside. "Stay here. STAY HERE."

They nodded their understanding. He opened the door and ran back outside into the fray. There was pandemonium as Kettle's team dispatched the drones. When enough of the drones were down, the crowd began to disperse, preventing them from firing on the remaining undead.

The dozen drones that were left began to grab fleeing Sienese. Kettle and his team infiltrated the crowd and took them down with bayonets and baton, one-by-one.

Kettle saw Peter. "Captain!"

Peter turned and saw Kettle. "What the hell took you so long?"

Kettle tossed him his assault rifle.

"Is anyone taking the bank?" asked Peter.

"No," shouted back Kettle. "Betancourt ordered all forces to converge here."

Kafka was down in the computer center with Yvette. She was rigging the computers with C4. When she finished, she executed the technicians in the room in cold blood.

"Our escape route has been cleared," said Kafka.

Yvette nodded and looked over at the fountain in the computer center that had been hacked to pieces with jackhammers, revealing an opening to the Bottini.

"How did you know they would abandon their assault on the bank?" asked Yvette.

"Because I put them on the defensive. They had to do everything in their power to protect the Sienese civilians."

"The explosives are in place," said Yvette.

"Then we go," said Kafka.

"What about your brother?"

"Don't worry. He'll come to us."

Chapter 15

"Take your team and storm the bank," ordered Peter. "I need a squad."

"Where are you going?" asked Kettle.

"If they were able to draw all of you out into the Piazza del Campo, I have a hunch they're heading back out the Bottini," explained Peter.

"Then I should go with you," insisted Kettle.

"Negative. If I'm wrong, you'll need every man possible to storm the bank. Get going."

Kettle nodded. He picked up his mini-com, "Alpha Squad, follow Captain Birdsall. The rest, converge on the bank." He looked at Peter. "Good luck, sir."

Peter nodded. "C'mon, men. Follow me."

He texted his coordinates to Betancourt and informed him where he was going. He walked over to the fountain with the statues of dogs spitting out water and brilliant reliefs of women and children all around. He fired his grenade launcher at the fountain and it exploded, flinging shards of stone.

"Into the hole!" Peter commanded.

"Captain Birdsall just texted that he is going into the Bottini," said Betancourt. "He thinks that Kafka is using the access at the computer center to make his retreat out the way we came. I want reinforcements at the access point where Kettle's squad entered the Bottini outside of town. I want boots on the ground and drones in the air. Kafka has to pop up somewhere."

Peter led his squad down the Bottini in column formation, as that was all the space would accommodate. Peter consulted his muti-tasker. "This tunnel runs south of Siena," he said, his voice echoing off of the smooth walls. "The tunnel from the bank runs north. The two intersect. We'll blast through the wall and intercept the northbound tunnel."

He hoped that in doing so, they'd either take Kafka by surprise or reach the intersection first and wait for him. They traversed the tunnel for some distance, Peter's multi-tasker using echolocation to map the tunnel system. The drones would've been perfect for such an operation.

They reached an area where the space widened and the ceiling rose higher. His multi-tasker indicated that this was where the two paths ran next to each other, separated by the wall.

"Stand back," ordered Peter. His squad stepped back, sloshing in the water, and he aimed his grenade launcher at the wall.

Before he could fire, there was a loud bang and the wall blasted inward, filling the tunnel with a cloud of dust and raining debris everywhere. Peter and his men were thrown onto their backs in the water.

A dark shadow passed through the dust and debris, moving quickly. One-by-one Peter's squad was executed by this unnaturally fast shade whipping around the tunnel.

When the dust began to clear, Peter saw a helmeted, lithe figure dressed in black standing over him. It snatched the rifle from Peter's hands before he could react and rammed the stock into his face, knocking him out cold.

Kafka grabbed Peter by the front of his suit and pulled him up, slapping the helmet off of his head. "You're coming with me, brother."

Yvette and a few other OIL operatives came through the opening in the wall. "Is that him?" she asked.

"Yes. I told you he'd come to us. They'll be expecting us to go north, but we're going south to Porta Camollia. Give me the clothes."

Yvette handed him a bag. He began to undress Peter. He then removed a regular outfit out of the bag and dressed Peter. When he was finished, he tossed the bag aside. "Okay, let's move. We don't have much time."

Lieutenant Kettle was entering the Palazzo Salimbeni. "Column formation, squad-by-squad. Once we enter the bank, fan out. Take out all drones."

They breached the bank building and entered the atrium. They took out approaching drones with headshots—one shot, one kill. Kettle checked his multi-tasker. "Beta Squad, this way to the computer center. The rest of you fan out and clear the building."

They crossed the halls and reached the outside of the computer center. They breached the center housing all of the mainframes. They neutralized several drones that were lying in wait.

"Well, that was easy," quipped Kettle. He saw the dismantled fountain. "The Captain was right. They escaped into the Bottini."

"Sir, look."

Kettle looked at the soldier who called his attention. "What is it, Private?"

"The computers are rigged with C4, sir."

"Oh, my God," said Kettle. It looked like about 200 pounds of it. He knew there was a timer somewhere, but there was no time. They had to evacuate. "Everybody—"

Before he could give the order, the computer center was wiped out in a flash of light.

Kafka and his entourage reached the node under Porta Camollia. He removed his helmet, placed it in a backpack, and shot a grappling hook up the vertical ventilation shaft. They climbed up through the shaft and surfaced at the southern gate amongst a crowd of panicking Sienese.

Kafka dragged Peter's unconscious body up and hoisted him upward, throwing one of Peter's arms around his shoulders. Yvette threw Peter's other arm around her shoulder and they dragged him along, the whole group dressed in civilian clothing, with the exodus of terrified hostages.

Kafka looked up and saw the saying carved into the arch above the gate: "Siena opens its heart to you wider than this gate." They pushed their way out with the crowd and past several overwhelmed Italian military.

"We lost contact with Lieutenant Kettle's unit," said Betancourt. "Farrow, is it a technical difficulty?"

Farrow looked pale. "I don't think so, sir."

"Son of a bitch," said Betancourt. "Any word from Captain Birdsall?"

"No," said Lieutenant Farrow. "We're tracing the location of his multi-tasker. It seems to be at a standstill in the Bottini within the city, sir."

"Get some men in there," commanded Betancourt. "If he's dead, I want to see the body."

"Yes, sir."

"In the meantime, we're monitoring the northern fork of the Bottini. The Italian military is monitoring the southern fork and the southern gate of the city as well as the other six gates. This Kafka isn't slipping through our fingers."

However, both Farrow and he were aware that no one knew what Kafka looked like, so the soldiers didn't know who to look for. They were canvassing the crowds to the best of their ability. Deep down, Betancourt knew Kafka was good—too good—to allow himself to be snagged.

***

04:23 HRS

The doors to the pirate church swung open and Kafka dragged Peter inside by the scruff of his shirt. Yvette followed with three other operatives, the last of which closed the doors behind them.

Kafka dragged Peter up the aisle and back into the sacristy. Belmont had the RGT apparatus fired up and was waiting for them.

"How did it go?" asked Belmont.

"According to plan," said Kafka.

"Exactly according to plan," added Yvette, exchanging a look with Kafka that would melt the polar ice caps.

"Who is our guest?" asked Belmont.

"My brother," said Kafka, putting Peter down on the tiled floor with his back leaning against the vestment cabinet. "Our first subject of interrogation with the RGT."

Belmont produced smelling salts and waved them under Peter's nose. Peter grimaced and began to stir. He looked around the room, uncertain where he was, and then he looked at the clothes he was wearing.

"We had to change you into civilian clothes like the rest of us, and then we walked right on past the Italian military with the crowd," gloated Kafka. "Your unit is probably still looking for us to pop out somewhere in the countryside."

Peter took note of the inhuman voice and the motorcycle-looking helmet. "You must be Kafka."

Kafka looked at Yvette and Belmont. "It appears my reputation precedes me." They chuckled in response.

"Where's Carl?"

"Excuse me?"

"Where is Sergeant Carl Birdsall?"

Kafka was amused under his helmet. Peter saw nothing of it. "What makes you think we have him?"

"Because you took my father and someone is controlling those drones," said Peter.

"Your father is fine. He's in a safe location," said Kafka.

"And Carl?" insisted Peter.

"Carl is dead."

"Impossible. Who's controlling the drones? Why is my father still alive?"

Kafka walked up to Peter and pulled him up with one arm under Peter's armpit. Peter was startled by his strength. "I want you to have

209

a seat, Captain." Kafka said that last word with bitterness. He took Peter over to the chair in front of the RGT.

Peter looked at the RGT apparatus. "We thought you blew it up with Captain London. There's no way I'm sitting there. You're just going to have to kill me."

Kafka clapped his hand down hard on Peter's right shoulder. Peter took a swing, but Kafka caught Peter's fist in his hand and squeezed. "Don't tempt me, Captain." He swung Peter around and slammed him into a metal chair. Then he nodded to Yvette, who began to flip switches and turn dials on the apparatus.

"The world will never believe that I was Carl," said Peter.

"On the contrary," said Belmont, "you were quite convincing."

"And who the hell are you?"

"Simon Belmont, terrorist extraordinaire, murderer, thief, and all around scoundrel. Pleased to make your acquaintance."

"They'll never believe that I ordered the execution of those people. They saw me protest. They saw me protect the children," said Peter.

"It doesn't matter," said Kafka. "They will begin to ask questions, and the army will have to explain itself. In other news, we destroyed the precious files holding all of the accounts of the Monte dei Paschi."

"They have backup servers in a remote location," said Peter. "You had to know that. Every major corporation does now-a-days. You were there for something else," said Peter, "and you must be American with military training and a lower rank."

"Why do you say that?" asked Kafka.

"Because you said 'the army,' not 'your army' or 'the Americans.' And you sneered at my rank, which means you must be of a lower rank and resent officers."

Kafka smiled terribly under his helmet. "Very good, Captain Birdsall. Now I must ask you to keep your head still and look into the retinal interface." He clamped down on Peter's shoulder holding him in place and held Peter's head facing forward with his other hand. His grip was like a vice.

"You work out?" Peter asked. "You're freaking strong."

"Hold still and be quiet," Kafka commanded.

The retinal interface fired up and soon images began to appear on the screen. They saw Peter flying backward after the wall blew in down in the Bottini. Then they saw Peter leading his squad into the Bottini in the Piazza del Campo. They saw him protecting the children as the drones feasted on the two women.

They saw Betancourt and his instructions to Peter outside of the walls of Siena. They went back and back and back. They saw the new training tactics in the airfield at Fort Bliss. Finally, after some time, they saw the exchange between Peter and Betancourt after Peter found out the kill chip in Carl's brain was activated. Kafka's grip loosened a little.

Then they saw Peter desperately searching for Carl, and the assault on the farm. Kafka felt Peter's hope that his brother was inside and his profound disappointment when he was not.

"Enough," spat Kafka, "turn it off."

Yvette nodded and switched the retinal interface off. The images on the screen vanished.

"This changes nothing," said Belmont.

Kafka had unknowingly released Peter. He was looking down, deep in consideration of what he just saw.

"Kafka," pleaded Belmont.

"On the contrary," answered Kafka, "this changes everything."

"I don't see how," said Belmont. "We need to study those tactics we saw. We need to learn about their weaponry, their formations."

"In due time," said Kafka, "but first he needs to be given the same chance I was given. The same chance Yvette was given."

Peter was watching the exchange with great interest. Something Kafka had seen moved him, but Peter was uncertain of what and why.

"You don't call the shots around here," said Belmont indignantly. "I determine who gets chosen for liberation, not you."

"I'd check your tone if I were you," answered Kafka menacingly. Yvette was looking at Kafka with great concern. Peter figured there was something going on between them.

He saw the opportunity and seized it. He grabbed the metal folding chair he was sitting on and smashed it into the retinal interface.

"Kill him!" Belmont shouted in outrage.

But Kafka held up a hand to Yvette. She froze where she stood. The other three operatives drew down on Peter. "Anyone who fires on this man will answer directly to me," threatened Kafka.

Just then, Barry Birdsall wandered into the sacristy. "Is-is that Peter? Peter, is that you?"

"Dad?"

Barry walked up to Kafka and put his hand on Kafka's shoulder. "Don't kill him. We've got our family back. No more killing."

Peter looked at Kafka and how he softened under his father's touch. Suddenly it all made sense. Why Kafka took his father, how the drones were being controlled, Kafka's reaction to what he saw in the RGT...

"Carl? Carl, is that you?"

"He cannot be allowed to live," demanded Belmont. "Do not forget who you are."

"I know who I am," said Kafka. He turned to face Belmont. "I'm someone who doesn't take shit from the likes of you."

"Kafka, what are you doing?" Yvette asked.

"I'm reminding Belmont whom he is speaking to."

"Remember the Cause," she prompted. "Belmont helped us both."

"And now he's going to offer the same courtesy to my brother."

"Jesus, Carl, it *is* you. What happened to you?"

"I have to wear this helmet to protect me from having the kill chip activated. This helmet is what's keeping me alive."

"I searched for you, Carl," Peter said, choking up. "I had nothing to do with the order to terminate you. Ramses gave the order. It came straight from the top."

Kafka looked down again. "I know that now…which is why I am giving you a choice. Join us. We have both been used by our government. They created OIL to justify passage of the Second Patriot Act. They want emergency powers, and now they are going to use the RGT secretly on everyone. It's not right, Pete."

"But, Carl, OIL? These are the ones who killed Mom."

"No, Pete. There was one man operating independently, and I killed him in this church. They gave him to me. They also saved my life when my own government was trying to kill me because I had become…inconvenient."

"If that's true, then let's go to the House Oversight Committee."

"They're likely in on it."

"Okay, then how about the media?"

"Come on, Pete. I hardly think a feature on the Tyler-Sklyer show is going to do it."

"So what's the answer then, Carl? You're going to go around blowing up banks? You killed Fiona. She cared about you."

"Bullshit," snapped Kafka, "she was spying on us, and Dad was taken into custody like a terrorist."

"And what about those women you had murdered, Carl? Did they deserve it, too?"

"I had to make a point."

"And what point is that? That you're a cold-blooded killer?"

"You had women executed?" Barry asked in disbelief. "Son—"

"I did what I had to do. The army set me up and tried to kill me. Now I set them up," snapped Kafka.

"You set yourself up," said Peter, "because as far as the world knows, the Automaton ordered those executions."

"I am no longer the Automaton," said Kafka. "He's dead anyway, and he took the army with him."

"Kafka, real cute," said Peter. "So what, you've transformed into something else?"

Kafka reached up and removed the helmet from his head. Peter and Barry gasped when they saw what was underneath.

"Jesus, Carl."

"I am changing, Pete. I am a killer. The Monte dei Paschi had an incredible historical archive. Did you know that throughout history there were others like me? But their societies killed them before their purpose could come to fruition."

"Purpose? What purpose?" asked Peter.

"I am the perfect killer, a harbinger for what is to come."

"You've gone mad," gasped Barry.

"I am the first wave."

"What the hell are you talking about, Carl? You've gone off the map on this one," said Peter.

Carl saw his doppelgänger lurking outside the window. It flashed jagged teeth in a feral grin, threatening to come in.

"Where do you think THV came from? What do you think its purpose is? To kill or convert every human on this planet. To create an undead army for the second wave."

"The second wave of what?" This time it was Belmont who asked the question.

The doppelgänger was now clawing on the glass with saliva dripping from its toothy jowls.

"Invasion," stated Kafka simply. "You each thought the RGT was to be used for your own purposes, to spy on the enemy. In the meantime, the Outworlders have been watching all of you this whole time. Gathering information. Biding their time."

"Yvette, kill him," Belmont ordered. "He's too dangerous to be left alive."

Yvette pointed her gun at Kafka, then Peter. "What do you want me to do?" It was unclear who she was asking, but she looked panicked.

One of the three other operatives in the room made a move, but Kafka grabbed the man's wrist, twisting his hand inward in one quick, deft motion. Before the man knew what happened, he had already pulled the trigger and shot himself in the chest twice. Kafka then grabbed the gun from the man's hand and turned to shoot the other two before the first hit the floor.

Peter watched all this, hopeful. These guys were doing all the work for him, killing each other rather conveniently. He hung back to see how it was going to resolve.

Belmont pulled a knife and came at Barry. Kafka crossed the space between them with incredible speed and snatched the hand holding the knife. He twisted the hand until there was a pop and a crunch and the knife dropped to the floor. It clanged on the tile, and Kafka grabbed Belmont by the neck and squeezed.

Belmont's eyes looked like they were going to pop out of his head. He reached up with his one good hand and grabbed at Kafka's hand in an act of futility. He dropped to the ground, slamming hard on his knees. He reached out to Yvette imploringly.

Yvette had tears in her eyes. She saw her savior Belmont kneeling on the floor, the life slowly being choked out of him. He was looking at her. She saw the knife. She looked at Kafka. Tears streamed down her face.

She walked over to the knife and picked it up. She walked over to Belmont. He understood. He relaxed a little, preparing to receive the knife. They had done this dance before.

Yvette kneeled on one knee, she looked into Belmont's eyes, his face turning purple, and she drove the knife into him with all her might.

Belmont had a look of confusion as he had realized that this time Yvette had not gone along with the ruse. This time, she had truly driven the knife through his heart. His eyes went from horrified to sad, and then to nothing. Kafka released his grip and Belmont hugged the tile.

"Jesus," said Peter in awe of what just played out before him. Carl was freakishly fast and strong. If Peter couldn't win him over, it was going to be one hell of a fight stacked in Carl's favor.

"Carl, you did good. We can work the rest of this out."

"This changes nothing, Pete."

"Come on, Carl, you don't really believe that you're the first wave of some kind of alien invasion."

The doppelgänger was now pounding on the window. The glass was cracking.

"Pete, I see them in my dreams. They make me look like a choir girl. They're perfect and horrible all at once, the stuff of nightmares."

"Carl, you need help."

"Fiona couldn't help me, Pete."

"And you killed her for it."

"She had it coming."

"She may have been involved with the RGT, but she had nothing to do with your termination."

"You don't know that."

"Carl, you never gave her the chance to explain."

"But I'm giving you a chance."

"A chance for what?" asked Peter. "To go on the run with you and your homicidal girlfriend here?"

"It is humanity who will be running," said Kafka ominously.

"What do you think I am or Dad is, or even Yvette? We're all part of humanity. Would you see us all destroyed?"

"I will protect you, all of you."

"How do you know these perfect beings will let you protect us?"

"It is the price of my work here."

"Will you listen to yourself," said Barry in exasperation. "You sound like a megalomaniac with these fantasies of grandeur."

"They're not fantasies, Dad," said Kafka. "They are premonitions."

"Come back with Peter," begged Barry. "He'll take care of you, set this right."

"He wasn't there to take care of me when I was almost killed by a bunch of cowboys from a bar or from the army when they activated my kill chip."

"Carl, you're right," Peter said. "I can't always be there for you. You have to stand on your own two feet and make choices, but you have to do what's right."

"It's too late," Kafka lamented. "There's no going home. I've murdered Fiona and Nolan and those women in the city."

Peter was halted by what he heard. "Nolan?"

"I blew the computer room when he and his team were inside."

Peter's face hardened. "It's time to make a choice right now, Carl."

Barry saw Peter's sudden resolve and begged Carl. "Please, son. There's still time to make it right."

"No," answered Kafka. "For the first time in my life, I have a purpose. I was made to do this, and the world will be forever changed by my actions."

"Then it's settled," said Peter.

Kafka pushed Barry aside. "It's settled. Dad, go inside."

Barry looked horrified. "Carl, surely you don't—"

"Inside," Kafka insisted.

"Listen to him," Peter urged.

Barry looked at them both, realizing that this was the last time he was going to see both of them together. He knew one of them was not walking away from this.

"Yvette, take my father out of here," Kafka instructed.

She nodded and gently guided him away and out of the church.

"So this is it," said Peter.

The glass shattered. The doppelgänger was coming in.

"I guess so," said Kafka. "I will try to make it quick, brother."

"Let's dance."

Peter rolled on the floor to one of the operative's bodies and snatched up a gun as Kafka leapt in the air. Peter rolled away in time as he felt Kafka's heel graze his cheek and slam into the tile.

He took aim and fired, but Kafka moved ever so slightly in different directions, dodging the bullets by millimeters. Kafka delivered a swift kick, sending Peter sliding across the floor and slamming into the wooden vestment cabinet.

Peter struggled to get up and moved his head to the right just in time as Kafka buried his fist into the cabinet door, punching all the way through.

Peter spun away towards the RGT apparatus as Kafka pulled off the cabinet door in an attempt to free his arm. Peter took the opportunity to grab another gun from another of the slain operatives.

He fired into the wooden cabinet door. Kafka's view was impeded by the door, and he didn't see Peter coming. As Peter emptied his gun, several of the shots hit Kafka in his body and arm.

Peter felt a blow to his head from behind and his gun went flying across the room. He turned in time to see Yvette's fist make contact with his face, sending him flying backward.

Kafka pulled off the cabinet door and flung it to the ground. He was hunched over and holding his side. Those shots took something out of him.

"Two against one, eh?" Peter said. "Glad to see you guys are playing fair."

Yvette saw that Kafka was injured, and fury exploded in her soul. "You son-of-a-bitch!"

She ran at Peter, but he dodged a foot stomp and kicked her legs out from under her. She hit the tile floor hard and was momentarily stunned.

As Peter stood up, Kafka came running at him. They made contact and broke down the door to the church. They rolled around by the altar, alternating the top position. Kafka pushed Peter off, sending him sliding into the wooden pews.

"Your girlfriend's quite the catch," said Peter standing up and brushing himself off. He looked up at the skeletons smiling down at him.

Kafka was up on his feet in one deft move. Shit. He was still fast. "She's out of your league, Pete. Just like Fiona. Doesn't that just burn your ass?"

Peter looked behind Kafka, his eyes widening. "Oh hell."

Yvette came running out of the sacristy with a submachine gun and open fired. Peter ran down the side of the church using the black-and-white striped columns as cover. Shards of the columns flew off and bullets whizzed through the gaps missing Peter by the skin of his teeth.

Kafka, something taken out of him, flew down the center aisle slower than he normally would have, which allowed Peter just enough time to reach the front doors first.

The only problem was that they were locked from the inside. Kafka flew at him with full force. Peter stepped aside in time for Kafka to fly through the doors, tearing them right off their hinges.

Peter ran through the opening and into the street as bullets shot past his ears. He jumped over Kafka lying stunned on the ground, and narrowly avoided crashing into a storefront in the red and yellow striped building across the street.

He ran up the dim street in the cool winter air, the sight of the striped houses making him dizzy. As he ran, he heard the roar of a motorcycle engine come from around the side of the church behind him.

Damn, that bitch was persistent.

He ran past closed outdoor restaurants with little tables and multi-colored umbrellas bearing the brand names of Italian beers and liquors. Yvette was closing the gap quickly.

Peter ducked down an alleyway and up the backs of houses. He passed under an arch as he heard the motorcycle tear around the corner and up the hill after him.

Bullets hit the ground at his feet and flew past him as he ran in zig zags, which made him harder to hit but allowed her to catch up quicker as he was covering ground more slowly.

Just as she was practically at his back, he jumped left into a doorway and she soared right on past him. He jumped out and ran in the other direction as he heard her take her hand off the throttle and apply the hand breaks. It was too narrow for her to turn around easily.

He bolted back down the alleyway and turned left in between two houses. As he re-entered the street he was previously on, he noticed a shadow dancing above his head in the waning moonlight. It was Kafka jumping from rooftop to rooftop, tracking Peter like a predator of the sky.

Instead of running back down the street, Peter ran across it and into another alleyway on the other side. That bastard would have to leap across the street to follow. Given his injuries, that would seem unlikely, thus buying Peter another few seconds.

He ran up another steep alleyway as he heard the growl of the motorcycle somewhere behind him, searching for him. Suddenly, a great shadow leapt in front of him, and Kafka hit the ground. He knelt where he landed for a moment, the exertion and the fall having taken something out of him.

Peter ducked between another couple of peach and pink colored buildings and re-emerged out onto the main street in front of a wine artisan shop. He looked up the street and saw Yvette perched on her motorcycle. Unfortunately, she noticed him, too, and began careening down the sloped main boulevard right at him.

The streets were largely empty, save for a few locals taking in some crisp early morning air. Peter ran to the side by an outdoor café. The place was vacant, locked up, and the umbrellas closed.

He reached over a wrought iron railing and snatched up an umbrella, pointing the tip at the oncoming Yvette like a joust. She saw the point coming at her but couldn't stop her own momentum. She tried to take aim at Peter with her submachine gun, but it was too late.

The point of the umbrella crunched into her chest cavity, knocking her off the motorcycle and sending Peter and the motorcycle flying into the café, crashing into the tables and chairs.

Peter opened his eyes. He was caught in the opening in between the seat and backrest of a chair, his right arm radiating pain as he tried to hoist himself up. It was broken. Blood trickled down the side of his face from a gash on his hairline.

He rolled over, taking some chairs stuck together with him. He agonizingly shimmied his way loose and slowly got to his feet. He saw lights turning on and faces appearing in windows.

He stepped out of the café and saw the body of Yvette lying on the uneven stone, blood running out of the right side of her mouth, her eyes wide open with shock, the last emotion that ran through her…before the umbrella did.

Peter took her submachine gun and walked down the street, his body aching and paining from all directions. He saw a smart car parked on the side of the road in a little nook next to a staircase leading up to an apartment.

He preferred a Mack truck, but this would do. He smashed the window with the stock of the submachine gun and opened the door from inside. He slid into the seat and closed the door gently.

If he was going to beat Carl, it wouldn't be mano-a-mano. He would need help and, unfortunately, this little shitbox was the only thing on hand. He pulled out the wires under the steering column and severed them with a shard of broken glass. He stripped the ends and began to hotwire the car with his good hand.

He heard a shrill screech, like an enraged banshee, in the distance behind him. Carl had found Yvette. Poor bastard. He tried so hard to meet a woman. When he finally did, Peter had to go and kill her. He felt awful. But in his defense, she was trying to kill him.

Soon Carl would be coming for him and, if he wasn't pissed off before, he was going to go nuclear now. The poor kid had gone crazy with all that talk of perfect beings and invasion.

He peeked above the dashboard and saw Carl's lithe shadowy form and four red eyes stalk down the hill past him. Peter reached down and crossed the wires. The engine turned over and he twisted the exposed tips together.

He put the car in gear and crept out of his spot slowly. He couldn't see in the waning darkness, a reverse twilight, so he turned on the headlights totally prepared to gun it.

There was no one there down the stretch of the street. Where did he—

Suddenly Kafka descended on the little car, his long limbs stretching over it like a spider overwhelming a morsel. Peter floored it and sent the car bowling down the street as fast as it would go.

Kafka was reaching into the broken window and grabbing at Peter, unfazed by his forearm being sliced by shards of broken glass. Peter was leaning inward avoiding the swiping hand.

Peter saw around Kafka's hideous form that the jetty was approaching fast. He sped past rows of multi-colored boats on either side of the road and onto the narrow cement jetty. Kafka looked behind him to see the sea rushing at him.

For a moment, the little car's engine gunned as it popped up on the lip, smashed through the top of the cement barrier, and flipped over the rocks on the other side. Peter and Kafka were weightless for a brief moment. The front of the car slammed the water so hard that the jagged glass on the broken car window severed Kafka's right arm, causing it to land in Peter's lap.

Peter was slammed forward against the steering wheel, knocking the wind out of him. The windshield spider-webbed around the impact of Kafka's face. Water rushed into the little car as it sank into the water.

Peter got his bearings, grabbed the submachine gun, and drifted out of his seat and to the surface of the water. The car sank, taking Kafka with it, but the water wasn't that deep. Peter hoped he was pinned under the weight of the car.

He climbed up the rocks to the top of the jetty where the cement barrier was smashed to pieces. He lay prone catching his breath as the sun rose over Monterosso, chasing out the monochromatic night and bathing the many colors of the town in golden light.

Peter heard splashing behind him and he turned around to see his mother climbing up the jetty one-handed. She looked up at him imploringly, the sight of her rendering Peter speechless.

She reached out for him, and he so badly wanted to take her hand. Then he reminded himself that she was gone. Peter grabbed the submachine gun and fired into his brother. Kafka was hit over and over, sliding down a little each time, but he kept coming.

Kafka grabbed Peter's right ankle tight and looked up at him. Peter wasn't able to classify the expression on his brother's face—hatred, betrayal, shame. It was horrible and made Peter's stomach turn. Kafka let go of Peter, and Peter delivered a boot to his face sending him rolling down and into the water.

After Kafka disappeared under the surface, Peter waited for some time, but his brother never returned.

Chapter 16

The Next Day
14:07 HRS

Peter sat in the debriefing room at Fort Bliss with his arm in a cast. As it ended up, he had also dislocated his shoulder from the impact of the joust with Yvette and was recovering from a mild concussion.

"So what you're telling me is that this Kafka was your brother, Carl?" asked General Ramses.

"Yes, sir. It was."

"I suppose that's why he broke your father out of Guantanamo Bay."

"What about my father, sir?"

"He's free to go," said Ramses dismissively. "Let's talk about the RGT."

"Yes, sir."

"The report...your report states that you were the one who smashed it."

"Yes, sir. That's correct. That was the apparatus they led us to believe was lost with Captain Fiona London."

"I see. And this Simon Belmont...he was the mastermind behind all of this?"

"Carl appeared to have worked out the finer points of their plan, sir. But, yes, Belmont was a high ranking member of OIL."

"Were there any others, Captain?"

"The girl, from what I could tell, was important but not one of the top ranking members."

"And this was the girl that made contact with your brother at the bar."

"That's correct, sir."

"Your brother took credit for the deaths of those civilians at Siena and Lieutenant Kettle and his team."

"Yes, sir."

"You saw his body slip into the water?"

"Yes, sir. I did."

"You are aware, Captain, that his body was never recovered."

"Yes, sir."

"And you said he wasn't wearing his protective helmet when you saw him slide into the water."

"Correct, sir."

"Did you have any indication why he did any of this?"

Peter hesitated for a moment. "With all due respect, sir, you did order his termination."

Ramses looked flustered. Betancourt sat there stoic as ever. "I'm not sure how that necessitates treason, Captain," said Ramses with no small degree of irritation.

"I guess he'd rather have lived a traitor than die an instrument of corruption."

"I'm not sure what you are referring to, son."

"It says in Captain Birdsall's report," interjected Betancourt, "that Belmont and his brother both claimed that OIL had some involvement with our military. If this is true, its implications are profound."

"Poppycock," said Ramses flippantly. "OIL propaganda designed to confuse and disillusion."

"The RGT program is implicated," stated Betancourt. "I don't suppose Congress would like to look into this matter further. It might affect their deliberation on the passage of the Second Patriot Act."

Ramses was glaring at Betancourt. "Will you excuse us, Captain Birdsall?"

"Yes, sir." Peter looked uneasily at Colonel Betancourt, who nodded. Peter rose, saluted both men, replaced his headgear, and stepped out of the room. He closed the door behind him and leaned against the wall.

Minutes passed slowly and, after a half an hour, the door finally opened. Ramses stormed out and stalked down the hall back to his office. Betancourt stepped out of the room.

"Sir."

"Captain."

"What happened in there?"

Betancourt gave a sly grin. "The General reminded me about the danger of vicious rumors and the deleterious effect it would have on morale and our programs."

"And what do *you* say, Colonel?"

"Me thinks he doth protest too much."

Peter smiled.

"We're going to issue a press release that the Automaton went rogue and you killed him, which in fact, you did," said Betancourt.

"Hey, why let the truth get in the way of a good story," said Peter, resigned to the fact that you can't fight city hall. "So what do we do now?"

"Well, you, Captain, have been promoted to Major." Betancourt gauged Peter's reaction. He was disappointed but not surprised. "This is a promotion. I thought you might have reacted differently."

"I just killed my own brother. Many good soldiers died in uncovering this plot."

Betancourt frowned. "And you think this promotion was meant to keep you quiet, and you're wondering if you're fighting for the right side."

"I know OIL is not the right side, sir. But I'm not sure that the army's involvement in RGT is right."

"You are a soldier. It's not your place to question," reminded Betancourt.

"But I'm a Major now."

"Well, Major Birdsall, unless you reach the rank of general, you cannot yet question General Ramses' intentions. First, Major Lewis and the Navajas cartel, and now this. You keep uncovering plots like this and one day I'll be taking orders from you." Betancourt cleared his throat. "And speaking of your brother, I've been given the order to broadcast the frequency that activates your brother's kill chip via satellite."

"Leave nothing to chance," Peter said.

"Yes, Major."

"Permission to flip the switch myself, Colonel."

"It's actually a button. This isn't the electric chair in some backwards Texas prison, Major. Are you sure?"

"Yes, sir. I want to see this through."

Betancourt considered Peter's request for a moment. "Granted."

"Thank you, sir."

"Follow me to the satellite relay station. Lieutenant Farrow is waiting for us."

"Lead the way, sir."

Peter followed Betancourt to the relay station. Lieutenant Farrow was standing behind a switchboard overseeing the communications officers.

Farrow saluted Peter. "Captain."

"He's actually a major now," said Betancourt.

"Congratulations, sir."

"Thank you, Lieutenant Farrow." Farrow looked confounded.

"I requested to give the order personally," said Peter.

Farrow looked at Betancourt for reassurance. "He said he wanted to see it through personally," said Betancourt.

"It should be me," said Peter.

"Awaiting your order," said the communications officer.

Peter reached over the man's shoulder and pressed the button himself. The video screen showed a representation of the signal uploading to the satellite and then disseminating over the globe. The communications officer looked awkwardly at Betancourt, who shrugged.

It was done.

Peter looked at the map of the globe up on the screen and hoped that wherever Carl was, this transmission gave him peace. That was why Peter wanted to press the button himself...

...he wanted to give his brother peace.

Chapter 17

One Week Later
Fundraising Benefit
Chateau Chevalier, Washington DC
23:00 HRS

"Be ready," said General Ramses biting into a mini quiche. He swallowed it, savoring the sounds coming from the jazz band. "We go online in twenty-four hours. We'll need the encryptions for the data streams."

"Don't you worry," said Jon Wolff, Assistant Director of the NSA. "Everything's in place. Once congress passed the Second Patriot Act, our cryptographers went into overdrive. We have some beautiful algorithms for you, new Suite A stuff, 920-bit elliptic curve."

"I have no idea what you just said," admitted Ramses looking around the room dimly lit by opulent crystal chandeliers, "but it sounds good to me. There's some concern that this data can be intercepted via satellite."

"Yes, I've heard about the extra-terrestrial concern," smirked Wolff.

"Yes, well, let's just say that the crazy ramblings of a certain rogue operative before his death made an impression on some of the brass."

"Aren't you the brass, General?"

"Just tell me that this data cannot be cracked," demanded Ramses impatiently.

"Maybe not by the Predator or ET, but perhaps by the Romulans."

"Great," huffed Ramses, "I'm talking national security and he's referencing old movies."

"Relax, General. It should be secure."

"Should be?"

"It will be. Besides, no one knows we are using this technology."

"Except for OIL," corrected Ramses.

"I understand that your man took care of that, and at great personal cost," said Wolff.

"Yes, he did. But we don't know if anyone else knows."

"Our cypher is near impossible to crack, even by space aliens."

"That's real reassuring, Jon. Now if you'll excuse me, I have to drop the bomb on Japan."

Jon shook his head at the crude reference to a bowel movement. Ramses excused himself and made his way across the crowded room of politicians, governmental officials, and socialites to the staircase.

He climbed the staircase to the second floor and walked down a long hallway. He passed a couple talking rather intimately in the hallway next to a painting of the French countryside. He found the men's room door on the right.

He opened the door and entered. He passed an attendant rearranging his towels, perfumes, and mints, and took the closest stall. He put down the paper guard on the toilet seat, pulled his pants down, and plopped himself down on the bowl in the nick of time.

He thought he heard the attendant lock the door. "Excuse me. There's someone in here."

A head popped up over the side of the stall, black as an oil slick with four red eyes. It was the attendant. When he smiled, he revealed pearly white fangs.

"YOU!" said Ramses, aghast.

Kafka flipped over the side of the stall and landed in front of Ramses, who tried to stand but was slammed back down on the bowl.

"Please, General, don't stand up on account of me."

"You're supposed to be dead! Help! Help!"

Kafka rolled his eyes. "Oh, don't waste your breath, General. I've taken the liberty of putting a 'do not disturb' sign on the door and posting a drone in a custodian's outfit outside so our meeting isn't…interrupted."

"How can you be here?"

"Well, I have a saying…well, it's actually more of a credo for me: what doesn't kill me makes me stronger."

"The chip. What about the chip?"

Kafka reached into his tuxedo breast pocket with a white-gloved hand and pulled out a small, thin, square chip with dried blood crusted around it. He tossed it into Ramses' naked lap. Ramses bobbled it a bit and took a look at it. "How?"

Kafka pulled back his greasy hair and turned his head to reveal a hole in his skull. "I dug it out myself with my finger. Not a very pleasant thing to do, but absolutely necessary under the circumstances."

"If you kill me, you won't make it out of here alive."

Kafka looked genuinely amused. "I don't want to kill you, General."

"Then what do you want?" snapped Ramses.

"I want you to live. I want you to launch the RGT program, and I want it to flourish."

"Oh, that's right," said Ramses contemptuously, "you and your alien overlords."

"If you weren't so concerned about it, why did I just see you chatting it up with the Assistant Director of the NSA? Let me guess...they're using KG-250 with a TCP/IP accelerator, Suite A algorithms...Am I getting warm?"

"Even if you could break the encryption," Ramses said, "what would you possibly do with data on millions of people's memories and experiences?"

Kafka shrugged. "Me? Personally, nothing. But my friends from outer space, well, they would just eat that data up."

"Why? For what purpose would they use the data?"

"That's for me to know and earth to find out, and it will soon enough," Kafka teased with a hint of menace.

"Why are you telling me all of this?"

"Because I know that you know that no one believes in this UFO theory of yours, and it's going to eat you alive to know that you have to go ahead with the RGT Program constantly wondering if I'm really crazy."

"Oh, I think we've established the answer to that question," answered Ramses.

"Maybe so, but you'll always wonder."

"So that's my punishment? To live in fear and guilt?"

"No," answered Kafka, "your punishment is coming. When it arrives, you'll wish I killed you with my bare hands in this bathroom."

"What about your brother?" Ramses asked, trying to deflect the attention off of him.

"Peter? He'll get his, too. Everyone will."

"Well if that's the case, then why don't you get out of here so I can finish my shit in peace?"

"Certainly, General. But first, a memento of our time here together." Kafka opened his mouth to reveal fangs, and he bit into Ramses before he could react, sinking his fangs into his shoulder. Ramses struggled on the bowl, attempting to pry Kafka from him.

Finally, Kafka pulled away. "One of my new tricks. Now I will always be with you, General. I will see what you see. I will haunt your dreams. We are now inexorably connected."

Ramses clutched his shoulder, "Get out! GET-OUT!"

When he looked up, Kafka was gone. He pulled up his pants and flushed the toilet. He burst out of the stall and threw the door to the outside hallway open. He peered down the hallway, but it was empty.

He went back into the bathroom and took off his jacket, throwing it on the sink platform and knocking over the attendant's tip bowl. He unbuttoned his shirt and took it off, placing it on top of his jacket.

He turned on the faucet for the hot water full blast and let it run into the sink. When the water was hot, he scooped some up in his right hand and washed the bite on his left shoulder. He grabbed some paper towels and dabbed at the two holes until the blood began to coagulate.

Then he turned off the faucet. The hot water had steamed the mirror above the sink. He was startled at the sight of a four-eyed smiling face drawn on the mirror at face level, overlapping his. The crude features smeared as the moisture on the mirror ran, creating an unnerving effect.

He threw the paper towels out and put his shirt and jacket back on hastily. He spilled out into the hallway and strode back to the staircase. He looked at the room and all of its occupants, social butterflies bouncing from clique to clique in almost random patterns.

He descended the stairs with heavy feet, holding onto the bannister, looking at Jon Wolff talking to one of the young female socialites, the one with the reality show…flirting was more like it. He couldn't blame Jon, given her reputation.

On his way down the stairs, he bumped shoulders with a passerby. He looked up to excuse himself and caught a glimpse of the man he bumped. An odd chill ran down his spine…

…he could've sworn the man bore an uncanny resemblance to him.

www.ingramcontent.com/pod-product-compliance
Lightning Source LLC
Chambersburg PA
CBHW071305210626
46818CB00015B/3000